more prais

HER SISTER'S TATTOO

"*Her Sister's Tattoo* is an honest and riveting po~~~ ~~~ti-war activists and the price individual~ ~~~ eir actions, no matter how ju ~~~ s and secrets can eat away aga ~~~ ie in their families, particular ~~~ the fear and exhilaration of pi ~~~

—Marge Piercy, ~~~ *Woman on the Edge of Time*

"Rarely has the political been more heartrendingly personal than it is in *Her Sister's Tattoo*. Within the story of these incandescent sisters, Meeropol contains a lifetime's worth of devastating choices and the remorse that inescapably follows. At a time when politics are again threatening to rip the American family apart, this might just be the novel we need."

—Andrew Foster Altschul, author of *Lady Lazarus*

"When their involvement at a Vietnam War protest escalates an already-violent situation, activist sisters Rosa and Esther must decide what lengths they will go to in support of their political convictions. Blood may be thicker than water, but in this family, politics may be thicker than blood. *Her Sister's Tattoo* explores the shades of gray in a world that demands black-and-white perceptions, demonstrating that the lines we draw in the sand between what we are and are not capable of doing are ever-shifting under the weight of our complicated humanity."

—Emily Crowe, bookseller at An Unlikely Story

"*Her Sister's Tattoo* is a story not just of two sisters but of our country, where politics have so often torn apart families, loved ones, and communities. This tenderly told novel brings humanity to all sides of struggle, lifting us with its grace, compassion, and hope for the future. I highly recommend."

—Rene Denfeld, author of *The Child Finder*

HER SISTER'S
TATTOO

a novel

Ellen Meeropol

🐓 Red Hen Press | *Pasadena, CA*

Book design by Mark E. Cull

Library of Congress Cataloging-in-Publication Data

Names: Meeropol, Ellen, author.
Title: Her sister's tattoo : a novel / Ellen Meeropol.
Description: First edition. | Pasadena, CA : Red Hen Press, [2020]
Identifiers: LCCN 2019040075 (print) | LCCN 2019040076 (ebook) | ISBN
   9781597098441 (trade paperback) | ISBN 9781597098557 (ebook)
Subjects: LCSH: Vietnam War, 1961-1975—Protest movements—Fiction. |
   GSAFD: Historical fiction.
Classification: LCC PS3613.E375 H47 2020 (print) | LCC PS3613.E375
(ebook) | DDC 813/.6—dc23
LC record available at https://lccn.loc.gov/2019040075
LC ebook record available at https://lccn.loc.gov/2019040076

The National Endowment for the Arts, the Los Angeles County Arts Commission, the Ahmanson Foundation, the Dwight Stuart Youth Fund, the Max Factor Family Foundation, the Pasadena Tournament of Roses Foundation, the Pasadena Arts & Culture Commission and the City of Pasadena Cultural Affairs Division, the City of Los Angeles Department of Cultural Affairs, the Audrey & Sydney Irmas Charitable Foundation, the Kinder Morgan Foundation, the Meta & George Rosenberg Foundation, the Allergan Foundation, the Riordan Foundation, Amazon Literary Partnership, and the Mara W. Breech Foundation partially support Red Hen Press.

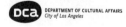

First Edition
Published by Red Hen Press
www.redhen.org

This book is dedicated to my Movement sisters,
with enormous love, in honor of those years
Beth, Rayna, Marilyn, Gayle, Karen, Di,
Lydia, Oceana, Dolphin, Dale

HER SISTER'S TATTOO

PART ONE

1968–1980

CHAPTER 1

Esther

The August air was charged with whiffs of marijuana and patchouli oil, the sulfur stench of asphalt softening in the heat, and the distant admonition of tear gas. Protesters overflowed the broad expanse of Woodward Avenue and spilled onto the sidewalk. Their chants ricocheted off the brick faces of the squat downtown Detroit buildings. And the excitement. Excitement had a peppery smell all of its own.

At the front of the demonstration, Esther let herself be pushed along by the zeal of the march, elbows linked with her sister Rosa on her left and their best friend Maggie on her right. Maggie lowered the bullhorn and handed it to Esther.

"Your turn," Maggie said. "I've got to save my voice. I'm on medic duty soon."

Shaking her head, Esther passed the bullhorn to Rosa, who raised it to her lips. "Hey, hey, LBJ! How many kids did you kill today?"

Esther joined the chant, her voice hoarse, a good kind of sore. To their left, three eight-foot-tall puppets dressed in military uniforms splashed with red paint swayed to the chants. The puppets bobbed and bowed to the National Guard troops stationed in front of Hudson's Department Store. Mama used to bring the girls to Hudson's every year for back-to-school shopping until a store clerk was murdered and

Mama swore she'd never again set foot in the store. The neighborhood had become too dangerous.

Beaming, Rosa squeezed Esther's arm against her ribs. "Isn't this great?"

Esther squeezed back. She loved it all, her sister's fireworks smile and the two elderly women shuffling next to them sharing a metal walker and the guy on the sidewalk cheering and waving his Detroit baseball cap, even though she could swear he was chanting, "Go get 'em, Tigers!" Most of all she loved feeling bonded cell to cell, not only to Rosa and Maggie, but to every single one of the tens of thousands of people in the crowd as they all marched for a single shared cause: ending the Vietnam War.

Rosa pointed the bullhorn toward a couple marching on the edge of the crowd. A sleeping infant snuggled between the woman's breasts, his white sailor hat shading his red cheeks and his mouth pursed with dreams of nursing.

"See?" Rosa said. "You could've brought Molly."

Esther shook her head. A demonstration was no place for a five-month-old. "That's not what Mama said."

Rosa rolled her eyes. "What'd she say?"

"That I should stay home, because what if I get arrested?" Esther waved at two men watching the march from a second floor window. They looked like father and son, with the same grim expression, the same stiff posture, forearms leaning on the sill. They didn't wave back. "I tried to explain that I'm protesting *for* Molly, for her future." Before their conversation Esther had the same qualms, but the minute Mama started saying those things, Esther pushed her own doubts away. "Mama wouldn't listen, just made that disgusted sound, that *phuff* noise, you know?"

"Mama forgets what it's like." Rosa paused to let five young men cut ahead of them. They waved pictures of their draft cards ignited with fire-engine-red paint. "She and Pop brought us to rallies and strikes all the time when we were kids. You've got to take risks for your beliefs."

"That's easy for *you* to say." Esther had agonized over bringing Molly. Their collective had been working for weeks with the national office of the Students for a Democratic Society aiming for the biggest anti-war march in Detroit history, building momentum for the protest at the Democratic National Convention coming up in Chicago in ten days. "It just didn't feel safe to bring Molly. Leaving her with the babysitter until Jake gets home from the hospital is a compromise." But Rosa didn't like compromises.

"People have to choose," Rosa said. "My priority is ending the war."

"Women can do both." Esther tried to sound confident, but some days that felt impossible. Like the night before, when Molly woke up at two a.m. and Esther tried to nurse her back to sleep. Molly wanted to play, grabbing at the origami peace crane mobile hanging from the ceiling. "It's just hard, you know, when Molly is up a lot at night."

"At five months, she should be sleeping through the night."

Rosa's scolding was drowned out by the five-piece military band playing "God Bless America" in front of the Army Recruitment Center. The recruiters and their buddies, several of them in military uniforms, shouted at the marchers: "America! Love it or leave it!"

Esther tugged at Rosa's corkscrew curl to bring back her attention. "Mama says that at five *years* you still woke up every night and demanded a glass of milk and a story."

Rosa stopped to confront the hecklers, her legs planted solidly on the pavement and fists clenched. "Ho, Ho, Ho Chi Minh. The NLF is going to win!"

Esther grabbed the strap of Rosa's bib overall cut-offs. Rosa let herself be pulled away from the recruiters, but she turned to Esther, her face furious. "Mama likes to dramatize everything, especially raising kids. You'd think it's the hardest thing in the world."

"How would *you* know?" Esther didn't even try to keep the sarcasm out of her voice. Rosa might be older, taller, smarter, but she didn't know squat about babies. "When did you become an expert on child-raising?"

"Stop it, both of you." Maggie rubbed her hand over her blond buzz cut. She turned to Esther. "Ignore her. You know how hyped she gets."

Esther studied Rosa's profile, only her nose visible through the mass of red curls. Esther had seen the ache on Allen's face when he played with Molly, but close as the sisters were, Esther had no idea if Rosa and Allen wanted to have children.

Sometimes she agreed with Rosa that ending the war was the most important thing on earth, for Molly and the little guy in the sailor hat. Other days, she felt herself pulling away from the collective. If she were stronger or braver, maybe she could do everything: be an activist and a mother and an artist. She had tried to paint her enthusiasm for the rallies and demonstrations and protests, but sparks of vermillion pigment on canvas failed to capture the energy, the thrill of it.

The baby in the sailor hat was fussing now, small fists hammering his mother's chest. His cries made Esther's milk let down. She untangled her elbows from Rosa and Maggie and pressed the heels of her hands tight against her nipples, hoping she wouldn't have to march with twin circles darkening her shirt.

As they reached the rally site, double rows of blank-faced National Guard troops lined the wide avenue, sunlight bouncing off their helmets. Rooftop cameras mounted on panel trucks with television station logos swiveled to catch the action. Esther smiled and waved to the soldiers.

"Don't wave." Rosa's lips pinched into a thin line. "They're the enemy."

"No, they're not. They're Danny."

Esther wondered if their favorite cousin wore a helmet like that. Twenty months earlier he had stopped by the sisters' New Year's Eve party to announce that he'd been drafted. Esther remembered his exact words: "I know you're disappointed in me. I'm not burning my draft card or moving to Canada. The war is wrong, but I'm going." Rosa asked how he could be a soldier if he believed that the war was wrong.

He stared down at his red basketball sneakers and answered, "I'm no chicken."

Rosa probably regretted what she said to Danny that night, her voice barely audible above the party chatter. "Fine. Go be a brave soldier. Kill people. Napalm babies." Danny just stood there looking at Rosa, his hand trying to smooth down the cowlick that tormented him.

"You don't mean that," Esther had told Rosa, then turned to Danny and touched his shoulder. "She doesn't mean it." Danny started basic training two weeks later.

The crowd spilled onto the sidewalk, around and through the curious onlookers, the parked buses with license plates from Illinois and Indiana and Ohio. Rosa stopped to high-five a skinny guy carrying a hand-painted sign saying POLITICIANS LIE; GI's DIE. The marchers pushed amoeba-like into Kennedy Square, flowing around the blue islands of police officers standing with arms crossed, batons swinging from their belts. They funneled under the red banner with human-sized block letters reading BRING DOWN THE WAR MACHINE, then fanned out onto the brown August grass.

Maggie approached a man wearing a red armband and distributing flyers. "Where's first aid?" she asked. The marshal pointed beyond the stage to a white canvas tent, its roof visible above the heads of milling protesters. He handed Esther a flyer and she glanced at the list of rally speakers and supporting organizations. The ink, tacky in the humid air, left fragments of print on her fingers.

Maggie tightened the red and white fabric band around her arm and checked her watch. "I'm on duty soon."

Esther wished Jake had also volunteered for first aid, but a pediatric residency didn't leave time for anything else. Their friends didn't understand and made fun of him. "Jake is a regular Albert Schweitzer of toddlerland," Rosa once sneered, "fighting the epidemic of ear infections." Maggie still had a year of RN training to go, but she had taken a street medic course and here she was in the trenches, ready to treat victims of police violence.

"We'll walk you over," Rosa said.

Onstage, members of the tech collective draped extension cords between the mammoth speakers and the microphones. The squawk of feedback added to the almost unbearable weight of the air, thick with moisture and crackle and heat.

The sisters followed Maggie into the first aid tent, where the harsh sunlight filtered into soft shade. "How's it going?" Maggie asked the medic on duty.

"Not bad. A couple of minor burns from hairspray flamethrowers. Beth is on her way in with a scalp laceration—some frisky cops on Grand River." He unclipped the walkie-talkie from his waist and handed it to Maggie. "I'm going to listen to the speeches, but I'll be around if you need me."

"Thanks. Beth and I will be fine." Maggie attached the walkie-talkie to her belt, then placed a liter bottle of sterile saline and a thick pack of gauze pads on the table. She waved at Esther and Rosa. "We'll talk this evening."

The sisters wandered past the stage and found seats along the fountain. Rosa rubbed at the blue ink on her hand. "Guess I won't need the Legal Aid number. Sounds like all the action was on Grand River."

"You sound disappointed."

"A little."

Esther gathered her hair into one hand and lifted it off of her neck. Sometimes Rosa was too much. "Well, I'm not disappointed. The march was fantastic and I can't wait to see the six o'clock news, but I'm really glad there was no trouble." Esther grinned. "Didn't you love that old woman's sign, ANOTHER GRANDMOTHER FOR PEACE? I hope we'll still be activists when we're that old, and our kids and grandkids will march with us."

"And how about that chant from the Bloomington contingent, for the student who couldn't come because his mother threatened to have a heart attack?"

"Five, four, three two one, Mrs. Goldberg, free your son," they sang together.

"I'm dying of thirst." Rosa kicked off her leather sandals. "Any juice left?"

Esther rummaged through the contents of the daypack: crumpled wax paper from their cheese sandwiches. Plastic bags with bandanas soaked in vinegar in case of tear gas attack. Legal Aid telephone number on a folded piece of lined yellow paper, the same number as the one scrawled on their hands. Torn strips of bed sheet and a can of red spray paint, ready for a last-minute banner. Six empty cans of apple juice. A brown paper bag? Where did that come from? Inside were four small apples, green and rock hard.

"No juice," Esther said. "What's with the apples?"

Rosa smiled. "In case things get heavy, like if we need to break some windows. If we're busted, we can always say, 'Why, officer, that's just a snack.'"

Break windows? Rosa wasn't serious, was she? Esther didn't have the energy to disagree. Rosa would puff up and play the more-radical-than-thou game and Esther would lose the argument, as usual.

Esther peeled her damp shirt from her chest and looked down at the silk-screened image. A Vietnamese woman, with a baby in a cloth sling over one shoulder and a rifle over the other, splashing through a rice paddy away from a landing helicopter. When the art collective chose her design for the rally image, Esther had been so proud, but when Rosa saw the design, she'd raised one eyebrow in disapproval.

"You see babies everywhere," she'd said.

"That's to balance you," Esther said. "Children don't exist in your world." Still, Rosa had helped her staple the posters to telephone poles and tape them to storefront windows.

The loudspeakers squealed, then the static started to divide into words.

Rosa squinted at the stage. "That's Tim Wright."

"Isn't he in jail?" Esther asked. Tim had been busted three days before when his guerrilla theater group interrupted the city council meeting.

"That's him," Rosa said. "No one can power up a crowd like Tim."

"I thought the National Office didn't want him to speak as often, so other people get a chance to be leaders."

"Let me up there. I'll talk about the war."

Esther grinned. "You'd be great, Rosie."

Tim Wright held the microphone close, angled down to his lips like a rock singer. "1968 has been a tough year. Last month alone, there were 813 combat deaths among US troops and over 6,000 soldiers hospitalized, the worst casualties since *Khe Sanh*."

Esther snuck a look at Rosa, who stared straight ahead. *Khe Sanh* was where Danny died. Esther squeezed her eyes closed to stop the prickling.

"But those numbers—awful as they are—don't tell the whole story. They don't include the more than 11,000 Vietnamese soldiers killed last month. And they don't begin to reflect what the loss of each of those lives means to their families." Tim held out his arm and a black woman joined him at the standing microphone. "This is Mrs. Marilyn Amos. Her son died on Hill 364."

"My family is against my being here." The woman spoke slowly into the microphone, staring out across the mostly white crowd. "But I'm marching with you folks today so other mothers' boys don't have to die."

Esther wiped her eyes. Jake said she took the war too personally, that she had to live her life and keep politics in perspective. He tried to make her laugh at herself, like the night before, when he'd suggested that they make the next edition of their anti-war newsletter a swimsuit issue and call it "Girls of the New Left." Esther knew he was just kidding, but it wasn't funny when he joked about women's liberation, so she made fun of his bald spot and then they started wrestling and that led to fooling around until Molly woke up and wanted to nurse.

Back at the microphone, Tim Wright's voice grew more urgent. "This year almost 300,000 young men have been drafted, more than ever before in US history."

"Hell, no. We won't go!" Rosa's yell joined thousands of others.

No one is drafting *you*, Esther thought, then stopped herself. Rosa did draft counseling and helped guys cross into Canada. Maybe she acted inflexible and harsh, but that was because she cared so much.

A woman with a red and white armband hurried by, leading a young man toward the first aid tent. She must be Beth, the other medic. The guy's shirt was bloody, as was the cloth he held against his head. He stumbled and almost fell. Beth steadied him with her arm around his shoulders and spoke into his ear. Esther tugged on Rosa's arm. "Come on. Maggie might need help."

Rosa grabbed her sandals and the sisters followed the injured man to the tent. He was young, just a kid really. He staggered inside and crumpled onto a stretcher as Rosa and Esther watched from the doorway. Maggie peeled the bloody cloth from the boy's head. It was someone's T-shirt, the peace symbol soaked deep red. The bleeding bubbled up under the blond surfer-boy curls at his hairline. Rivulets hugged the contours of his face, spreading across his forehead, flowing along his nose, streaming into his mouth. He spat blood.

"What happened?" Maggie tore open a package with her teeth and pressed the gauze pads against the boy's forehead, then handed him a tissue.

He wiped blood from his lips. "A bunch of us broke off the main march. We walked along Grand River. We were in the street, singing, holding signs. These mounted police showed up in front of us. They yelled at us to get back on the sidewalk."

"How many cops?" Rosa asked.

"A dozen? Maybe more. We told them we had a right to march in the street. Fucking cops just charged us. No reason."

Rosa moved next to his stretcher, kneeled down close. "What happened then?"

"One cop came right close to me. He held his billy club over my head and said it was my last chance to get my ass on the sidewalk. When I didn't move, he swung his club down on my head. Hard. I fell. I couldn't see, but I heard horses' hooves stamping all around me. People pulled me away from the horses. Someone gave me his shirt." He pointed to Beth. "She came and helped."

Rosa frowned. "Anything else?"

"They used tear gas. Lots of it. One canister exploded right in front of us." He looked at Maggie. "I'm bleeding like stink, aren't I?"

"Scalp wounds always look worse than they are. Did you lose consciousness when he hit you?" Maggie asked. "Pass out?"

He shook his head, sending a new gush over Maggie's hand. She taped the bandage to his forehead. "You need stitches. We'll clean you up, then send you to the ER." Maggie pointed to a liter bottle of sterile saline. "Open that for me?"

Esther poured the saline on clean pads, grateful to have something to do so she didn't have to look at the boy's face. Maggie wiped the blood from his eyes.

"What about the other people back there?" the boy asked. He touched his fingers to his scalp, examined his blood.

Maggie gathered up a supply bag from the table. "I'll go."

Beth nodded. "Good idea. There's another medic there, but she may need help."

Rosa touched the boy's shoulder. "We'll get those bastards for you."

"Get real, Rosa," Maggie said.

"I'm going with you," Rosa said. She stood up, swaying visibly. She planted one hand on the kid's stretcher; the other clutched the thick central tent pole.

Esther grabbed her sister's shoulder. "You okay?"

Rosa steadied herself on the table edge. "Must be the heat."

"Or the blood," Maggie said. "Stay here. I don't need you fainting in the street."

"No way." Rosa took their backpack and followed Maggie into the square. Esther trailed after Rosa, past the marchers listening to the speeches in the sun, tagging along as usual, even when she didn't really want to go. But she couldn't let Rosa go into danger alone.

Two blocks down Grand River, they heard the shouting. People leaned out of second and third floor apartment windows watching the street below. Rosa and Maggie ran toward the action, with Esther close behind. They passed an empty police cruiser parked half on the curb, tilted at an awkward angle. The sun flashed off the metallic paint and Esther saw her face reflected there, warped by the curve of the trunk. The cruiser's strobe lights flickered in time to the jumpy beat in her chest.

The air grew harsh with the acrid weed-killer smell and Esther's eyes started to sting and burn. After seven or eight marchers ran past them back toward Woodward holding bandanas over their noses and mouths, Maggie pulled a mask from her medic bag.

"Shit. My throat hurts." Rosa unzipped the pack and grabbed the plastic bag with vinegar-and-water-soaked bandanas. She handed one to Esther and held one over her nose and mouth. Tossing the pack to Esther, Rosa started running down the street to catch Maggie. "Hurry," she called behind her.

Esther slung the pack over her shoulder and followed more slowly. The tear gas haze was thicker ahead. Clouds of it, or was that just her eyes, blinking and weeping and stinging? A small crowd, maybe three dozen people, mostly young, swarmed the middle of the street. Facing them, standing between the protesters and the rally in Kennedy Square, six mounted police held their batons high in the air. One officer yelled through a bullhorn, "Get back on the sidewalks. You have no street permit for this location." A few onlookers watched from under the green-and-white striped awning of a restaurant across the street.

A young woman wore two Vietcong flags safety-pinned together instead of a shirt. The red tops covered her chest, the blue bottoms hung below her waist, and the yellow stars hovered, half and half, over her heart, front and back. "Let us through," she shouted at the cops. "We have the right to march."

Esther stood on tiptoe, trying to see past the horses' broad rumps and braided tails. One cop swung his baton wildly, threatening the flag-wearing woman. This was going to be ugly and Esther didn't want to be there.

She caught up to Rosa. "Let's go back to the square. It's too dangerous."

"You go if you want. I'm staying." Rosa ran to the left, around the line of horses, toward the demonstrators.

Esther lost sight of her sister and stood frozen on the sidewalk, torn between going back and going forward. Sticking close to Rosa and Maggie sounded like a good idea. But how could anything be safe, with angry demonstrators and angrier cops ready to fight? She wanted to be home. If she were hurt, what would happen to Molly? Could tear gas poison breast milk?

A scream, someone in pain. Was it the flag-wearing woman? Was it Rosa? Esther ran in the direction her sister had gone.

Maggie kneeled on a small square of lawn in front of a three-story apartment building. A woman sprawled on the sere grass, motionless. Her head rested on a boy's lap, ponytail skewed to the side, the stain of her blood on the boy's khaki shorts. The boy sobbed, rubbing at his eyes with both fists. Rosa stood between Maggie and the street, staring at the scene. Esther squatted next to the boy and handed him her bandana. She showed him how to hold it over his face, then took another one from the backpack.

The boy's words were muffled behind the cloth. "This lady lives on my block. The cop hit her, on purpose." He looked down at his lap where his neighbor's bloodstain grew large on his shorts.

The sounds of yelling and chanting grew louder. A pop, then another, and the gas cloud grew thicker, denser. The crowd started to shift along the far side of the street, spreading out around the phalanx of policemen.

Maggie fiddled with the dial of her walkie-talkie but got only static. She tore off her mask, tried again, then shook her head. Coughing, she turned to Rosa and Esther. "They're probably blocking our channel. Can you go back for help? This woman needs an ambulance."

Esther looked around. "Where's the other medic?"

"She *is* the medic." Maggie pointed to the woman's armband. "Cops like to target us." She replaced her mask, adjusted the stethoscope earpieces, and began inflating the blood pressure cuff.

From the street came the dull cracks of wooden sticks on heads and the answering shouts and screams. Esther stood up. The mounted cops were turning, herding the demonstrators in the direction of Kennedy Square.

The boy cried louder. "Make them stop."

"I'll go back for help," Esther said. She tightened the bandana over her nose and mouth.

Rosa stepped off the curb into the street. "Fucking pigs," she shouted at the cops. "Leave the people alone."

Esther grabbed Rosa's arm, pulled her back onto the sidewalk. "Don't get them pissed at you. Come back with me."

"We *have* to stop them before they kill someone." Rosa reached into the backpack for the brown paper bag. She grabbed the four green apples. She put one in Esther's hand, pressing her fingers around it.

Esther stared at her sister.

"Help me do this," Rosa said.

Esther looked into the street, then down at her feet, at the sidewalk. Clumps of grass grew in the thin lines of dirt through the jagged cracks. How had she—the quiet sister, the artist, the mother—ended up at the edge of a street fight facing the rear ends of six police horses, rockhard apple in hand?

In the street in front of her, one of the cops shouted a couple of words, quick and sharp. A command, it sounded like, and then all six policemen attacked. They leaned out over the protesters, truncheons swinging.

"Now," Rosa said. She threw her apple hard at the officers.

Rosa's face was so fierce that Esther had to look away. She studied the apple in her hand. Her fingertips searched the apple skin, seeking a soft spot, probing for a worm hole. Maybe it wasn't that hard. Not like a rock, not really.

Rosa threw a second apple and reached for the third.

An officer stood tall in his stirrups and leaned way out over the crowd. He raised his baton above the flag-wearing woman. It smashed down on her head with a dreadful crack, and she sank to the street.

Rosa grasped Esther's chin in her hand, brought Esther's gaze to her own face. "Throw with me, Esther. Now!" Rosa said. She pulled her arm back, ready.

Esther hesitated. It was the right thing to do, wasn't it, to stop the cops from hurting people? She squeezed her eyes shut and hurled the apple as hard as she could, at the same instant Rosa threw hers. She pictured their twin green spheres flying into the turmoil on the street, together, in the same graceful trajectory. Well, maybe not exactly the same: Rosa's probably flew straight and true, while her own wobbled a little and fell short. But still together, like sisters, together, even if they didn't agree about everything anymore.

A horse screamed, sounding astonishingly human. Esther opened her eyes. The horse sidestepped wildly. The officer on its back, already leaning over with baton high, seemed to teeter in the air, then lose his balance. He yelped and tumbled off the saddle, disappearing into stamping hooves and brown rumps.

Two cops dismounted. Another grabbed the bridle of the skittering horse. Had the horse been hit by an apple? *Oh my god.* Did they do this? Did *she* do this?

Esther hadn't actually seen what happened, and now she couldn't see what was going on behind the horses. Empty space grew between the two groups in the street, each circling around their injured members on the ground. The protestors dragged two people out of the street toward Maggie on the grass. Rosa and Esther moved away from the street too, back closer to Maggie. Sirens whined in the distance. Esther peered down Grand River as the sound grew louder, closer.

"I guess *their* walkie-talkies weren't jammed. Want to bet those ambulances won't help this woman?" Rosa said.

Maggie looked up from her patient. "You look awful, Rosa. Like you're going to keel over. Go back now and get help. Please."

Rosa tugged Esther's arm, leading her toward the apartment building. When they reached the shrubbery along the brick facade, Rosa leaned over the thick branches of a rose bush and puked.

Esther rubbed Rosa's back, fingering the row of bumps along her spine. Rosa was never sick.

"It's just the gas," Rosa said.

"Or the excitement," Esther said. "That was crazy."

Rosa's face lit up, the sick look gone. "Crazy-wonderful. We stopped them, didn't we?"

Did they? "We'd better get help for Maggie."

"This way." Rosa wiped her mouth on the back of her hand. She sidestepped along the side of the apartment building, between the shrubs and the brick wall.

Esther followed. The bushes scratched her arms and hands and face. The gas stung worse. Behind the building, a gravel parking lot connected to a narrow alley behind the next building. They ran through packed-dirt backyards ringed with weeds, around rusted jungle gyms with chain-link swings and sandy sliding boards, past plastic wading pools turned over to drain. At the next side street, they cut back to Woodward, then sprinted the two blocks to the square.

Esther's lungs burned as if the air was on fire. The blaze filled her chest, overflowing into her throat and eyes and nose. She concentrated on breathing, on following Rosa, on Molly, who should be waking up from her nap, who usually woke up cranky and needing to nurse. On anything except the horse screaming and the officer going down.

Back at the white tent, they reported to Beth. The older medic had returned. He called for an ambulance, then pointed at Rosa. "You look green. Sit down and stay put." He grabbed a supply bag and followed Beth out of the tent.

Rosa collapsed onto a metal folding chair. The stretcher was empty, the surfer boy gone. Esther pulled another chair next to her, close, and positioned so they could see the stage. The Secretary-Treasurer of the UAW was speaking about union support for the anti-war movement, but Esther couldn't concentrate. She stared at the lamppost just outside the tent opening, festooned with rally posters taped in overlapping layers. They were her posters, but she felt no swell of pride this time. She felt nothing at all.

The crowd chanted, "End the war." Esther tried to join in but her lips were thick and prickly, almost numb, and couldn't form the words. She bent forward, hugging her chest and letting her hair fall over her knees. Rosa's arms enveloped her. She pictured Rosa's red curls and her own brown ones nested together. Rosa smelled of vomit. Esther swallowed a sob.

"You okay?" Rosa asked.

"Scared to death. I was sure the cops saw us, that they would come galloping after us with pistols drawn, shooting. Weren't you terrified?"

"I was so psyched. I've still got goosebumps." Rosa held out her bare arm, the gingery hairs stiff with excitement.

Esther twisted one of Rosa's curls around her index finger. As a little girl, that gesture always made her feel safely tethered to Rosa but it wasn't working now. She let it go and hugged her knees.

Maggie and the medics returned. Their injured colleague was en route to the hospital, still unconscious. Maggie didn't mention anything about green apples or horses or an injured officer.

Esther whispered in Rosa's ear. "I don't think Maggie saw what we did. Should we tell her and the others?"

"Dunno. Let's listen to the speeches."

"No." Esther stood up. Rosa would never leave in the middle of the excitement, but at that moment Esther didn't care. "I'm going home. I need to see Molly."

"I'm coming too."

Esther stared at her sister's face. Rosa leaving a demonstration early? Impossible. She must be sick.

CHAPTER 2

Rosa

Rosa and Esther found seats in the last row of the bus. Their bare legs stuck to the vinyl and the air reeked of old socks. Rosa held the pack and flipped the frayed strap back and forth, echoing the drumbeat thumping through the open window. As the bus jerked away from the curb into traffic, cutting off a rusty VW bus with flower decals, Rosa searched the faces of the soldiers standing at attention along the edge of the park. One guy looked a little like Danny—the pointy chin. Could have been Danny, if things had gone differently. The uniforms whizzed by. Rosa closed her eyes. Woozy.

Esther rested her cheek on Rosa's shoulder. "I hope Molly's okay. I've never left her with the sitter for this long. I wish Jake and Allen had come with us today."

Rosa frowned. As much as she loved him, she was glad Allen hadn't come to the protest. He would have tried to stop her, and she felt *good* about their actions. They'd stopped the pigs from busting heads, at least for that moment. Allen was smart and savvy and active in the Black Panthers, but he preferred his battles in the courtroom rather than the streets.

And Jake was useless. Rosa turned to Esther. "Yeah. If someone had a diaper rash, Jake could help."

"Don't be mean." Esther leaned back against the cracked vinyl seat and fanned herself with her T-shirt.

Rosa shrugged. Mean or not, it was the truth. Jake was hard to recognize these days. What happened to the guy who wanted to bring free healthcare to the poor? Why wasn't he starting a free clinic, or at least volunteering with Maggie?

Fifteen minutes later, they were in Esther's neighborhood. It felt a continent away from Kennedy Square, from everything that mattered. At the door to the apartment, the sour-faced babysitter thrust Molly into Esther's arms.

"She refused the bottle," the babysitter accused. "You should give her formula so she's used to it. That's what I did with my babies."

Molly's face was purple from screaming. She smelled yeasty, curdled. Rosa turned away, into the kitchen. She leaned over the sink and drank from the faucet, then splashed cold water over her face.

"Rosie," Esther called from the living room. "Would you pay Mrs. B. for me? There's cash on the dresser."

Walking by the living room, Rosa watched Esther kiss Molly's stinky neck, then lift her shirt and help the baby latch on.

"Poor Monkey," Esther murmured. "You're starving."

Rosa found the money. Leaving the bedroom, she glanced into the little end room, once Esther's studio. A dusty easel held an unfinished painting. Esther was letting her talent go to waste. Art could *move* people, change minds and goose them into action.

After Mrs. B left, Rosa stood in the doorway to the living room watching Esther stroke the wispy hair plastered to Molly's scalp, rusty-red like Rosa's.

"I'm famished," Rosa said.

"There's tuna. Make us sandwiches? And turn on the news."

At the sound of her mother's voice, Molly pulled away from the breast without letting go. Esther's nipple glistened, pulled like taffy by Molly's suck.

"Ouch, Molly. Stop it."

Rosa turned away, toward the kitchen. No babies for her. She squeezed the tuna fish oil into a bowl for Mustard, Esther's yellow kitten, then made sandwiches. They sat thigh to thigh in front of the television. Molly nursed. Esther ate. Mustard jumped onto Rosa's lap and licked her sandwich, untouched on the arm of the sofa.

A young anchorman with outsized ears orchestrated the network coverage of the demonstration. Film clips of speeches alternated with live feed of confrontations between demonstrators and police at the end of the rally. Protesters thrust V-fingered peace signs out the half-open windows of the jail-bound buses.

"We shouldn't have split early." Rosa imagined herself leading chants from the front of the bus, talking to reporters, convincing ordinary citizens watching TV that the war was wrong. She missed the electric charge, the wonderful chaos.

"I'm glad we did," Esther said. "What if we'd been busted?"

Rosa pointed to the screen. "Shush."

Paramedics ran with a stretcher toward an ambulance. Lights flashed. An injured police officer, blanket tucked to his chin. A close-up of his helmet hooked on the IV pole, bumping up against the saline bottle. Someone led a horse away.

The reporter stood to the side. "On Grand River Avenue, a few blocks from the rally at Kennedy Square, demonstrators attacked mounted police officers. Officer Martin Steele lost control of his mount and was thrown. The officer is in serious condition at City Hospital with a spinal cord injury."

"Demonstrators attacked the cops?" Rosa yelled at the television set. "What about cops cracking heads?" She picked up her sandwich and looked at it, then put it back down. Her stomach still didn't feel right.

The anchorman introduced a wire service photographer who been eating at a restaurant on Grand River. "We bring you an exclusive interview to shed some light on the tragic consequences of today's street fight."

"Street fight?" Rosa grabbed two fistfuls of her hair in fury. "They were beating up unarmed citizens!"

"Did you see anyone taking photos?" Esther asked, switching Molly to the other breast.

"Shush."

"I was at lunch when a skirmish developed between mounted police and demonstrators," the photographer said. "I stood under the restaurant awning and took photos of the fighting. That's when I noticed two curly-haired young women. A redhead and a brunette, acting furtive. When they threw the rocks, my camera was ready."

"Furtive?" Esther asked.

"They weren't rocks," Rosa muttered.

His photograph filled Jake and Esther's fifteen-inch television screen. Two young women with pale oval faces and electric hair. One with eyes squeezed closed. Each with one arm extended, fingers splayed, frozen in the act of letting go.

Neither sister spoke. Local coverage transitioned to international news. Soviet tanks swarmed the streets of Prague. Rosa felt dizzy.

Esther turned to her sister and touched her arm. "It's worse than I thought," she whispered. "What have we done?"

"Don't think about it." Rosa wiped a tear from Esther's cheek with her thumb. She wanted to cry too, which was totally unlike her. But she *wouldn't* cry. There was too much work to do.

"Don't *think* about it? That cop is hurt. And it's our fault. We hurt him."

"They started the fighting. Besides, we can't help him now. We've got to figure out how to proceed, how to make a plan. Like Pop taught us."

"What *about* Mama and Pop?" Esther said. "They never miss the six o'clock news. They'll be so freaked out. Should we call or go over?"

"You go," Rosa said. "I need to talk to Allen. Strategize."

"Why wasn't Mr. Black Lefty Lawyer at the demonstration, anyway?"

"He's in the middle of a trial. The Sanders case—that Haitian guy the cops beat up walking home from the store with a bag of baby formula? Allen says a court victory would make more difference than any march." Rosa wasn't sure she agreed with him about that—they had argued about it the night before. But Allen would know what to do about this.

"But our parents," Esther pleaded. "Please come with me."

Rosa shook her head. "Priorities. We have to move fast, before they bust us."

"How will they know who we are?"

Rosa rolled her eyes. Sometimes Esther was so innocent. "Come *on*. We're well known in this city. They'll have an ID in an hour, if they don't already. Take Molly and get out of here." Rosa started toward the door, hesitated. She turned back, leaned over the couch, and put her arms around Esther and Molly. "It'll be okay."

"I'm scared," Esther whispered. "What if that cop is hurt bad?"

"What about all the injured and slaughtered Vietnamese? Think about this as an opportunity to make people understand about the war."

"*You* think about all that." Esther turned her face away. "You go right ahead and plan strategy and write a press release. I have a diaper to change. Then, I have to face Mama and Pop alone."

Rosa let herself out of the apartment and walked down the block to the bus stop. Maybe the cooler evening air would steady her stomach. She probably should have gone with Esther, but she couldn't face their parents. Especially Pop.

Pop hadn't always been so rigid, so negative. He used to be passionate about politics. His union's Labor Day parade was Rosa's earliest childhood memory. She must have been four or five, standing on the curb, marching in place and waving a small union flag. Pop was on the end of the front line, next to the fellow holding one pole of the large red banner: SHOEMAKERS AND REPAIRERS AMALGAMATED. He swerved from formation and scooped Rosa up, leaving Esther bouncing on Mama's lap on the lawn chair with unraveling green and gold plastic webbing. Rosa finished the parade on Pop's shoulders, her cotton candy grin memorialized in a black and white photo with scalloped edges in the family photo album. Every year they went to the parade, and then the union picnic. When they got home, Pop would have a serious grown-up talk with his daughters about how the union was picnics and good wages now, but it wasn't always so easy. About strikes and scabs. About his best friend, Bernie, interrogated and beaten by the union-busting cops until his heart gave out and he died in his jail cell.

At home, Allen was pacing back and forth in the living room, still in his courtroom clothes. The local news played in the background. He opened his arms and Rosa walked into his bear hug. Her throat swelled, ached with relief.

"Did you see us?"

He nodded, his beard rubbing against her hair. "You were hard to miss."

"It was crazy. The pigs were cracking heads. We stopped them." She pictured the woman in the Vietcong flag shirt, blood soaking the bright fabric.

He didn't respond and Rosa leaned back to study his face. Sometimes Allen could be a bit of a fuddy-duddy. But he knew the law.

"Are we screwed?" she asked.

"I'm surprised they're not here yet. You'll probably be arrested tonight, both of you." Allen kissed her forehead, then squeezed her harder.

"I've been busted before. No big deal."

Allen shook his head. "Assaulting a cop is different than spray painting slogans on university buildings."

Fire flared in Rosa's chest, warring with the wooziness and the doubts. "I feel bad that he got hurt, Allen, but we did it for the Vietnamese. If the DA charges us, if there's a trial, we'll talk about the war, how wrong it is. You'll get someone really good from your firm to defend us. This could be an opportunity to educate people about what our government is doing over there." Another wave of nausea stopped her words and she closed her eyes.

"Maybe." Allen rested his face on the top of her head, so his words half-disappeared into her hair. "I hope so."

CHAPTER 3

Esther

With Molly wrapped snug against her chest, Esther let herself into her parents' overstuffed apartment. She sidestepped around the tall ceramic cylinder packed tight with umbrellas, Pop's walking stick, and a fishing pole with the frayed line in knots. Mama always apologized about the crowding, sorry that they couldn't afford a house, even after Pop opened his own shop. Whatever savings they managed were spent sending the girls east to camp every summer.

Esther lingered in the long hallway Pop called the gallery. Every inch of wall space was covered with images: childish drawings in plastic frames, art museum prints curling at the edges, Mexican bark paintings, and the intricate woodcuts of coal miners or farm workers that Bernie's widow sent every Chanukah.

She stopped in front of her favorite painting, a framed print by an Italian artist she'd never heard of. Rows of grim-faced workers walked straight toward the viewer, like they meant business. In the front row, a barefoot woman in a long skirt carried an infant. Growing up, Esther liked to sit on the floor against the opposite wall, hugging her knees, and look up into the woman's unwavering eyes.

Rosa used to tease that the woman was her fairy godmother. "If you love her so much, what's her name?" Rosa asked when Esther was eight or nine. "Hannah," Esther had answered, having no idea where the name came from. But it sounded strong, like a pioneer. Rosa laughed and made the cuckoo sign, pointer finger circling her ear. "Hannah's not an Italian name," Rosa said, but she didn't rag Esther about her again.

Now, Esther touched Hannah's determined chin. Did she worry that her baby would be hurt if their protest got violent? Did Hannah have someone—a mother or a husband or a sister—to watch the kid if she were arrested?

Who would take care of Molly, if *she* were arrested?

Forcing herself away from the painting, Esther paused at the kitchen. In March of third grade, when their grandmother Leah moved in, Pop pushed the sofa into the kitchen so Leah could use the living room as a bedroom. Leah took over the bathroom too, filling the bathtub with live carp to make fresh gefilte fish for Passover. When Rosa complained about having to wash up at the sink, Pop's eyebrows bristled and he made them sit at the kitchen table and listen up. Grandma Leah was born in Russia, he said. When she was sixteen, her father was forced into the Czar's army and there was no food. He starved to death and Leah joined a secret cell to overthrow the Czar. Her twin sister Tovah was frightened that she'd get the rest of the family killed, but Leah argued that the peasants should own their land. Tovah adored her sister and joined the group, standing guard while Leah and her friends printed anti-government leaflets.

"A printing press was as subversive as explosives," Mama told them. "One night, the Czar's guard caught Leah with pamphlets stuffed under her coat. It was February, freezing cold, just a few weeks before the Czar's soldiers gunned down hundreds of protestors at the Winter Palace."

"Wow," Rosa had said.

"What happened to Grandma?" Esther asked.

Their grandmother was convicted of treason and exiled to Siberia. The girls loved the part of the story about how Tovah smuggled her sister out of the labor camp, in the bottom of a cart filled with firewood, pulled by their uncle's nasty-tempered mule. Esther studied the world map on her classroom wall; there was no way they could have traveled that far by mule cart. But Mama insisted. "That's how Leah came to America."

"Your grandmother was a freedom fighter," Pop said. "You should be proud."

"Where's Tovah now?" Esther asked in a small voice.

"There was typhus on the boat," was all Mama said.

"We gave you Tovah as a middle name, in honor of her," Pop added.

If only Grandma Leah were still alive. Maybe she could've helped explain to Mama and Pop what happened today. Esther rubbed Molly's back through the wrap cloth and entered the living room where her parents sat in deep silence on the sofa. The blank television was still pinging as the tube cooled. Mama's cheeks were shiny with tears.

"What were you thinking?" Pop asked without looking up. His hands lay in his lap, palms up, his arthritic fingers stiff and stained with shoe polish.

Esther stood facing her parents. "The cops were beating people. It was horrible and we *had* to do something."

"The cops are often brutal," Pop said. He looked up for a moment, then back down at his hands. "But I taught you girls to plan, to think, not to act crazy on some *cockamamie* impulse."

Esther wanted to explain that she hadn't wanted to do it either, that it was all Rosa's fault. But the sisters always stood together. "Rosa thinks it's an opportunity to educate people about Vietnam."

"Rosa thinks? What do *you* think?" her mother interrupted, jabbing her finger toward Esther's chest. "You have a baby. What about Molly?"

Esther hesitated. How would Rosa answer? "Isn't this what you guys always taught us?" she asked Pop. "When we see something wrong, don't we have to fight to change it, to make things better? Like you did when you fought for your union?"

How could Pop not understand?

He shook his head, hard. "We taught you girls to anticipate the effect of your actions. Not to act like hoodlums, assaulting an officer."

Molly squirmed and whimpered. Esther patted her back and jiggled side to side to comfort her.

"We didn't mean to hurt anyone. We had to stop the cops from beating innocent people." She wasn't good at this. Rosa was the one who argued with Pop.

When she and Rosa were younger, their family was all on the same side. Mama and Pop sent them to Loon Lake Camp every year to enjoy New England summers with other kids from left-wing families, kids like Allen and Jake. But when Rosa started college, she began quarreling with Pop about everything, from the revolutionary potential of students versus workers, to black power and guerrilla theater tactics. Mama and Esther tried to make peace between them, but they failed and the arguments raged. These days, when they were all together, Esther tried to redirect dinner table conversation to Molly, to what she and Rosa had been like as babies. It rarely worked; instead Pop and Rosa continued to fill the room with their loud voices until Esther and Jake made excuses about Molly's bedtime and escaped.

"Feh," Mama said. "All you've done is hurt that policeman. And yourselves. And Molly." She paused before adding, "Tell Jake I can watch the baby while he's at the hospital."

"We will do what we can to help," Pop said. "But you're in big trouble this time." His fingers clenched and unclenched. "Unless Rosa's lawyer boyfriend is pals with the judge."

Pop's right eye fluttered. Was that a wink, when he mentioned the judge? Esther searched her father's face. Maybe secretly he was on their side, but couldn't let Mama know because she was just too scared?

"We'll call your cousin Joel," Mama said. "He's a lawyer downtown."

"Allen is a great lawyer, Mama, and he's political. It'll be all right."

"Sometimes you can't make it right. You shouldn't have gone to that demonstration. You should have stayed home with Molly." Mama's voice was raspy and raw, her words dragged over glass shards. "Your Pop's right. This is big trouble."

Esther knew better than to talk back when Mama was in her dire-predictions-of-doom mood. No matter how innocent her sentence started out, somewhere between a daughter's lips and Mama's eardrum the words ignited and blazed. Usually Rosa was the flammable sister.

This time, maybe Mama was right.

Halfway down the block from the bus stop, Esther spotted the police car in front of her apartment. She hesitated, briefly considered turning around and—doing what? Running where? Two cops stepped from the cruiser and blocked the sidewalk, holding their billy clubs two-fisted, horizontal across their bodies at holster level. For one wild moment, Esther imagined they might twirl them like batons, toss them into the air like the girls on the high school team and catch them with split-second precision. Get real, she told herself. They're much more likely to smash your head with the wooden clubs. She swallowed a nervous gulp, circled her arms around Molly, pulling damp warmth against her chest, then walked toward the policemen.

The taller officer rested his left hand on his holster. "Esther Green?"

She nodded, pointed to his gun. "You don't need that."

He didn't move his hand. "You're coming with us to the station."

"I have to nurse my baby."

"Should've thought of your baby when you attacked that cop."

She opened her mouth to argue, then thought better of it. "Please?"

His partner shrugged. "You've got ten minutes. And we're coming in with you."

CHAPTER 4

Jake

The yellow kitten wove in and out around his ankles. Jake chugged stale coffee, read the instructions on the back of the spaghetti box, and worried. Esther's backpack was on the table and an uneaten tuna sandwich on the arm of the sofa. She must have already come home from the demonstration and gone out again, in a hurry. She usually left him a note. Something was wrong.

No doubt that something was connected to the two policemen who were waiting at the curb when he got home. They asked for Esther but wouldn't say what they wanted. When he looked through the slats of the Venetian blinds a moment before, their cruiser was still double-parked on the street below.

Should he start the spaghetti now, or wait for her to get back? He was famished; on surgery rotation he never managed lunch. He ate the sandwich, ignoring the places where the kitten had nibbled, and rummaged in the cupboard. Where did she keep the canned clams? When he heard the apartment door open, he tossed the box on the counter. Good, she could take over making dinner.

Two cops flanked Esther. Molly was fretful, working up to a meltdown. Jake looked from one officer to the other, then at Esther, trying to control his expression and his breathing.

"What's the problem?" he asked.

"Ask your wife," the tall cop answered.

"Help me with her." Esther struggled with the infant wrap. Maggie had learned to tie the *khanga* in the Peace Corps in Togo and insisted it was the best way to calm a fussy baby, but sometimes the fabric twisted with a diabolical mind of its own.

Jake extricated Molly while Esther settled in the rocking chair. "It's okay, Monkey," he whispered. "Dinner's coming." He turned to the cops guarding the doorway. "Would you give my wife some privacy while she nurses?"

The tall cop tapped his watch. "Ten minutes." He followed his partner into the living room.

Jake sank back against the counter. Dread found its familiar home in his stomach, where it roiled and soured on the brink of nausea. He opened his mouth, then closed it without speaking. He picked up the spaghetti box, stared at the gibberish instructions and then back at Esther.

"What happened?"

"I guess you didn't see the news." Esther reached for Jake's hand and pulled him close. "There was a street fight, mounted cops beating up demonstrators. It was awful. Rosa and I threw apples at them."

"Apples?"

"Little hard ones." She rested her head against Jake's hip. "We must've hit a horse. A cop was hurt."

Jake stared at his wife. That sounded like Rosa, but Esther?

"How did they know it was you?"

"A newspaper guy took our picture. It was on the news."

"Oh, baby. What's going to happen?"

"Don't know. I told Mama and Pop. They'll call some lawyer cousin. And Rosie went home to talk to Allen." Esther paused. "If I'm not back when you have to leave for work, call my mother. Or Mrs. B."

"Molly and I'll be okay. I'm worried about *you*." Jake kneeled on the floor next to the rocker and put his arms around her. Together they listened to Molly's small sounds, the sucks and sighs, until the tall cop appeared in the doorway.

"Time's up."

"But I only nursed on one side."

"Like I said, you should have thought of your kid before assaulting a police officer." He grabbed Esther's arm and pulled her up. "Let's go."

Esther kissed Molly's forehead and handed her to Jake. "She's probably still hungry. There's breast milk in the freezer. Then call Allen. He'll know what to do."

After Esther left, escorted by a cop at each elbow, Molly immediately began to fuss. Jake took a bottle of breast milk from the freezer, and put it in a pot of hot water to thaw. He paced with Molly, jiggling her as he circled the kitchen; sometimes that calmed her. This was all Rosa's fault. *She* could take risks. *She* didn't have a baby depending on her. Dragging Esther into this was reckless. Negligent, really. Just what you'd expect from Rosa.

Molly cried louder. She didn't usually need to be burped anymore, but he couldn't think of anything else to do while the milk thawed. Patting her back, he walked through the living room, kitchen, bedroom, then negotiated a tight turnaround in the little end room where Esther had pushed aside her paintings to make space for the crib they rarely used. The canvases were dusty and abandoned. He couldn't remember the last time he'd seen a work in progress on the easel. Certainly not since Molly was born, maybe not the whole pregnancy. But that wasn't Molly's fault; that was Rosa's influence. "You've got talent," Rosa had urged Esther. "Use it for the movement. Posters and T-shirts and banners change more minds than framed paintings hanging in a fancy museum."

Pacing the long hallway, he wondered if he should have insisted that Esther finish her art degree, even though it would have meant her staying in Ann Arbor while he moved to Detroit to start his residency. He had been relieved at her decision to move with him. His brain could master the science of medicine just fine, but his hands needed Esther's body to study the art of it. His fingers learned anatomy on her flesh. He explored the resistance of the veins inside her elbow for the best IV sites, palpated the bones and tendons of her ankle joints, investigated the valleys between her ribs for imaginary chest tube placement. Still, they could have managed it if Esther stayed in Ann Arbor that extra year; it wasn't like they had much time together anyway. By then, Rosa was already in Detroit with Allen. Maybe a year apart would have broken Rosa's spell and avoided this mess.

Molly's complaints escalated. Jake found a clean rubber nipple and attached it, then sprinkled a few drops of milk onto the inside of his wrist to test the temperature. He sank into the rocking chair with Molly.

No, if it hadn't been for Rosa, none of this mess today would have happened. Esther was usually reasonable and responsible. When she was under Rosa's influence, she became someone else, someone reckless, unpredictable. And look where that landed her.

Molly choked, coughed, and spit up onto Jake's shirt. Poor kid, she'd probably picked up on all the stress of the afternoon even though Esther had the sense to leave her at home. Babies were intuitive. Molly probably understood that their contented family life was threatened. Jake wiped her face with the kitchen towel, offered her the bottle again. This time she drank slowly, sucking herself to sleep in his arms. He put her in the cradle in their bedroom and rocked her.

"Don't worry, Monkey," he whispered. "Nothing bad will happen. I won't let it," he promised.

Big talker, he scolded himself. A stronger man would have intervened, not just watched the cops take his wife away. Allen would have done something. What right did *he* have to promise his daughter anything? His promise was worthless. Bad things happened to little kids, all the time.

No. He stopped himself. In comparison to meningococcemia or malignant brain tumors, how bad could this be, throwing apples at cops? Still, he dreaded telling Esther's parents that she'd been taken downtown, presumably arrested.

First he'd figure out that spaghetti. One of these days, after he finished his residency and had a real job, he'd learn to cook. Once he had some food in his stomach, once he could think straight, he'd phone Allen, see what wisdom Rosa's legal eagle had to offer. Then he'd call Esther's parents, reassure them that Esther and Rosa would be fine. He'd make arrangements for Molly. It would probably all be settled by tomorrow.

CHAPTER 5

Esther

Rosa was already in the holding cell, pacing back and forth across the cement floor. Esther sank onto the metal bench and let her face fall into her hands.

"I can't believe this. What's going to happen?"

"They'll arraign us," Rosa said. "Probably tomorrow morning, Allen thinks. Then we'll post bail and go home." Rosa sat down, tucked one foot under her bottom and swiveled to face Esther. She put her hands on Esther's shoulders and looked into her face. "Don't worry. We've got some good ideas about our defense."

"Not that," Esther said. "I mean what will *happen* to us? Will we go to prison? I have Molly, remember?"

"Lots of women with children go to prison." Rosa waved her hand at the five other female prisoners, dressed in tight miniskirts and low-cut blouses. "I bet some of these women have kids." She frowned. "I wonder why they segregated us from the other demonstrators."

Esther didn't care about the other demonstrators or the other women. She slipped her hand under her T-shirt and touched the tight ache in her right breast, hard with milk. "I feel so damned lopsided. If I try to stand up, I'll tip over sideways."

"What?"

"The cops only let Molly nurse on one side. They said she was taking too long."

Rosa finger-combed the snarls in Esther's hair. "Calm down. Our job now is to develop a strategy. To contrast this one injured cop with thousands of mangled and murdered Vietnamese people."

"But what if Jake hadn't been home? What if he was on call tonight? What would have happened to Molly?" Esther sniffed the stale urine scent and her eyes filled. The cell was no place for a baby.

Rosa drummed her fists against her thighs in a rapid beat. "I wish Allen would get here so we can start working. He promised to bring one of the senior attorneys in on this. Someone really political, I told him. And not a white male."

"I talked to Pop." Esther stroked Rosa's arm, feeling the small bumps of gooseflesh. Rosa couldn't be chilly in this steam bath, and how on earth could she be excited? But skin didn't lie. Esther pulled back, rubbed her hand on her jeans. "Pop will find a lawyer, someone who can get us out quick."

"Allen's got this. You know his father was in prison for a few years when he was a kid and Allen survived, didn't he? The important thing now is to bring the war home, make people pay attention." Rosa pressed her lips into a determined line.

Whenever Rosa made that face, Esther and her parents would exchange looks, half-warning and half-amused. Esther had no patience now for Rosa's disappearing lips. She crossed her arms over her chest, pushed against the sore breast. "You don't understand. I have a baby."

"Listen." Rosa stroked Esther's cheek. "I want to go home too. I feel like I'm going to barf any second. I promise you we'll get out of here and you'll get back to Molly and the four of us will work together, just like we always have."

They *had* been a good team. Esther was the youngest, the last of the four to get to Ann Arbor, but she fit right into the daily routine of handing out flyers to students crossing the Diag between classes, of planning rallies and organizing teach-ins. She loved the intense atmosphere of the

Fishbowl, the glassed-in lobby of the social sciences building where competing political factions set up literature tables and argued vigorously. Her art classes were fine, but the real education was the politics, learning to analyze what was happening in the world, talking to students about how to end the war and fight racism. It was Rosa and Esther, always together, and Jake and Allen, right there with them. It would be wonderful to feel that certain again, about how to make things right in the world.

The sisters dozed on and off all night in the cell, leaning against each other to minimize touching the slimy damp of the cement wall. Esther's full breast alternately throbbed and dripped.

In the morning, two cops escorted Rosa and Esther to conference with their lawyers before their arraignment. Allen and Jake met them at the door, Molly in Jake's arms.

A guard shook his head at Jake. "No kids."

The other guard pursed his lips into a fish-face for Molly. "I've got a six-month-old at home," he told Esther, then turned to his partner. "Ease up. It can't hurt."

"Tell that to Steele. I bet he knows about hurt." But he turned away and didn't stop Esther, Molly, and Jake from joining Rosa and Allen at the table with the two lawyers.

Esther winced at the initial sharp pain of Molly's suck, followed by waves of relief as her milk let down. She nodded to Dwayne, the lawyer from Allen's firm. Allen said Dwayne was smart, but he didn't look impressive. Under his rumpled jacket, his white shirt was coming untucked. At least Joel, the downtown lawyer Pop hired, looked the part in his crisp three-piece suit. Joel was a distant relative, the son of Uncle Max's cousin. When Esther moved back home to Detroit, Mama had tried to persuade her to take a typing job at his office instead of working at the cooperative bookstore. Mama said Joel was smart, but she trusted him because he was family. Esther hoped he knew more than business law and tax loopholes.

Esther twisted one of Molly's wispy red curls around her index finger, while the unfamiliar legal phrases tumbled senselessly in the air. She concentrated on the pull of Molly's mouth, rhythmic as tides, and on Jake's hand on her back, his fingers circling the hard knob of each vertebra. Across the scarred wooden table, Rosa and Allen huddled with Dwayne and Joel, arguing about coercive charges. Whatever those were.

Finally Esther held up her hand. "Slow down, guys. I'm lost." She turned to Joel. "What happens now?"

"You'll hear the full indictments and enter a plea of not guilty. Later, Dwayne and I will meet with the prosecution team and work out a deal."

"No deals," Rosa said. "Allen, tell Esther about the necessity defense."

Allen turned to Esther and Jake. "In certain circumstances the court will accept the argument that a person may violate the law in order to prevent injury. Rosa thinks that she can convince a jury that your action was justified by the necessity of drawing attention to the genocide of the Vietnamese people."

Dwayne shook his head. "Won't work. The only way to win with the necessity defense is to prove that your action prevented imminent harm. Not potential damage at some unspecified time to unnamed foreigners halfway across the world. I suppose you might be able to make a case that stopping the mounted police was necessary to prevent harm to the *demonstrators*. But not to the Vietnamese."

"The harm is damn imminent for the Vietnamese," Rosa said.

"That's not what he means." Allen rested his index finger gently across her lips and Rosa didn't slap him away or yell at him. Amazing how her fiery sister would accept disagreement from Allen that no one else would dare offer.

Esther reached for Jake's hand under the table. He hadn't spoken a word during the meeting, but she could feel his anxiety. Jake's younger brother died of leukemia when he was five and the family never recovered. Jake rarely talked about it, but sometimes his little boy fears seemed to take over. "The world can be a monstrous place," he had told Esther once when she called him an old worrywart. Molly wasn't the only one who needed her at home.

This situation would make anyone into a worrywart. When they were led into the courtroom, Esther ran the palm of her hand along the curved grain of the railing, imagining all the people who had sat on these benches. The dark oak was sticky and swollen in the humid August air.

Esther and Rosa stood facing the judge, Allen between them, and flanked by the other lawyers. Esther kept sneaking glances at Jake sitting two rows back, rocking Molly against his chest, back and forth on the wooden bench. The arraignment seemed perfunctory and pale compared to the moment she could hold her daughter again.

Then the clerk started reading the charges. "Assault, with an enhanced penalty for interfering with a police officer in the performance of his duty. Reckless endangerment in the first degree, creating a grave risk of death."

Esther felt slapped. The other times they'd been busted, there had just been one or two charges, like trespassing or criminal mischief.

"They're throwing the book at you," Allen whispered. "It's all about intimidation, so you'll plead to lesser charges."

It's working, Esther thought.

When the charge of conspiracy was read, the lawyers exchanged glances. But Esther couldn't ask what that meant, because then she heard the charge of attempted murder and she had to grip the railing. Attempted murder? They didn't try to kill anyone. The courtroom air grew heavy. What could the penalties be for those charges? Reckless endangerment couldn't be too bad, but conspiracy? Attempted murder? She shivered in the warm room, then leaned slightly forward to see her sister. Rosa stood stalwart facing the judge, dwarfed by the tall witness boxes. Allen's hand was steady on the tender curve at the small of her back. Rosa's face was pale under her red hair, her eyes closed, hand covering her mouth.

"Esther, he's asking for your plea," Joel whispered in her ear. "Say 'not guilty.' You can change it later, if you want to. After we hear what they offer."

"Not guilty," she said.

"I'm going to expedite this case," the judge said. "Motions due in two weeks. Trial to start the third Monday in November."

CHAPTER 6

Rosa

"Don't worry. We'll figure this out." Rosa led Esther and Jake into the living room. She lifted a stack of heavy books sprouting yellow lined papers from the sofa and looked around for a place to put them. Similar piles lined the top of the bookshelves, jammed between empty Chianti bottles with candle stubs and drips of hardened wax.

"There's no place to sit, Allen," she called. "Come move your mess."

"It just *looks* disorganized." Allen grabbed the files and glared at Rosa on his way to the den.

"Should I put the barley in the oven to heat up?" Without waiting for an answer, Esther took the casserole from Jake and walked into the kitchen.

Rosa followed her. "Need anything?"

"A potholder?"

Rosa used a dishtowel to make room in the oven. She hoped Esther appreciated the effort she'd made with this meal. A whole chicken sizzled, surrounded by roasting potatoes and carrots and onions. That was as domestic as she got. The four of them used to eat together frequently—spontaneous meals of pasta or stir fry prepared between an afternoon of writing leaflets and an evening meeting—while they argued tactics or danced around the kitchen to the Supremes. That happened rarely now. This time Rosa had called two days ahead of time to invite them and suggested a babysitter for Molly so they could focus on the issues without interruption. She even borrowed a tablecloth from Mama.

She'd been making an effort to be patient with Esther, too. In the two weeks since their arraignment, she called her sister every day. "What are you thinking about the trial?" she'd ask. Or, "Listen to this about the necessity defense. I think we've got a good chance." Esther appeared to listen, but she didn't seem convinced, no matter how compelling Rosa's arguments, how relevant the case law. Tomorrow morning the DA expected Esther's decision about her plea. Tonight was Rosa's last chance to change her sister's mind.

Allen handed a glass of wine to Esther, another to Rosa.

"Cheers." Allen raised his glass and clicked it against Jake's coffee mug.

Rosa smiled at the two men. Best friends since summer camp, but so different. Skinny Jake, hair thinning on top even at seventeen, had always been brainy and quiet. Burly Allen, sporting a beard in defiance of camp rules, had been too heavy to be a stellar athlete, but was still the first person chosen for Capture the Flag teams.

"To ending the war. And to working together," Rosa added, clinking her glass to the others. "We're family. You guys are practically brothers."

"I could use a brother," Jake said. "These charges are scary."

"They're *trying* to scare us," Rosa said, leaning forward. "Which is why it's so important to fight back. What are you going to tell the DA tomorrow, Esther?"

Jake answered quickly. "Joel recommends that Esther take the DA's offer. Plead guilty to the lesser charges. Pay the fine and get on with her life. Our lives."

"If you do that," Rosa said, "you'll have to testify against me."

Esther buried her face in Jake's neck. Allen frowned at Rosa and stood up. "Let's eat. I'm starving."

Rosa tried to look apologetic. She'd promised Allen to go slow, not push Esther too hard. But she couldn't help it. This was too important. Still, he was probably right. "Sorry. I'll put the food out."

"Can I help?" Jake stood up.

Rosa noted Esther's small smile. Their women's group had spent the entire last meeting discussing the politics of housework. Rosa insisted that men must be *forced* into doing their share of laundry and cooking and cleaning. "You wouldn't expect slave owners to volunteer to help in the fields, would you?" Esther argued that their men weren't slave owners and they could change. She must've primed Jake to prove her point.

"Listen," Rosa said when they were seated around the table. "Our defense is much stronger if we stick together. I want a jury trial. I *know* I can make people on a jury understand."

"It's all about you, isn't it?" Esther passed the platter of chicken to Jake. "What I want, what I *need*, is to take care of Molly."

"Don't you understand? This is about more than one baby." She reached across the table and seized Esther's chin, capturing her gaze. "I can't believe you won't fight this with me. Won't stand up for the principle. Don't you remember our vow?"

How could Esther forget the final night of their last summer together at camp, when the four of them met at midnight at the Peace Crane sculpture? They pledged to dedicate their lives to each other and to changing the world—joining with their parents, Leah, and all the other freedom fighters through history.

"Of course I remember, but this is different." Esther whipped her head side to side, trying to loosen Rosa's grip. "What's the principle here? Our inalienable right to hurt horses and cops? Besides, sometimes you have to compromise."

Rosa refused to let go of Esther's chin, not when her sister was breaking her heart. She pushed back tears and tried to control her voice. "You can't compromise about the war."

"And you can't bully me into this." Esther swatted Rosa's hand away, then reached for her glass.

Rosa watched Esther's hand tremble, sloshing the red liquid against the glass. This must be hard for her too. Maybe her mind wasn't totally made up. If only Rosa could find the right argument to convince her.

"So every woman with a baby abandons the movement?" Rosa said, trying to keep her tone low-key. "That's it? No more activism, no more responsibility for changing the world? Just changing diapers?"

Rosa felt a little guilty saying that. She could see how Esther struggled trying to balance Molly and meetings. Maybe she herself didn't make it easier, always pointing it out when Esther begged off an action, instead of offering to help with childcare. In the future, she would help more. But this trial was different. Esther had to understand. They *had* to work together on this.

"I'm not talking about everyone," Esther said. "Just about what feels right for me. And I'm not abandoning the movement, you know. I'm just choosing to avoid prison. Not all activists have to go to jail. Besides, we're guilty, remember? We did it. Don't you ever think about that cop?"

Of course Rosa thought about the cop. And these days her emotions seemed to be on heightened alert. She teared up at the smallest things. "I try not to," she said. "The cops were brutal and we had to act."

"Get real." Jake jabbed his finger, glistening with chicken grease, at Rosa. "You think you're Bernardine Dohrn or Angela Davis? Well, you're not."

"I wish I were! They make a big difference. I bet *their* families are proud of their actions."

Jake's laugh was rough. "You didn't bomb a napalm lab or defend the barricades in Paris or storm the Pentagon, Rosa. You're proud of throwing rocks?"

"Apples."

"Apples. At a horse, a poor dumb beast. Street fighting like a thug is nothing to be proud of."

"Not street fighting, exactly. More like a spontaneous act of rebellion, motivated by profound love for the Vietnamese people."

"Get a grip, Rosa. You're not Che either." Jake swiped at the grease on his hand.

Damn him. Jake could be so condescending. "*You* get a grip, *Doctor.* This is serious stuff. The DA takes it seriously. Look at the charges."

"The charges do increase the political significance." Allen's voice was low, soothing. Under the table, he rested his hand on Rosa's thigh. "Conspiracy is what they charge when they really want to nail you big time. We could set important legal precedent here."

"Precedent?" Jake said. "For the right to throw apples?"

"I'm talking about political targeting," Allen said. "Because Rosa and Esther are known activists, leaders in the movement. Plus, we do have some other investigatory avenues to explore, things that could blow holes in their case."

Jake looked skeptical. "Like what?"

"Like the photographer, the hero of the day, sitting across the street. If it was so clear to him what Rosa and Esther were doing, why didn't he try to stop them? Or warn the cops? See, he didn't take it too seriously either, until the horse was hit and the officer thrown. That might help us." Allen helped himself to more barley casserole.

"You can't have it both ways." Esther pushed her plate away. "One minute, you're acting out of revolutionary fervor to save the defenseless protestors against the armed cops. In the next breath, it's just a little tossed apple, Officer, merely a prank. Which one is it, Rosa?"

"Whatever it takes. This is war."

"I don't want war," Esther said. "War is what we're *against.*"

It's not that simple, Rosa thought. Sometimes the battleground felt so big it made her chest ache. How could they ever right all the wrongs? Maybe Esther was right—maybe she *was* trying to do too much. But how did you choose what to fight? And how did you accept giving up some battles? It made her stomach clutch and dive, and for a moment she thought she would throw up all over the faded lilacs on Mama's best tablecloth. She took slow, shallow breaths, and tried to make her voice quiet.

"We don't have to agree about everything, Esther. Let's just stick together, like we always do."

"You mean, let's do it your way." Esther folded her napkin and tucked it under the edge of her plate. "I can't do that. Not anymore. Not with Molly."

CHAPTER 7

Esther

The afternoon before Rosa's trial, Esther answered a knock at the apartment door to find Maggie brushing a frosting of snow from her hair. Her smile looked as bogus as a snowman's crooked grin of pebbles.

The morning after the awful dinner at Rosa and Allen's apartment, Esther had changed her plea to guilty and accepted District Attorney Turner's deal. In the two months since, she barely left the house except for her part-time job at the bookstore, where she was assigned to unpack boxes rather than sell books at the counter. She stayed home from the weekly women's group meetings and she hadn't heard a single word from Maggie or any of the other women in the SDS collective. She tried not to blame Maggie for her silence; everyone knew Maggie was Rosa's best friend. Just a few months ago, Esther had thought Maggie was her best friend, too.

"I guess sisterhood isn't *that* powerful," Jake had observed. Esther argued with him, but her heart wasn't in it. Maybe he was right.

Maggie wiped her glasses on her scarf, succeeding only in smearing them. "Hey. Can I come in?"

Esther took a step back so Maggie could enter. Esther touched her finger to her lips. "Molly's sleeping."

Maggie nodded and followed Esther silently into the living room.

At least that response was better than Rosa, who usually raised her voice at the request to be quieter, insisting that babies had to learn to sleep through talking and music and meetings.

"How's Molly doing?"

What kind of answer did Maggie want, pleasant or honest? Esther sat at one end of the sofa hugging a hand-me-down pillow with orange blossoms. "Fine. She's crawling. Still not sleeping all night, though." Maggie loved kids, claimed that the only negative to being a dyke was the difficulty making babies. But she hadn't come over to discuss Molly's developmental milestones. "What's up?"

Maggie rearranged herself at the other end of the sofa, tucking one leg under her. The tip of her tongue peeked between her top and bottom teeth, like it always did when she was nervous. "I can't stand this," she said.

You can't stand it? Esther wished she could sob her misery into her old friend's arms. She didn't trust herself to speak past the lump in her throat, so she just shrugged and waited for Maggie to continue.

"This is really hard. I'm sorry that my support for Rosa means not being here for you. I want to help."

"Help *me*?"

"Both of you. Rosa is just as miserable as you are. Not that she'd ever show it."

"Did she send you here?"

Maggie shook her head emphatically. "She'd be furious. This is my idea, because I want you and Rosa to work this out. So you don't have to testify against her tomorrow."

Esther put her foot on the rocking chair next to the sofa and pushed. The squeak of the springs, rusty under the denim-patched pillow, was loud in the silent room. Soon Maggie would leave and Molly would wake up from her nap. Esther would bundle her in the plush rose-colored snowsuit with bunny ears that Mama bought in preparation for Molly's first Michigan winter. Dressing a baby girl in pink was conforming to gender stereotypes, but Esther loved the slippery feel of the fabric and the hopeful color. They would walk to the neighborhood park and Molly would ride the baby swing, squealing with delight at every rise and fall of the arc.

"Is there anything I can do?" Maggie asked.

"Talk to Rosa, because she's the only one with a choice now. I have to tell the truth about what happened. I mean, how can that be wrong, telling the truth? We *did* it, you know?"

"Rosa sees it as a betrayal. Besides, is there only one truth here? There are no possible nuances of motivation or necessity?"

Esther let herself sink back into the sofa, so weary. If only she could disappear into the lumpy old stuffing. "The truth is that we caused an accident and a cop was hurt."

"He's not hurt that bad. Rosa says that—"

"He's paralyzed," Esther interrupted. "That's pretty bad. Listen, I know you want to help. And I know Rosa is a force of nature. It's impossible to say no to her. If I didn't have Molly, I probably couldn't do it. But I do have Molly, and I'm going to tell the truth tomorrow."

"Can't you try one more time to talk with each other?"

Trying to talk with Rosa when she was determined was a complete waste of time. Maggie must know that after all these years. Feeling so isolated and alone these days, Esther was growing equally as resolute. Whenever she pictured her sister, she saw the black and white television image of Rosa's face. An ashen oval framed by high voltage hair.

Esther shook her head. "Won't do any good."

"She'll never forgive you." Maggie's mouth moved stiffly, as if forming the words took great effort.

Esther stood up. "I know that."

"Please try once more." Maggie was begging. "I'm scared. If anyone can persuade Rosa, it's you."

How peculiar that Maggie would say that. She was usually so smart about people. Esther never had much influence over Rosa. She had always been the little tag-along, the follower, the faithful sidekick. And now, when the stakes were so high for both of them, Esther felt even smaller. No. Despite Maggie's wishful thinking, Esther had absolutely no influence on her big sister.

Esther spoke before Jake was through the door. "Maggie was here today."

"What did she want?" Jake tossed his coat on the rocking chair and leaned down to kiss Molly's forehead.

"Just for me to change my mind and not testify tomorrow."

"Great, so they slap you in jail? You've got a deal with the DA. Does Maggie remember that detail?"

Esther didn't answer.

"Did Rosa send her?"

"Maggie claims not. She says Rosa is miserable."

Jake sat on the sofa and put his arms around Esther, gathering her and Molly against his body. "I hope she is. Serves her right, treating you like a traitor."

"Rosa can't help it. She can't believe that anyone, me or you or Allen or Maggie or anyone, could disagree with her on something this important. I admire that about her, how unshakeable she is."

"Well, I don't." Jake emptied his pockets onto the coffee table. Stethoscope, reflex hammer, dog-eared laminated card with pediatric emergency dosages, two-inch tall blue plastic monkey that opened its arms and legs and squawked when you squeezed its back. At the sound, Molly opened her eyes, pulled away from Esther's nipple, and reached for the monkey.

"*You're* the Monkey," Jake said to Molly. "Let me wash this first, then you can play."

"Well, I do admire her," Esther repeated, loud enough for Jake to hear over the splash of the kitchen faucet. "I just wish she didn't demand everyone's agreement."

"Everyone's obedience, more like it." Jake squeezed the monkey twice and handed it to Molly, who brought it to her mouth and sucked on the head. "I can't believe you guys come from the same parents. How did you turn out so different? She's warped."

Esther shrugged. "She thinks I'm the one who's warped."

"Well, I'm starved." Jake held out his arms to Molly. "I'll play with her while you make dinner. And tomorrow we'll see what the jury thinks about who's warped."

It's not the jury's opinion I care about, Esther realized as she opened the refrigerator for the leftover brown rice.

When she heard Jake and Molly's laughter from the living room, Esther dialed Rosa's number. The empty rings of the telephone echoed in the dark hallway.

CHAPTER 8

Rosa

"One more word from you and I'll hold you in contempt of court."

The judge's words landed like spittle on Rosa's cheeks. She ached to wipe her face. Instead she sat up straight in the witness stand, willing her hands to stay clenched in her lap. She returned his stare, imagining her own olive skin facing off against his purple complexion. Maybe he would burst a blood vessel. Imagining that worked better than picturing him walking naked down the street, the emperor without clothes—that's what her lawyer suggested if she felt intimidated by the courtroom ceremony, the robes and office. But she would *not* be intimidated.

She ignored the judge's threat and turned to the jury, trying to keep her voice even and reasonable. "It's not just me on trial here. Our *country* is on trial. Because our rich and powerful nation, built on principles of freedom, is committing genocide in Southeast Asia."

The judge banged his gavel.

"I am a citizen." Rosa did not shout. She kept her gaze on the members of the jury. "I have the right to speak."

The bailiff smothered her words. His hand was thick and sprouted coarse dark hairs. She tore it away from her face and yelled, "The citizens are against this war. You can lock me up, but you can't jail dissent!"

Two officers dragged her from the courtroom into a small room.

She put her head down on the metal table and bit her lip to keep from sobbing. She needed a clear head to figure this out. It was no big surprise that District Attorney Arnold Turner was prosecuting her case personally. He was running for Congress on a law and order campaign. Convicting her and scoring a stiff sentence would win votes. Allen seemed to think that was a bad omen, but Rosa was elated.

"See, Turner is ambitious, and he sees this case as important. People are watching us," she argued with Allen and Dwayne at the lunch break. "Our action was small, but it had big consequences. We can make important points here about the war."

But each day of the trial, the judge looked more sour. Each day DA Turner's expression grew more confident, his smile wider, his gestures more flamboyant. Her own lawyer seemed to shrink, his sandy hair and pale skin fading into the blond oak of the defense table. He dug the knuckle of his right index finger into the soft flesh near the corner of his mouth, chewing the inside of his cheek.

In their apartment that night, she raged at Allen. "Dwayne is a spineless chicken. Can't you get Kenny Cockrel, or someone like that?"

"Dwayne is trying to get you off, Rosie," Allen pleaded. "You're being unreasonable."

"You can worry about reason. I care about justice."

"These charges are *serious*." Allen rubbed his hands over his beard, and she thought she saw him roll his eyes, too.

Was even Allen giving up on her? She understood that there was a fine line between standing strong and sounding self-righteous, pompous, even. But sometimes the old slogans were all that kept her going. She let her head rest on his shoulder.

"I know they are," she whispered. "And I'm scared."

The charges weren't the only serious problem. She had missed three periods. She'd been too busy to mark the calendar, so it could have been more. It was probably just all the stress. The trial wasn't going well and she was the problem. She knew that. Dwayne kept advising her to control her face, to stop interrupting Turner's theatrical declarations about conspiracies and traitors and giving aid to the enemy. But she *couldn't* keep quiet when the DA lied.

At the lunch break on day three, Allen put his hands on Rosa's shoulders. "This is bad. And the worst testimonies will come tomorrow: the crippled cop's and Esther's. So, you'd better decide right now. You can minimize the damage. Or you can make political pronouncements. Your choice."

Her choice? The jury seemed to have already decided. None of them would meet her eyes. They didn't seem interested in the plight of Vietnamese peasants, only concerned about one injured police officer. Maybe her best option was skipping out. Leaving town. Disappearing.

She hadn't decided yet, but she definitely needed more information. She used the public phone in the back hallway to call the number Tim Wright had provided. That evening, Dwayne and Allen worked late at their office preparing for the next day in court. Rosa was supposed to join them. Instead, she changed into a black tee and long black skirt and slipped out of the apartment, climbing through the side window that opened into the narrow alleyway.

Catching the hem of her skirt on the window latch, she lurched forward and scraped her knee on the brick wall. She bit her lower lip to keep from crying out and stood still for a moment in the near darkness, blotting the pinpoints of seeping blood with the cotton skirt. Then she crept quietly around the trash cans at the rear of the apartment complex and through the thick rhododendron bushes into the next street. She was pretty sure the plainclothes cop in the dark green sedan didn't see her leave.

Her contact was waiting as promised at the back door of the Black Orchid Café. He leaned against the chipped brick wall, long legs in Frye boots. They sat in his rusted Toyota, with The Doors singing loud on the radio, and pretended to neck while he went over the instructions. She hadn't decided whether to disappear, but she memorized his words.

"You won't be able to come back here," he said. "To Michigan. For any reason."

She stared at the brown birthmark on his cheek, a splash of milky coffee, hoping an onlooker would interpret her disbelief as passion. "Never?"

"Never."

Her stomach clenched. She took shallow breaths so she wouldn't vomit. She had to get out of there, into fresh air. "I'll let you know tomorrow."

The next morning, Rosa looked around the courtroom and forced herself to face the truth. This trial was a losing game, played entirely by the prosecution's rules, with all the cards stacked in their favor. Allen was right. It was going to be a bad day: the photographer, the injured cop, and Esther. Her parents sat expressionless in the third row, their shoulders just touching. Esther wasn't with them. They must be keeping her separate, so she couldn't listen to the testimony.

Esther hadn't spoken to her in weeks. It felt like betrayal, but Rosa knew that wasn't really what Esther *meant*. Rosa kept thinking back, remembering all their political work together—camp and Ann Arbor and everything. Didn't Esther feel just as strongly as she did about what they were trying to accomplish? Maybe it was Rosa's own fault for keeping their cousin Danny's secret, trying to shield Esther from the truth.

Rosa had never shared Danny's last letter with anyone: not Esther, not his parents or sister Deborah. Nobody. Written just days before he died, it was smuggled out of Vietnam by a buddy who delivered it in person months later. Rosa could barely recognize Danny in that letter, describing incidents that never made it into the newspapers. How the US soldiers threw wounded Vietnamese women from their helicopters and watched the bodies tumble into the jungle below. How they tossed handfuls of candy from their truck to the village children running alongside, timing it so that the kids were run over by the next vehicle in the convoy.

In the last paragraph, Danny admitted he was hooked on heroin. Danny, who would never even smoke weed, was shooting heroin two or three times a day. Dope was everywhere, he wrote, easier to score than chewing gum, and it made the bad images recede into the jungle. He had gone to the military shrink for help. But there was no methadone. No treatment. No help.

Maybe she should have shared his letter. At the time she told herself she was protecting Esther. Now she wondered if she was protecting herself because of how mean she had been to Danny about going to war.

Elbows planted on the oak table, Rosa rested her head in her hands. When she tried to imagine going away and never coming home, her head spun. The courtroom swelled and vibrated in orange waves. She was queasy all the time now. She pictured Mama and Pop losing their bail money and she almost threw up. She hated deceiving Allen, but her Black Orchid contact warned that if Allen knew her plans he would be an accomplice. He could be charged as an accessory and slapped with a year or two.

Never come back?

Still, it was probably better than waiting around for the inevitable verdict. She looked up as the bailiff's barbed wire voice called Esther to the stand.

CHAPTER 9

Esther

"Don't mess up," Joel Mattson told Esther in the witness waiting area. "Your suspended sentence is contingent on your cooperation today."

She tried to listen, but a black speck was lodged between the lawyer's front teeth. A poppy seed, or a fragment of pepper from a polished brass pepper mill twisted over a white tablecloth at some ritzy restaurant? Lunch paid for by her legal fees, by Mama and Pop. Esther tried not to dislike him. After all, he was family. It wasn't his fault that she was about to testify against Rosa.

"Why can't I sit inside?" she asked him. "Listen to the trial?"

"You're sequestered until after your testimony. So that you aren't influenced by what other witnesses say."

"I'm going to tell the truth no matter what anyone else says."

Joel seemed clueless about how much she dreaded this day. "Everyone's nervous," he told her, but Esther knew differently. Her feelings went way beyond nervous. What did Joel know anyway? His legal practice was mostly real estate closings and wills.

Concentrate, Esther told herself.

Rosa always accused her of daydreaming. She didn't understand that when an artist daydreamed, it wasn't the same as goofing off. When Esther daydreamed, her imagination shifted into sixth gear and carried her into a zone where textures and shapes and colors shimmered. In that place, with her senses open wide and ultra-sharp, ordinary life was transformed into contours that became images and drawings.

Of course, Rosa had an answer for that too.

"You're not even doing art anymore," she had accused Esther on the day she accepted the District Attorney's deal. "You're not an artist or an activist. You're just a cow."

Esther knew that Rosa didn't really mean that; she was just angry. Everyone knew that breastfeeding was best for the baby and for the ecology of the world, plus it was way cheaper than formula. But she had to admit that Rosa had a point. Esther still cared about the war, and justice, but these days she thought about changing the world so that babies wouldn't have to grow up and go halfway around the world to kill other children. She would probably become one of those women who joined Another Mother for Peace, or even the League of Women Voters, instead of being a revolutionary like Rosa.

"DA Turner is calling for you, Esther." Joel touched her arm. "You're on."

The room spun when she stood up and she grabbed the table. Joel took her arm. "I know this is hard for you," he said. "And you might be thinking about changing your testimony. So I should mention one new thing, just a rumor, really, but I heard that if you back out, Turner plans to claim that it was *your* apple that actually hit Officer Steele's horse. He has some witness who'll say that. I heard it might be Rosa, but like I said, just a rumor."

Esther shook her head. "I'm screwed whatever I do. Don't worry. I won't change my mind. I'm telling the truth about what we did."

Courtroom 404 was in the new wing of the courthouse. The amphitheater-style room had a modern, airy feel. It could have been a classroom, an Intro to Sociology lecture. Esther had expected mahogany paneling and heavy drapes the color of dried blood.

From her seat in the witness box, the jurors looked somber. Their faces were closed up tight with lips pinched and eyes blank or looking away. Esther searched the rows. What did these citizens think about the war? Could they imagine being in a crowd marching down a hot street, fighting to change the world? One juror looked like a friend from her eleventh grade gym class, a girl who barely opened her mouth to smile or speak because her teeth were so crooked. Even her friend-lookalike wouldn't meet Esther's gaze.

Rosa sat at the defense table between Allen and Dwayne, refusing to look in the direction of the witness box. Good thing, because Esther didn't think she could hold her gaze if their eyes met. Rosa's lawyer must have given her the same speech Joel recited, about how dressing conventionally in court made a good impression on the jury. Rosa wore a white blouse under a loose blue cotton jumper. Her hair was gathered in a matching grosgrain ribbon and she had attached a gold circle pin to the rounded Peter Pan collar.

Aunt Miriam and Uncle Max gave Rosa that pin for her thirteenth birthday, wrapped in pink flowered paper. Uncle Max had raised his eyebrows and announced that if she had a Bat Mitzvah, her gift would have been a fat check. For once, Rosa managed to ignore the taunt. She thanked them for the gift, rolling her eyes when Aunt Miriam said Rosa should try to be a real lady like her cousin Deborah. "Nothing looks as sweet and innocent as a circle pin," Aunt Miriam had said. That evening, Rosa tossed the pin into the tumble of discarded comic books in her top bureau drawer, along with the panty girdle from Aunt Miriam the year before, still in its cellophane wrapper.

Esther stifled a smile. If the jury had X-ray vision, if they could see beyond the gold-plated circle, through the blue jumper and cotton blouse, they would be shocked. Because tattooed on Rosa's left breast was a small red star, a quarter-inch in diameter. Esther knew that tattoo well; it was the twin of hers. Getting matching tattoos had been Rosa's idea, two summers before when they hitchhiked to San Francisco with Maggie.

At first Esther had been appalled. "Tattoos are for sailors and gang members."

"That's going to change," Rosa said. "You'll see. These tattoos will identify us as revolutionaries, will prove our commitment to the whole world."

Esther had giggled. "To whatever subset of the world we show our tits."

Maggie had tried to reason with them about dirty instruments and infection and self-mutilation, but Esther didn't worry about pain or disease. She just wanted to capture the delicious moment and make it last.

A tattoo is forever, she had thought. Like a sister.

After Esther was sworn in, the DA stood in front of her for several seconds without speaking. Close-up, Esther could see the violet veins snaking under the skin of his nose, the kind of complexion that would have evoked a nudge in the ribs from Mama, with a whispered reference to excessive drinking. She searched the gallery for Mama and Pop and Jake but couldn't find them.

"Mrs. Green, please describe to the jury the events of August 17, 1968," the DA said. "Take your time, and tell us everything that happened."

How could she explain to these strangers how alive she felt marching down Woodward Ave. with thousands of demonstrators, how simultaneously exhausted and flooded with energy? Each time she tried to lock eyes with one of her peers on the jury, they looked away, toward the lawyers or the judge or Exhibit A, an enlargement of the photograph placed on the easel at the front of the courtroom. Esther had never seen it so large, easily four feet square, so that every detail was blown-up out of normal context. It was a little grainy, but there was no doubt about the identity of the two young women standing with arms outstretched, hands open, fingers extended. There was no doubt that they had just thrown something. In the smaller photograph, the one that had been shown on television and printed in the newspapers, Esther had never noticed the sheen of wetness that gleamed on her cheeks.

She had not seen that her eyes were squeezed tight, but Rosa's were wide open and luminous, ignited by the afternoon sunlight.

Esther tore her gaze from the photograph. "Rosa and I could smell tear gas during the march. So when we got to Kennedy Square, we went with our friend Maggie to the first aid tent, to see if they needed help."

"That would be Margaret Sternberg?" the DA asked.

"Yes. She was trained as a medic."

"What did you find at the first aid tent?"

"A young man bleeding from his head."

"What happened next?"

"The injured guy said that mounted police were beating protesters on Grand River."

"Please simply describe what you saw, Mrs. Green, without hearsay or opinions."

"I *saw* him bleeding. I *heard* him ask the medics to go help his friends on Grand River. Maggie said she'd go, and my sister and I went along to help."

"That's Rosa Levin, the defendant?"

"Yes." Esther glanced at Rosa. Rosa wouldn't look at her.

"What did you see when you got to Grand River?"

Esther remembered the scene frozen into a painting. It had been an afternoon of strong colors—the blue and white city cruiser with spinning roof lights barely detectable in the bright sunlight, the striped green and black awning across the street, the sleek tan rumps of the horses, the brown blur of the wooden batons swinging arcs in the air, pea-soup air that was thick with clouds of tear gas, the bloody T-shirt and the sewn-together Vietcong flags.

"I saw mounted police, about six or seven of them, facing a crowd of demonstrators. I saw the police hitting people. The whole area stank of tear gas, you know? A woman was on the ground, unconscious and bleeding." Esther remembered the boy too, rubbing his eyes.

"What did you do?"

"Maggie asked us to go back to the square and get help, because her walkie-talkie was jammed."

"Objection." The DA turned to the judge. "Mrs. Green is making an assumption."

"Sustained."

Esther nodded. "The walkie-talkie wouldn't work. The injured woman needed an ambulance."

"So you left?"

"We started to. Then the cops began beating people harder, and Rosa said we had to try to stop them."

"Stop them how?"

Esther hesitated before speaking. "By throwing apples, small green apples."

"Where did the apples come from?"

"Our backpack. We also had sandwiches and juice."

"Did you pack the contents of the backpack, Mrs. Green?"

"Yes. All except the apples."

"So how did these apples get into your backpack?"

"Rosa said she brought them."

"Why?"

"As a snack."

"So, you claim that this was just two girls tossing a snack at some police officers, is that it? Tossing apples to try to stop half a squad of mounted officers in their work protecting the citizens of Detroit?" The DA's voice was incredulous.

Esther shook her head. "I don't know. Rosa said we should try. It was horrible, what the policemen were doing."

Rosa in the street had been shiny like steel. *Help me*, Rosa had said. *Throw now.*

The DA lowered his voice to a soft whisper, but it still filled the courtroom. "Can you explain to the jury why you threw those apples, Mrs. Green?"

"I wanted to stop the cops from hitting people, cracking their heads. I never meant to hurt a horse, or an officer."

Esther wanted to sob. There was no right way to tell this story. No way to explain that she didn't want to do what Rosa said, and she did want to, both at the same time. No way to stop remembering every diamond-sharp word Rosa said. *We have to stop them. Help me.*

"You never meant to hurt anyone." The DA sighed loudly. "What did you and your sister do next?"

"We ran back to the first aid tent, told them about the unconscious woman. The medics called for an ambulance and asked us to stay in the tent while they went to help Maggie on Grand River."

"Then what?"

"When the medics returned, we caught the bus home." Esther's voice drifted off and she looked down at her lap. She remembered how her milk let down on the bus, thinking about Molly. The idea of her milk feeding the Vietnamese baby on her T-shirt had tickled her fancy, and for a few seconds, she forgot what they did in the street.

"Just a few more questions, Mrs. Green." The DA's voice had a listen-up-here edge. "Are you medically trained? A doctor, or a nurse?"

"No."

"So when you went to Grand River with the medic, it wasn't really to offer first aid to injured demonstrators, was it? Did you go because you knew there was fighting there, and you wanted to throw rocks?"

"No, that's not true. I went to help. And I never threw a rock."

"Excuse me," the DA said, smirking at the jury, "a very hard green apple, the size, shape, and solidity of a rock." He shook his head before continuing. "How do you feel about your older sister, Mrs. Green? Are you afraid of Rosa?"

"Of course not. Why should I be afraid of her?"

"Your sister Rosa is a committed activist, a self-proclaimed revolutionary leader. Are you ever frightened of her zeal?"

"I admire her commitment."

"Do you always follow her lead?"

"I can think for myself."

"Is your sister the leader in political matters?"

Esther shrugged. "I guess so. She's older."

"Did you follow her lead last August 17 on Grand River?"

Esther looked down at her hands. They were strangers folded in her lap. She couldn't feel them at the ends of her arms. Her neck wouldn't work either, so she could not turn and look at Rosa at the defense table. She didn't need to look; she knew how tall and straight her sister was sitting.

"Mrs. Green. Please answer the question. Did you follow Rosa's lead on August 17?"

"I don't know."

"Was it Rosa's suggestion to throw rock-hard *apples* at the mounted police?"

"I guess so."

"Did Rosa bring the apples to the demonstration and put them in your backpack?"

"Yes. But we never meant to hurt anyone."

The DA's voice boomed. "*You* might not have meant to hurt anyone, but you cannot know what your sister planned."

Oh, but she did know. She had always known. All their lives, until the last few months, people joked that Rosa and Esther could have been twins, even with the dramatic difference in their hair color. Rosa made fun of those comments, but Esther had always loved the idea.

People probably wouldn't be saying that anymore.

"Did your sister Rosa bring the apples, hand them to you, tell you to throw them, and then herself start aiming them at the officers and their horses?"

Esther tried to imagine what Rosa was thinking. She didn't trust herself to look at her, but she didn't have to. Esther had spent her whole life studying her older sister, trying to avoid disappointing her. Rosa would be ferocious with rage, blazing with it, just like on Grand River on that awful afternoon. She could feel Rosa's gaze on her chest. Rosa's eyes burned twin holes through Esther's clothes, sizzled her tattoo, charred her flesh.

"Please answer the question, Mrs. Green. Did your sister Rosa Levin do those things?"

"Yes," Esther said. "She did."

CHAPTER 10

Jake

"Yes. She did."

Esther's three words punched into Jake's sternum. Sitting next to him, Mama clutched her throat. She must have felt it too, the calamity of those three true words. Jake had encouraged Esther to accept the plea bargain. It was the right thing to do, for Molly, for their family. For herself, damn it; it was high time Esther stopped doing everything Rosa told her to. Still, when Esther spoke those three words in the courtroom, Jake wondered if he had been terribly wrong.

"That will be all, Mrs. Green. Thank you." The DA's voice was cheerful. If he was pleased, it couldn't be good news for Rosa. Jake barely heard Dwayne's cross-examination, taking Esther through her years of shared activism with Rosa, in Ann Arbor and Detroit. None of it mattered after those three awful words.

The bailiff helped Esther out of the witness box and down the steps. Jake tried to catch her eye, but Esther studied her feet as if she couldn't walk without visual assistance.

"One moment, Mrs. Green," the judge said.

Esther halted. Jake held his breath.

"Have a seat." The judge pointed to an empty chair at the end of the prosecution table. "You are no longer sequestered."

Jake wanted to stand up and object. Why does she have to sit with them? That's not standard procedure; it's harassment. She's done, he wanted to yell, so let her sit here with her parents and me where she belongs. But Esther let herself be escorted to the DA's table.

Next to Jake, Mama took Pop's hand. Pop lifted her fingers to his lips, briefly. Jake closed his eyes. He had never before observed any physical intimacy between Esther's parents. Things must be even worse than he thought.

The wire service photographer's testimony echoed his television interviews. He set the scene with the scorching heat and the shade of the restaurant awning. He had just finished his sandwich and was smoking a cigarette when he heard the commotion on the street. Jake's attention wandered as the photographer answered questions about angle of vision and camera distances. It had been right to leave Molly with the sitter, but his chest ached for the comfort of her small warm weight.

On cross-examination, Rosa's lawyer tried to focus on the violent behavior of the cops. "Did you take any photographs of the altercation between the mounted police and the demonstrators?" he asked. "Of the police hitting citizens?"

"A few," the photographer admitted.

"Where are *those* photos? Why weren't *they* in the newspaper? Why aren't *they* enlarged so the jury can see the whole picture?"

"Not my job," the photographer said. "I take the photos. The wire service decides which ones to distribute and the papers choose what to publish."

Jake had to admit that the DA was good. He primed the jury with evidence from the injured cop's commanding officer, the paramedic first responders, the vet who treated the traumatized horse, the fourth-year resident on duty in the Emergency Room. Next came the spinal cord trauma specialist who had been called in from his Upper Peninsula fishing camp to operate late that night. Jake knew the guy from his neurosurgery rotation in med school, and it was bad luck for Rosa's case. The neurosurgeon spoke to the jury in his husky voice, sharing secrets of the most intimate workings of the human body. On a large diagram, he pointed to the three crushed vertebrae in the officer's spine. "These things are difficult to predict, but with a complete T11-L1 injury, most likely Officer Steele's legs will be paralyzed for the rest of his life."

Finally, an attendant in clean white scrubs pushed a wheelchair into the courtroom. The injured officer sat motionless, wearing his uniform and a neck brace under his bland and sad expression. Neck brace? The trauma was to his *lower* spine. If Esther were sitting next to him, he could whisper-rant about courtroom theatrics, about having the guy wear a collar when the injury was nowhere near his neck. Theatrics or not, the tactic seemed to work, judging by the sympathy visible on the jurors' faces.

The judge agreed to the DA's request that the officer be allowed to give testimony from his wheelchair, due to his significant injuries. "Officer Steele," the DA said, "could you tell us what you and your squad were doing on Grand River Avenue on August 17, 1968? Take it slow and easy."

"My squad was assigned periphery duty that afternoon, patrolling a neighborhood adjacent to the demonstration. We came upon an offshoot of the march. These individuals did not have a permit to use the street." Officer Steele's mild expression tightened slightly. "We advised them of the situation. We requested several times that they move onto the sidewalk. They refused to comply. They began shouting abusive comments at us."

"What kind of comments, Officer?"

"Epithets like 'pig,' sir." The police officer seemed comfortable in the courtroom, conversing with the DA as if they were relaxing together with a beer at a bar down the street. Jake envied that kind of ease. He had observed it in some physicians at the hospital, wondered where it came from.

"And then what happened, Officer?"

"More demonstrators joined the group in the street. Despite multiple warnings and the deterrent use of tear gas, they did not disperse. Instead, they attacked us."

"Attacked you how?"

"The perpetrators swarmed into the street, surrounded us. They yelled threats."

"How did you respond?"

"We defended ourselves with our billy clubs, sir. To secure the street."

"How were you injured?"

Officer Steele shook his head slightly in the neck brace. "I'm sorry, but I can't remember. The doctors say I might never regain those memories. My buddies tell me that rocks were thrown at us and my horse was hit. They say that when I fell off, I landed so hard they could hear bones break."

Jake looked at the defense team; why didn't they challenge that testimony as hearsay? Jake knew it wasn't likely that bystanders could hear the vertebrae crack, but it made a strong impression on the jury, a damaging impression. Their faces mirrored the DA's expression of shock. Esther felt it too. Jake knew by the way her shoulders sagged, collapsing into herself.

He studied the sisters' backs at the twin tables facing the judge. When they were younger, their torsos were almost identical: Rosa a bit taller, Esther slightly rounder. They didn't resemble each other anymore. Esther slumped at the far end of the DA's desk. Jake hadn't noticed before how much pregnancy weight she still carried. Rosa sat erect between Allen and Dwayne at the defense table. She didn't move, but her body radiated energy. Rosa had always been like that, even as a teenager. Before Allen fell in love with her, he once called her a matchstick, tall and skinny with a flaming head. Not that he ever would, or even really wanted to, but Jake couldn't help wondering what it would be like to hold that voltage in his arms.

Officer Steele was excused and wheeled out of the courtroom. Jake wondered if he had kids. If he used to hurry home from work in time to read *Babar* at bedtime, deeply inhaling the scent of shampoo in their damp hair as they sat together on the sofa. He bet that was what Esther was thinking about too.

Jake wanted to take Esther away. Away from the courtroom. Away from Rosa. From danger. Just Esther and Molly and him. Safe.

CHAPTER 11

Allen

Waiting for Jake or Esther to answer their doorbell the next afternoon, Allen admitted to himself that he probably shouldn't have come. He could have telephoned with the news, or even asked Rosa's lawyer to tell them. But that didn't seem right after all the years of friendship. Didn't seem right even now, when their friendship was dead, *had* to be dead.

He and Jake had been through rocky times before, like that last summer at camp when they were both counselors, when Allen really noticed Rosa for the first time. She was two years younger, and any romantic involvement between counselors and campers was strictly forbidden. For a while, Allen suspected that his best buddy also had a crush on the skinny redhead, who stood up in the middle of a campfire program and asked why everyone was singing a silly song about a purple people-eater when their country was testing nuclear bombs over Bikini Atoll. Even back then, Rosa was ablaze, and most of the guys were attracted to her.

Over the last few years, he and Jake hadn't made much time for each other. They were both so busy, with the pull of their professions and then Jake's fatherhood. Rosa proclaimed that Jake had sold out his activism for a white coat and stethoscope, but Allen couldn't think of any guy he admired more. That made this visit even harder, knowing his news would likely end their friendship.

Jake answered the door. He hesitated, then stood back, a wordless invitation to enter. Esther was sitting on the sofa nursing Molly. Allen wished this were a social visit, so he could ask to hold the baby. He had wanted to ask so many times but never did, and now he probably never would. He felt Esther's eyes on his face, searching for the reason he was there. Maybe worrying that she had goofed in court the day before, said something bad enough to make the DA change his mind about the plea agreement.

"Have a seat," Jake said.

Allen sat on the arm of the easy chair, still in his coat. He buried his face in his hands.

"What's wrong?" Esther asked.

Jake sat next to her, put his arm around her shoulders. Jake was protecting his family and Allen admired that. But it made him feel so alone.

"You look serious," Jake said. "Did something happen in court today?"

"Rosa no-showed." Allen worked to keep his voice steady. "She's gone."

"Gone?" Esther looked at Jake for help.

"Underground," Allen said. "She knew how badly the trial was going. I wanted to tell you in person. That means the trial is over, at least for the time being." He hesitated. "This has been awful for all of us, but especially you, Esther. I'm profoundly sorry."

Esther opened her mouth—to speak, to scream?—then sat silent, mouth agape.

"There's more." Allen felt his eyes begin to burn. He blinked several times, but it didn't help. "Rosa is pregnant."

"I should have guessed," Esther whispered. "She was nauseous a lot. And so pale. When did she tell you?"

"She didn't. I found the phone number of the clinic on the pad next to the telephone, with three exclamation points gouged into the yellow paper. I called the clinic, said I was Rosa's husband. I told them Rosa couldn't remember the brand of prenatal vitamins they recommended." Allen heard how small his own voice sounded. He hated lying, even when it was necessary. "She didn't tell me she was leaving either. I didn't know until I woke up this morning. Her side of the bed was empty."

He rubbed his eyes, his beard, but couldn't wipe away the hopeless torrent of loss. He had to get out of there. He stood, glad he had never taken off his coat.

Jake moved awkwardly toward him. "I'm really sorry, Allen."

Allen held up both hands, palms out. He couldn't bear Jake's sympathy. "Got to go."

"Let me know if you hear from her. Please?" Esther called after him.

"Or if we can do anything," Jake added. "For you."

Allen pulled the apartment door closed behind him and crumpled against the wall in the unheated hallway. Closing his eyes, he relived his argument with Rosa after court the day before. Her leaving was partly his fault. He should have known better than to try to offer advice when she was so distraught.

"Maybe you could tone it down a little," he had said on the way home. "You know, show some sympathy for the cop?" He had looked out of the bus window, as if it was just an offhand comment. He wanted to take her in his arms and banish her anger and hurt. Sometimes he wished she were the kind of woman who would let him do that. The kind of woman who would admit that she felt sorry about the cop's injuries, that she felt wretched and hurt and betrayed that her sister would testify against her.

"I can't." Rosa's voice, when she finally answered, was tiny. "I thought you, of all people, would understand what's at stake here."

"Your freedom is at stake. I understand that."

Rosa compressed her lips into a tight white line. "How can I live with myself if I don't fight every inch? Who would I be?"

"You'd be yourself, Rosa Levin, free and ready to fight another day."

"No," Rosa said. "You're thinking like an arrogant lawyer. Not like an activist."

"Why arrogant?"

"Because you act like you know everything. You think it's all about manipulating the judge and jury, maneuvering the case law. The Olympics of Head Games, won by the team that comes up with the best bullshit. But you're wrong. This trial is about taking a stand. Like slave revolts or Selma." She paused. "What's at stake is who I am."

Later, in bed, Rosa had been more tender than usual, and she cried after they made love. At first he wondered if maybe she was sorry about their fight, but then he understood that something very bad was going to happen. He pushed the premonition away by licking the tears off her flushed cheeks and ears and neck and holding her until her breathing slowed into sleep.

The chill woke him up the next morning. Whenever Rosa got up first, she flung the covers off and never remembered to pull them back over him. That morning, he woke up cold, and Rosa was gone.

CHAPTER 12

Esther

After Allen announced that Rosa was pregnant and had gone underground, and after Allen left their apartment, Jake took Molly into the bedroom. He put her in the crib and began singing to her. Esther stood alone in the living room.

Profoundly sorry, Allen had said. The two words swirled around her, reverberated and gathered speed. They ricocheted off the walls and the syllables elongated. The sound swelled into the desolate stretch of coast the year Mama and Pop picked them up at camp and drove to Maine. They spent a soggy week in a rented cottage listening to the seagulls and the endless foghorn. Pop fished, standing alone in the surf, his slicker flapping in the wind. Esther and Rosa watched him from the rocking chairs on the porch, tucked in with quilts while the fog transformed them into ghosts.

How could Rosa leave when things were so unresolved between them? How could she not say goodbye, not tell Allen he was going to have a kid? Esther wished Allen had let her hug him. They could have cried together about losing Rosa.

Esther tried to imagine her sister pregnant. Could she have a baby underground? Or an abortion? Would pregnancy change how Rosa felt about the idea of going to prison? Was that why she left? Esther tried to picture the events of the last few months unfolding in a different way. Would she have acted any differently if she'd known Rosa was pregnant?

Over the next weeks—weeks with no word of Rosa—Esther speculated endlessly about those questions. While she folded laundry, she worried if Rosa had clean clothes and a warm place to sleep. While she fed Molly, she pictured Rosa nursing a newborn on the run. While the cops questioned her about Rosa's whereabouts, she tried to picture Rosa and a whimpering infant wandering the narrow streets of an unknown city. What did underground really mean, anyway, when it wasn't some romantic escapade, but day-to-day life with a baby? Even harder, probably, with a mixed-race baby. Would she face prejudice? And how would she even afford to *have* the baby without accessing her health insurance?

Thanksgiving that year was a mournful holiday. Mama made Danny's favorite stuffing, but it was dry and hard to swallow without him there to take a third portion. Esther tried to eat the pumpkin pie Rosa loved so much, but it wedged like sweet cement in her throat. Mama and Pop were mute. Aunt Miriam and Uncle Max were broken. Rosa would have sparked the conversation around that table, would have brought up the genocide of the Native Americans while waving a huge drumstick in the air, keeping everybody engaged and arguing at once. After dinner, Esther washed dishes and Jake held Molly on his lap and read *Goodnight, Moon* over and over. Deborah chased her toddler daughter around the dining room while her husband Bubba watched the football game. As they got ready to leave, Mama hugged Esther for a long time.

"I'm so sorry," Esther said. "It's my fault."

"Shush. Rosa brought this on herself."

Esther shook her head. "Maybe. I don't know."

Riding the bus home, Esther stared out the window at the city streets dark with rain.

"Wasn't Allen invited?" Jake asked.

"Sure, but he told Mama he wasn't celebrating anything this year."

"I'm worried about your parents."

Esther stroked Molly's sleep-limp hand. "Yeah. They seemed subdued."

"Subdued? More like catatonic. They may never recover."

We may never recover, Esther thought.

December 11 was the one-year anniversary of the day Danny stepped on a mine near *Khe Sanh*. Esther sat with Molly on the shag rug in the living room building a tower, counting out each wooden block as she placed it on top. On *one* and *two*, Molly watched, her arms flapping like chubby wings. On the count of *three*, she swooped, both hands swatting, sending the blocks tumbling onto the rug. She rocked forward, leaned her hands on the floor and laughed, a deep rumble starting in her belly and bubbling up through her toothless mouth. Then she settled back, lifted her hands, and waited for the next tower.

Danny would have loved the game, but he never had the chance to meet Molly.

The last time Esther saw him was at his sister Deborah's wedding, spiffy in his dress uniform, out on a weekend pass between Basic Training and Vietnam. Esther had always had mixed feelings about Danny and Deborah's family, even though Danny was her favorite cousin and Aunt Miriam was Mama's only living sister. The two families were close, despite Aunt Miriam being the kind of person who always left out the crucial ingredient—on purpose—when you asked her for a recipe. Mama and Miriam disagreed vehemently about religion and politics, so they compromised by alternating holidays between the two households. One year they held a traditional Seder at Miriam and Max's house, and the next a secular celebration of liberation at Mama and Pop's. Crazy, but they never missed a year.

Danny's military uniform wasn't the only problem with Deborah's wedding. Esther hated the showy ice sculptures and hand-sequined dresses and imported orchid arrangements. Rosa said she couldn't stomach watching Danny accept the back slaps of the older men, who talked about their wars over cocktails decorated with small paper American flags. And then there was the bachelor party, which Jake and Allen described in detail, with a stripper shimmying out of a cardboard cake. Worse of all, the sisters agreed, was the rehearsal dinner at the ritzy suburban country club that had only started admitting Jews a few years earlier, and still routed people with dark skin to the service entrance. Allen refused to attend but insisted that the rest of the family go.

"Hypocrisy," the sisters whispered to each other when Bubba and Deborah stood under the *chuppa*, the small bulge of pregnancy mostly hidden by the satin folds of her dress.

A few months later, when Danny stepped on a land mine, Esther never quite forgave Deborah, even though logically Danny's death had nothing to do with the awfulness of the wedding. That winter, Esther started working on a series of collage paintings: Segmented plastic worms wove in and out of lace wedding veils. Yellow spatters of napalm on torn strips of tuxedo alternated with ripped muslin painted with rice fields and jungle scenes.

She started a new alphabet block tower for Molly. Would she ever make art again?

An envelope shot through the stamped metal mail slot. It rode into the room on a chill draft and settled on the rug, bumping into the letter "B." Picking it up, Esther recognized her sister's handwriting. She lunged for the door and yanked it open, ran down the hall to the stairs, but there was no one there, and no postmark. Back in the apartment she found Molly sprawled on the rug, whispering nonsense syllables to herself. The room was silent except for the purr of the yellow kitten. Esther opened the envelope, unfolded the single sheet of paper, and read.

Dear Esther,

I never expected you would go through with it. Testify against me like that. How could you betray everything we believe in, everything generations of our family believed in? You are a traitor to yourself, to me, to Mama and Pop, to Leah and Tovah. You are a coward.

I'm ashamed of you.

Your daughter will grow up ashamed of you.

We are no longer sisters.

Stunned, numb, Esther refolded the paper in thirds, rubbing her thumbnail along the crease to sharpen it. She had to hide the letter. She would think about Rosa's words later, figure out how to dull their edge, but Jake would never understand or forgive. He would hate Rosa even more.

Molly had fallen asleep on the rug and Esther covered her with a blanket. She knew just the place for Rosa's letter. She took a small rectangular box from the desk. The fabric cover was red, embroidered with a stylized Asian scene—curved wooden bridge, willows dipping their branches into the faded blue water. Inside nested four smaller boxes with the landscape replicated on their covers, each tiny box stitched with a quarter of the scene. Ten-year-old Esther had been enchanted when the gift arrived from her Japanese pen pal. Rosa had been envious.

Esther opened the box with the weeping willows and removed a four-inch coil of braid. Three colors of hair braided together: red, deep brown, and gray. Rosa, Esther, and Leah.

Grandma Leah had died during breakfast when Esther was sixteen. Leah had had a mild stroke several months earlier, but was getting stronger and her speech was coming back. That morning she was sitting at the kitchen table, her chair pushed up close so cereal drips wouldn't stain her chenille bathrobe. Esther sat next to her at the breakfast table, looking down at the geometry book in its brown paper cover resting on her lap. She spooned milk-limp Wheaties into her mouth while memorizing the formulas for volumes of cones and cylinders for her third period test.

There was a clunk and Esther looked up to see Leah's head resting on the green-checked oilcloth. Her forehead landed on the paring knife and a streak of blood pushed through the smashed banana.

In the rush of activity and tears and the ambulance, what Esther remembered most was her mother fussing about the cut on Leah's forehead. Mama had been half-dressed for work with fuzzy bunny bedroom slippers over her stockings. "Is she still bleeding?" Mama kept asking. "Get me another bandage for her forehead."

Rosa took a bus home from Ann Arbor, and the next morning the sisters had a few minutes alone with their grandmother's body in the burgundy family room at the funeral home. Rosa used Leah's tiny sewing scissors, shaped like a silver heron, to snip off a generous lock of hair. Then she solemnly cut a similar length from her own red mane, and from Esther's deep brown curls. The sisters made three braids, fastened at each end with a strand of hair. They tucked Leah's braid into the left sleeve of her cornflower blue blouse, up out of sight.

"Say goodbye," Rosa said.

"I love you, Grandma Leah," Esther whispered. "I'll never forget you."

Then it was Rosa's turn. "Too bad you hooked up with the Mensheviks." She spoke into the wrinkled ear, with authority born of the Comparative Revolutions course she was taking.

"What's that mean?" Esther asked.

"Not revolutionary enough."

"Like me?" Esther asked. It wasn't fair that Rosa was named for a revolutionary and all Esther got was a Persian queen no one remembered from one Purim to the next.

Rosa raised one eyebrow, a gesture she had appropriated from Uncle Max in sixth grade and practiced until it was perfect. She leaned again close to Leah's ear. "You cared about your world. You were a freedom fighter. I'll never forget you."

Esther had been so impressed at her sister's words, so envious of everything Rosa was learning. Just Rosa's luck, to arrive in Ann Arbor at the perfect time. When the four black students in Greensboro sat in at that lunch counter six months after Rosa got to the university, Rosa organized support pickets. That sit-in sparked a whole movement, and Rosa was right in the middle.

Esther wrapped the braid around her pinky finger, admiring the contrasting colors. She slid it back into the tiny fabric box and then into the larger one, wondering if Rosa still cherished her braid, or if it was part of her life left behind. She folded the awful letter again so it would fit under the lid, and buried the red box in the back of the bottom desk drawer.

She wiped the tears from her cheek with the corner of the baby blanket and then rearranged it to cover the rusty fuzz on Molly's head, protecting her from the chill creeping under the door.

CHAPTER 13

Jake

On the bus ride home from the hospital, Jake worried about the ten-year-old in sickle cell crisis in intensive care. He found Esther in the rocking chair, holding Molly and weeping. He dropped his coat on the floor and kneeled next to her.

"What's wrong? Did something happen?"

"Molly's hair. How can I stop thinking about Rosa when I'm reminded of her every time I look at my baby?"

"We could dye her hair? Shave her head?"

Esther sobbed harder and buried her face in Molly's neck.

Jake stood up and turned toward the dark window facing the street. "This city isn't healthy for you. Our friends don't talk to us. You barely leave the house."

"People look at me like I have a fatal disease and it's contagious. The bookstore cut my position. Even my *sisters* in my women's group won't talk to me. Everyone's on her side."

Jake wished he knew what to say. He was furious with Rosa but still found himself looking carefully at redheads on the bus, scanning women's faces as he walked through the crowded ER waiting room.

"Even Maggie won't return my phone calls. I heard she has a new girlfriend, but that never affected our friendship before."

"Let's move," Jake said. "Go someplace new."

"Go where? This is home."

"We'll make a new home. The three of us."

Esther shook her head. "How could I do that, Jake, how could I leave my parents? Then they'd have no one; no daughters, no grandkids, nobody."

"They've got each other," Jake said. "And Miriam and Max. You'll visit often, with Molly. I'm worried about you, about us."

He picked up his jacket from the floor and hung it on the wrought-iron coat tree from Goodwill. He was fond of Esther's parents; they had become his family, too. His own parents barely survived the death of his brother, then died in a fiery car crash a month after he started med school. He suspected they waited until he was set on a life course before ending their pain.

Leaving town was definitely the right thing to do, but Jake wasn't anxious to see Esther's reaction to his news. He wasn't sure how to tell her.

She looked at him funny, tilted her head to the side. "What is it?"

"I've been looking into transferring to another residency program," Jake admitted. He hadn't said anything about his plans, in case he wasn't accepted. Esther couldn't deal with another disappointment.

"Without discussing it with me?" she asked.

"I wasn't sure it would work out." Not a good reason, he knew that. "I got a call today from the University of Massachusetts. They offered me a place and I took it."

"Boston?"

"The western part of the state. You'll love it."

"No I won't. I'll hate it. How could you make a big decision like that on your own? We're equal partners. Haven't you learned anything from the women's movement?" Esther squeezed her eyes closed and leaned down to Molly again.

"It could be just for a few years," Jake offered, then stopped. He understood that the conversation was over. She was right; he should have talked to her. But she hadn't been easy to talk to in the past couple of months. "I'm sorry."

She probably wouldn't love western Massachusetts, not at first. But something had to change. If they left Detroit, maybe it would break Rosa's spell. Esther would learn to be happy with just Molly and him. They could move there for a year or two, while he finished his residency. Maybe Mama and Pop would sell the store, come live near them. He kneeled again next to the rocking chair, put his arms around Esther and rested his head on her breast. Molly looked at him.

"Don't worry, Monkey," he whispered and stroked her cheek. "I won't get in the way of your dinner." He inhaled Molly's milky fragrance. For a split second he remembered the patchouli oil Rosa wore, how she had dabbed some just under his nostrils during his first clinical rotation, when he admitted that the smell of sickness made him nauseous. He pushed the thought away. This was home, the safe place he and Esther had created with Molly. He had to protect that place, despite Esther's inevitable reaction.

"One other thing," he said.

"What other thing?" Esther asked.

"We've got to leave the past behind. Start over with a clean slate."

"What are you saying?"

"Promise me that we won't tell Molly about this stuff. About Rosa or the demonstration or the trial."

"Not talk about my sister?"

"Rosa will never forgive you. Our only way forward is to leave her behind."

"How can I do that?"

"How can you not? This is very important to our family. Promise?"

Esther didn't say no, and Jake pretended not to notice the flooding of her eyes. He knew how hard this was for Esther, but it was the best way. At least he hoped that twenty years from now they'd talk about how they made it through these awful times. His knees hurt on the hard floor, but he knelt a moment longer in the nest of her unspoken promise, savoring the milky aroma of shelter.

Two weeks later, their living room was a muddle of cartons and trash bags stuffed with books and clothes. Packing up the apartment was challenging. Molly had mastered crawling and couldn't be trusted for a single, unobserved second. While Esther emptied the front closet, Molly played in a makeshift playpen of cardboard boxes. Jake packed books into cartons and tried to gauge Esther's frame of mind.

"Here, Mol." Esther picked dust bunnies off a soft fabric ball and rolled it to Molly, who startled at the jingle of the bells stitched onto the surface. Then she laughed and grabbed for the ball. Esther scooped the sleeping cat from the open carton labeled "Art Supplies" and turned back to the closet jumble. She gathered a handful of old paintbrushes, the bristles stained with shadows of color, and flung them into the trash.

At the noise, Jake looked up from a stack of paperback novels. "What are you doing?"

"I'm finished with art."

"That's nuts. That's why we're moving. So you can get your life back."

"I can't paint anymore."

"You've got to." Jake reached into the trash bag to retrieve the paintbrushes. He handed them to Esther with a flourish. "Please."

Stroking the velvety bristles back and forth against her upper lip, she looked absent, like her mind was elsewhere. Jake picked up a brush and stroked his own face with the soft bristles. He wanted to touch Esther like that now, with the whispery graze of brush on skin. He half-closed his eyes to blur the present image, to remember Esther at camp.

The summer of 1960, Jake hadn't planned to work at camp again, but his hospital orderly position fell through at the last minute. Loon Lake was desperate for counselors and he needed work. During the second week of the session, he sat alone at the edge of the ball field eating an apple and watching his campers play nobody-wins softball.

Camp was boring and he wished he had looked harder for a job in the city. He shoved the apple core into his mouth and licked the juice from his fingers. It had gotten Jake teased before, the way he ate every last bit of the fruit, seeds and core and all.

Esther plopped herself on the grass next to him. "Aren't you afraid an apple tree will grow in your stomach?"

"No." He started to explain why that wouldn't happen, how his stomach enzymes would prevent germination and the small amounts of arsenic in the seeds wouldn't hurt him either. Then he realized Esther was flirting.

Within a week, Jake had entirely forgotten about Rosa and couldn't stop thinking about Esther. One day, she missed free swim and Jake went looking for her. He found her painting in the art room, so entranced that she had lost track of time, so involved that she rested the wet bristles against her face. He laughed and told her she looked dazzling with a turquoise mustache. He tried to rub the paint from her upper lip with his thumb, faltered, then kissed her mouth instead. She smelled of turpentine.

He explained it all to Allen that night in the counselors' bunk: Esther was too young, but he could wait for her to grow up. He had big plans—college and med school and free healthcare for the poor of the world.

Molly's chortles turned into complaints. Jake rescued the ball, wedged in the crack between boxes labeled "Pots and Pans" and "Posters and Letters", and tossed it to her. Molly ignored it, her complaints escalating into demands. Esther was still staring at the apartment wall and Jake dabbed at her cheeks with an old cloth diaper, soft beyond absorbency.

She pressed her face against his hand for a moment, then picked up Molly. "Nap time."

"I'll keep working."

After Esther left the room, he wrapped the paintbrushes in the cloth diaper and slipped them into a corner of the "Art Supplies" box, tucked among drawing papers and misshapen tubes of paint. When Esther got over this, when she was herself again, she'd want her brushes. He taped the box shut and stacked it against the wall with the others.

When he moved "Desk Supplies" to the pile of boxes, a legal pad lay exposed on the blotter. It had Rosa's writing on it with bulleted reasons why Esther should reject the plea bargain and stand trial with Rosa, fight for the good guys. Rosa must have left it the last time she visited: before storming out of the apartment, before inviting them to dinner with Mama's tablecloth, before Esther accepted the DA's deal, before the trial, before Rosa disappeared. Jake tore off the page, but the impressions of Rosa's arguments still gouged the yellow paper. He ripped off the next two sheets, crumpled them, and threw them across the room into the trash.

He stood up and stretched, then wandered down the hall to the bedroom doorway. Esther and Molly were curled up together on the queen-sized mattress on the floor. The Venetian blinds sliced the weak winter sun into thin lines across the quilt. In sleep, Esther looked a decade younger, almost like the girl he fell for at camp. But the specter of Rosa lingered. How did she sneak into his apartment, her electricity palpable, to demand his attention even when she was disgraced, in hiding? Jake felt foolish talking to a phantom, but he couldn't stop himself.

"I don't know where you are right now, Ms. Queen of the Underground," he whispered. "And I don't care. We're leaving. And if you have any thoughts of reclaiming your sister, forget it. You're toxic, Rosa. Poison. Stay away from my family."

CHAPTER 14

Esther

Unpacking the last of the moving boxes, Esther glanced at Jake across their new living room. He tried to hide his frustration, but Esther could tell he was disappointed in her. It hadn't been easy to transfer his residency mid-year, even pleading family emergency. They had only been in Massachusetts for three weeks, rattling around in an old farmhouse Jake rented at the edge of a small town, in a valley between forested hills.

Esther hated it.

"You'll adjust," Jake said.

"You just don't get it, do you?" She shook her head. "This place is like a foreign country, like another galaxy, like Mars."

"Even after all those summers at Loon Lake?"

She pointed at the black square of window. "Does that look like summertime in New Hampshire to you?"

"Spring will be here soon," he said. "At least we're out of Detroit, the three of us safe and together."

Getting away from the icy looks and occasional muttered comments from ex-comrades was a relief, but who *was* she without her past? "That's easy for you to say. You have your work, your patients. There's nothing for me here."

"Then make something for yourself. Go back to school. Finish your degree."

Their arguments always ended at this same place. Jake meant well, but he had no idea how lost she felt. She took the last mug from the deep corner of the carton. Unpacking was marginally easier than packing. Crumpling the newsprint wrapping into a ball, she tossed it into the pile in the corner of the room. The yellow kitten raised his head, batted the air briefly, then let his nose sink back onto his paws. Mustard hadn't been his playful self since the move, and she couldn't blame him.

"Finally!" Jake shouted, ripping open the cardboard flaps of a large carton. "Records! I can't wait one more second for music."

Esther couldn't bear the thought of listening to the soundtrack of their old lives. She had managed to hide the box of LPs among the stacks of unopened cartons. Until now.

He hugged his favorite The Doors album to his chest. "I've been hearing 'Light My Fire' in my dreams." He slipped the vinyl record from the sleeve and turned toward the turntable.

"No," Esther said.

"You want Joan Baez instead? Okay." He started flipping through the albums again.

Jake knew all about Esther and Rosa's long-standing argument about Joan Baez versus Bob Dylan, about which songwriter spoke for their generation. Esther preferred Baez, the human side of protest. Rosa argued that Dylan was their prophet. Now *that* was protest music, Rosa used to proclaim, singing Dylan's "The Times They Are a-Changing" with her long arms undulating to the rhythm.

"No Baez either," Esther whispered. "I can't listen to *any* of our music anymore." She stood in her bathrobe in the middle of the living room, among emptied cardboard boxes tumbled like Molly's blocks. "Just the thought of it makes me feel boneless." She looked down, letting her tangled hair cover her face. "I have no scaffolding."

Jake put his arms around her. "We'll figure this out, Esther. But I can't live without music."

Why couldn't Jake understand how that music made her feel? Esther leaned against him. And it wasn't just the music. Tomorrow was Molly's first birthday, and how could they possibly celebrate without her family, without Rosa?

Icing a birthday cake late the next afternoon, Esther counted off the months on her fingers. If Rosa had been just pregnant on August 17, say three months along at most, and if she didn't have an abortion, she should have a baby right about now.

"You might have a cousin out there somewhere," she told Molly. She scattered a handful of Cheerios onto the wooden tray of Molly's highchair and sat at her desk tucked in the kitchen alcove. Every single day since Rosa's awful letter arrived, she had mentally composed her answer, revised it, and then trashed it. Today she had to get it on paper. For Molly's future and her own peace of mind.

Dear Rosa,

It's been three months since I got your letter. I'm still stunned.

The postmark was smudged but I figure you wrote it right before you left town. I doubt I could find the courage to mail this, even if I knew how to find you, which I don't. But maybe you'll get the message anyway. I used to think that we should have been twins; we understood each other's unspoken thoughts so well.

I know you're furious with me. But I don't deserve the things you said in that letter. "Coward. Traitor. No longer sisters." Those are rough words even for you. Brutal words. Impossible words.

When I read your letter, I can picture your face. Your lips so rigid they seem to disappear. When we were little, I used to worry when you got angry and blazed your eyes and lost your lips. I was afraid you would burn yourself up. End up a spent volcano of cinders on the floor. Guess I wasn't so far off.

I know. I know. If you were here you'd tell me to stop painting pictures in the air. I guess you'll get what you want, because I'm feeling pretty earthbound right now and I can't imagine ever painting another picture.

You've lost a lot too. I have no idea what it's like, being underground. I don't really know what that means. Are you in Detroit or far away? Do you know that Mama and Pop may have to sell the store? To pay my court costs and civil damages

and lawyer's fees, but mostly for your bail, which was forfeited when you left. Pop is
so stooped over and so thin, I can see the shape of his bones under his skin.

When she was a little girl, Pop's back had been straight and strong and he knew everything. His union picnic was the high point of every summer. There were puppet shows about the struggles between workers and owners. The three-legged race was her special time with Pop, their legs tied together with burlap strips making their gait impossibly, hysterically lopsided. Then, every year, just when she had almost given up on it again, the fire engine would finally pull up in front of the shoemakers' union hall, load up all the kids, and drive around the block with children piled on the ladders imitating siren noises.

Mama and Pop refuse to talk about the store, like they refuse to talk about you,
and about pretty much everything else, except Molly and when am I going to give
her a little brother or sister. I'm not ready for that yet, but I heard that you're
pregnant, that Molly will have a cousin. Congratulations, Sister.
Do you think our children will ever know each other?

What she really wanted to ask was harder to put into words. She wanted to know if having a child, experiencing in her blood that profound and awful responsibility, made Rosa understand Esther's choice and stop hating her. Esther had no idea. She used to think she could predict what Rosa thought, know what she would do before it happened, but no longer.

One of the things I've learned from all this is that even if we sometimes felt like
twins, we're not. When we were in jail that first night after the arrest, that's when
I knew how very different we were. You were so high on the whole experience. You
went on and on about Martin Luther King's Beloved Community, and how the
women in our cell were our sisters. When I looked around, all I saw were hookers
and thieves.
You didn't seem to notice the smells that night, the sour urine and dank stench
of dirty feet. You kept right on talking about that line you love so much, the one
Tim Wright liked to quote. How each of us has to figure out a way to live our lives

that doesn't make a mockery of our values. You were so fired up, Rosie. You were incandescent and I admired you so much. Me, I was just scared. I couldn't stop thinking about Bernie, snatched from the picket line and beaten to death in jail. I kept imagining Molly growing up without a mama.

You're my big sister and I've always listened to you, always followed your lead. But not this time. You and I made different choices, but that doesn't make me a coward and you can't disown me, no matter what you said in your letter. We'll always be sisters.

Love, Esther

P.S. We've moved to Massachusetts. In case you care.

Esther folded the letter in thirds, then in half again. She dug around in the back of the bottom drawer for the red Japanese box. The folded yellow paper fit perfectly on top of Rosa's letter. At the slam of Jake's car door in the driveway, Esther buried the box under old greeting cards and stationery and firmly closed the drawer. She checked the clock; he was right on time. The three of them would celebrate Molly's birthday with her first taste of chocolate.

"Your daddy's home." Esther scooped another handful of Cheerios for Molly.

"Dadadadadada," Molly repeated, her face serious.

Jake brought a frigid blast of air into the kitchen. He set a bottle of Chianti on the countertop and nuzzled Molly's belly with a bristly porcupine puppet. "Happy birthday, Monkey." He turned to Esther. "You, too."

"It's not my birthday."

"You did all the work." He hugged her and presented a large paper bag.

"Brrr." She wiggled away from his cold coat, felt the shape of the bag and stiffened. "No records."

Jake planted a loud raspberry kiss on Molly's neck. "We need music. If you can't listen to our old records, we'll try something new. Something old, actually." He pulled four albums from the bag. "Broadway musicals. From that second-hand record store downtown." He kissed

Esther's forehead. "These might be slightly scratched, but at least they won't remind you of Detroit."

That evening they listened to "Kiss Me, Kate" while they cooked spaghetti for dinner and toasted Molly's birthday, clinking their jelly glasses of red wine in celebration. They took photographs of Molly tasting her first bite of chocolate cake, her puzzled response to the sticky sweetness, then the dawning of delight. While Jake washed the dishes and sang along with Yul Brenner, Esther waltzed Molly around the kitchen to "The King and I."

At bedtime, the three of them squished together in the rocking chair and Esther nursed Molly to the mournful melodies of *Carousel*. She tried not to dwell on the image of Rosa all alone in a strange city with a new infant. When Molly was finally asleep, Jake put on *Porgy and Bess* and they slow-danced among the empty boxes. Esther rested her head on Jake's shoulder and swayed to the simple ache of the music, happier than she had felt in months. She could have danced until breakfast.

CHAPTER 15

Rosa

Rosa walked faster, dodging the onslaught of holiday shoppers. She cut in front of a guy with a greasy blond ponytail, slid into a bus station phone booth, and closed the glass doors. He gave her the finger and turned toward the booth with the smashed window at the Trailways counter. Rosa swiveled on the stool so only her back was visible to anyone nosy enough to watch. She pressed the receiver against her ear and held down the button with her mitten while she waited for Maggie's call.

Her toes were icy, her sneakers soaked from the slush on the downtown sidewalks. She missed her Earth Shoes, left behind when she snuck out of the apartment without waking Allen thirteen months earlier. Wearing bright red basketball sneakers was no doubt a violation of rule number one of surviving underground: don't call attention to yourself. Rosa grinned into her mitten. Her parents would agree with that principle, and both of them would disapprove of her choice of footwear.

"Never wear red," Mama had always taught her. "It clashes with your hair. Redheads should never wear red or orange."

"Never buy used shoes," Pop had always insisted. "Used clothes, furniture, whatever else is fine, but not shoes. Your feet work hard and deserve the best." Of course, she and Pop disagreed about what was best. Pop scorned her Earth Shoes, even though he admitted that the leather was quality goods. He had been furious when she declined his offer of a new pair of sturdy shoes from his downtown store. "My shoes aren't good enough for you anymore, college girl?" Rosa had kissed the top of his shiny head. Then she mailed off a pencil tracing of her foot and a check for thirty-five dollars for shoes guaranteed to fit like footprints in wet sand. "Highway robbery," her father muttered every time he saw them.

Funny how their voices replayed in her head all the time now, when she couldn't hear the real thing.

She checked her watch. Three minutes after the hour. It was already dark. She hoped Maggie wouldn't be too late. These monthly phone calls were her umbilical cord to her old world. Well worth the hassle of arrangements, the classified ad she placed every month in the shoppers' guide back home. Offering an item of baby equipment for sale "barely used." Always red. The area code disguised as the price, so no one would know what city or state Rosa called home at the moment, but Maggie could tell where to call that month. Even with the precautions, they never spoke longer than five minutes—that made it harder to trace the call if Maggie was followed to her randomly chosen phone booth.

Not that their phone calls were always pleasant. The month after Emma was born, Maggie had reported that Mama was furious.

"About the name," Maggie said.

"What's wrong with Emma?"

"You're not supposed to name a baby after a living relative," Maggie said. "Bad luck or something. Emma is too close to Esther."

"Too close?" Rosa couldn't believe what she was hearing.

"They start with the same letter. Your Mama insisted that the initial stands for the true Hebrew name. She said you've put a death hex on Esther." Maggie sounded uncertain.

"I don't believe in that crap and neither does Mama; she's just freaked out about everything. Besides, Esther is already dead to me, and I'm not changing Emma's name. Mama will just have to live with it."

Rosa wished Maggie would hurry up and call. If she didn't pick Emma up by five-thirty, the day care center would add a dollar late fee for every fifteen minutes. Even without the delay, it was a long day for a nine-month-old, and Rosa hated to lose precious moments of evening playtime.

She winced to remember how she had disparaged her sister for being a few minutes late to a meeting. How hard could it be to organize yourself with a baby? she had criticized. It was just a matter of setting priorities, wasn't it? If she ever saw Esther again, Rosa would acknowledge that she had been a little bit wrong, just about that.

Sometimes, when the two of them snuggled on Rosa's mattress, Emma all powdery-sweet after her bath, Rosa couldn't help thinking about Esther and Molly. Why hadn't Esther ever explained what it was like? How cuddling your baby split your chest open and let in a tornado of doubts and worries. Why hadn't Esther told her how astonishing it felt to feed a child from your own body? The power of that sweet sucking mouth. Those impossibly unspoiled fingers.

Maybe Esther had tried to tell her.

Every single day for the past thirteen months, Rosa had ruminated about her choice. Which was better for Emma? Going to prison, or going underground? Every single day, she replayed those four days in the courtroom and what came after. And sometimes, after Emma was asleep, Rosa let herself think about Allen, enormous in his absence. Missing him was bad enough, but taking Emma away from him was worse. Usually when his ghost image joined her on the mattress on the floor, Rosa had to get up, make tea, smoke a joint, anything to banish him.

Rosa let the phone ring four times before answering with the code word. "Tattoo."

"Your Pop's dead," Maggie blurted.

The words slammed into Rosa's throat. She couldn't speak. Strained to catch her breath. Not possible. He was still young. Not yet. Not now. Not before she had time to patch things up between them.

"I'm so sorry," Maggie said.

"How?"

"A massive coronary. He died instantly."

His heart? He never had heart disease. Sure, his blood pressure was a little high, but he took pills for that. Was it stress? Stress could lead to a heart attack, couldn't it? Was this her fault?

"When's the service? I've got to see Mama. I have to be there for Mama."

"You can't come, Rosa. They'll be waiting for you." Maggie paused. "Your Mama has Miriam. And Esther and Jake are in town."

"I *have* to."

"It's not safe. Pop wouldn't want you to risk prison. Think about Emma."

"I have to say goodbye."

"Say it long distance. Pop won't know the difference." Maggie's words were tough but her voice was soft. She promised to comfort Mama and report everything that happened at the memorial service.

Rosa couldn't recall the rest of the conversation, except that she never got around to revealing her own disturbing news. That was probably just as well. She had already delayed telling Maggie until it was too late to do anything about it. Rosa was embarrassed about giving in to loneliness and lust, trying to be quiet on the living room sofa so they wouldn't wake Emma in the curtained-off sleeping alcove. Mortified that she'd forgotten to use her diaphragm. Maggie would have lots to say about that too.

She sat for a moment in the stillness of the phone booth thinking of Pop. Now she could never fix the way things between them had gone sour. It had really started her freshman year at college, when he had argued with every new idea she brought home from Ann Arbor. She remembered how his face grew mute with disdain when she described their campus protest against Kennedy's actions during the Cuban missile crisis. He'd hurled her treasured mimeographed copy of the Port Huron statement—with its revelation of participatory democracy—onto the floor of the living room.

"Student power?" He spit the words. "*Mishegas.*" Craziness.

She never gave up trying to make him understand. Politics were more complicated than just unions and workers these days. The world was more complex, with Black Power and the Women's Liberation Movement and gay rights. But Pop didn't want to talk about abortion rights or racial divisions. He refused to discuss the issues that mattered to her. Like the day she was tabling on the Diag for a women's sympathy picket in support of the Woolworth's lunch counter picket in Greensboro. A crew-cut student with the engineering school logo on his shirt sauntered up to her flanked by two buddies.

"There's an awful lot of cunt around here today," he said, smirking at his six-foot buddy to his left.

Rosa thought she must have heard him wrong. "Pardon me?"

"I said there's a lot of cunt here."

Without stopping to think about it, Rosa punched crew-cut in the face, missing his nose but connecting to his left cheekbone with a satisfying crack. He socked her back just as fast, his blow landing on her upper arm, and then turned to leave without touching his face. He walked away, laughing with his cronies. She clutched her arm, trying not to cry with the pain.

The red splotch turned blue to green to yellow over the next ten days. The X-ray at the health services center showed no fracture. Two weeks later, when the sling was removed and the soreness faded, she signed up for a beginner's karate class. She called Pop that night, even though it wasn't Sunday with the lowest rates, and told him proudly about her decision, leaving out the details of what the guy said.

"Karate? That's not politics." Pop's contempt was clear. "Better you should forget this *cockamamie* women's lib stuff. Study history. Learn how to organize the working class."

So what if Pop didn't approve of self-defense classes, or the abortion work, or the rape crisis center? Deep inside, he was still really proud of her, wasn't he? Pop had shaped her politics. Pop and Loon Lake.

A sharp knock on the glass of the phone booth brought Rosa back to the present. "Sorry," she muttered to the scowling businessman. She hurried to pick up Emma, Pop's face swimming in front of her eyes.

CHAPTER 16

Esther

In the front row of the union hall, Esther sat between Mama and Jake with Molly asleep on her lap. Stroking Molly's back, she listened to Pop's buddies tell stories about union elections and strikes, about scabs and head busting. She wondered if Rosa was hiding in the crowd, incognito in a teased blond wig, or oversized sunglasses and a butch cut. She must be; how could she stay away? At least Allen must be here somewhere, paying his respects. He couldn't be that selfish, could he?

Who was she kidding? *She* was the selfish one. She hadn't seen her parents since she and Jake drove their rented U-Haul trailer out of Detroit on a frigid February morning ten months earlier. They had swung by the shoe store to say goodbye, waving as Mama and Pop shrunk in the distance. She had planned to visit much sooner, for Molly's birthday in March, or maybe Passover, but once she left it was hard to contemplate returning to that place. With Rosa who-knows-where, Mama and Pop had needed her even more and she let them down. And now Pop was gone.

While Pop's friends spoke about his commitment and leadership, Esther twisted around in her seat, searching the crowd in the back of the Union Hall. Rosa must be here somewhere. The Feds must've expected

Rosa too, because Esther identified three undercover cops in the crowd. They weren't hard to spot; they really did wear trench coats.

Molly woke up cranky when the mourners sang "Solidarity Forever," giving Esther a perfect excuse to wander through the crowd looking into faces, searching for her sister. At one point she thought she caught a glimpse of Maggie near the cloakroom, but whoever it was had vanished by the time Esther elbowed her way to the corner of the hall.

She paced back and forth across the lobby, murmuring Dr. Seuss rhymes to keep Molly entertained. In the grim months between August and December, Pop had loved reading the fantastical stories to Molly, who giggled with glee at his silly faces. Those were the only times Esther saw her father smile in those days. But she had been too selfish to bring Molly back to visit him, too chicken to face Mama and Pop and their enormous losses, too cowardly to try to make peace in their ruptured family.

She had never been good in the family peacekeeper role, especially since Rosa's big fight with their parents during her senior year of college. When the sisters came home for their holiday break that December, Rosa told their parents that she could only stay home a few days, that she and Allen were delegates to a national student activist conference in Ann Arbor. Mama and Pop could've been Republicans for all their support and understanding. But Rosa left anyway, right after Chanukah, just like she said she would. Esther had stood between their parents on the frosty front porch and watched Rosa skip down the steps, long red hair bouncing, to join Allen waiting on the sidewalk. She ran with him to the bus stop, one hand swinging her backpack and the other brushing snow from Allen's beard.

"College know-it-alls," Pop had muttered, turning away from the street toward the warm house. "Allen at least should know better." The icy cloud of Pop's disapproval fogged his glasses.

Esther had grabbed his arm. "Rosa says this new organization is much more than just student rights. This is part of a worldwide movement and it's really important."

Pop did not turn around. Eighteen-year-old Esther waited on the snowy front porch, watching until the bus pulled away from the curb in a blur of exhaust. She wished that she could be on it with them.

Rosa was still leaving her behind, and now Pop was gone too.

When the service was over, Jake caught a flight back to Massachusetts and Esther stayed. The next day, Bubba and his friends moved Mama's furniture to the spare bedroom in Max and Miriam's apartment. Mama and Molly played hide-and-seek on the bed while Esther filled the walls with pictures from Mama's old apartment, jumbled remnants of her family's life. No way they would all fit. Esther lugged the leftover artwork to the locked wire cage in the apartment complex basement, saving her favorite for last.

The Italian painting was too large for the bedroom wall, but the serious faces and drab browns and grays seemed at home in the dim shadows of the storage locker. Sitting on a carton of Pop's union organizing pamphlets that Mama refused to discard, Esther met the determined gaze of the barefoot woman holding her baby. There was a new sadness in Hannah's eyes, as if the frame were a window, or a mirror. As if the painted heroine could see right into Esther's heart and was ashamed for her.

After lunch, Esther unpacked Mama's collection of porcelain cocker spaniels. Mama never had the bizarre hobby when Esther and Rosa were girls, but over the past few years her collection had grown to cover every horizontal surface. Bubba and Max hung shelves and Mama carefully arranged the dogs in small "families" while Esther tried to keep Molly from grabbing at the delicate figures.

Later, while Molly napped and Mama rested, Esther went to clean the old apartment, grateful for a few minutes alone. She wandered around the home where she'd grown up. She stroked the scuff marks on the hallway floor where she and Rosa practiced broad jumps, ran her fingers across the holes in the walls where the dozens of pictures hung. The white glove treatment, but instead of dust or dirt she was searching for particles of family history, motes of memories. She couldn't find any leftover fragments of her past until she opened the refrigerator and saw the jar of Spanish olives in the back corner of the bottom shelf.

Rosa invented the olive game when they were little. Mama would give them a bowl with four fat Spanish olives with pits, two for each of them, and the goal was to make the olives last. Esther was good at waiting, and she hoarded her first olive whole in her mouth, so at first she didn't understand why Rosa always won. Then one day she got it. Rosa cheated. Rosa ate both of hers while they still had flavor, then snuck Esther's second olive from the bowl. When Esther finally gave in and chewed her first olive for the tiny remaining burst of salt, Rosa screeched, "I won, I won," and opened her mouth to reveal Esther's second olive, whole and smooth.

Even after all these years, even though there was no way she could have known about the olive game, even with Rosa gone, even though Pop always grumbled that they were too expensive, Mama kept a jar of colossal green olives for her daughters. Esther sat on the floor in front of the open refrigerator, resting her forehead on the vegetable crisper drawer.

After supper, Deborah came over. She hugged Mama, then her own parents, handing Max her daughter, Sarah, six months older than Molly. When the two toddlers were ensconced on the couch with their grandparents, surrounded by picture books and puppets, Deborah crooked her finger at Esther, mimed drinking a cup of tea, and pointed to the kitchen.

A few minutes later, Deborah looked up from her steaming cup. "I need your help."

"What's wrong?"

"Bubba lost his job and I'm pretty sure he's seeing another woman."

Esther put her hand on Deborah's shoulder, an uncomfortable gesture. Deborah was always the aloof cousin, a haughty contrast to Danny's impish fun.

"I'm pregnant again," Deborah whispered. "And I can't have this baby. No money. Soon maybe no husband. Do you still have that contact?"

Esther hadn't used the Waltonville number in over a year, but she found it scribbled in pencil on the inside back cover of her address book. The guy answered the same as always, making an appointment at a grungy motel, never the same place twice. Surprising that he hadn't been closed down. Some of the women in Esther's women's health collective had worried that it was too dangerous, both for the woman and her accomplice, but the sisters argued that it was necessary and right. They called him the Butcher, but there wasn't anybody else, and they didn't know firsthand of anyone who had actually died, just some nasty rumors, and you couldn't believe everything you heard. Especially if you had no better choice.

Two health collective members always escorted their clients for the procedure. They told themselves they went together for security reasons, in case something went wrong, not because they were scared. This was the first time Esther made the trip without Rosa, and now she knew the truth.

Deborah didn't speak on the drive, but when they pulled into the motel, she put her hand on Esther's arm. "Thank you." She mouthed the words without sound.

Walking across the gravel parking lot, Esther wondered who the Butcher really was, and whether he did this work for money or altruism. Rumor had it that he lost his license, something about a home birth that went very wrong. He opened the door on the first knock, stepped back to let them enter.

Drawn Venetian blinds darkened the room. The desk had been pulled into the center of the room, with folded blankets and pillows arranged on top of shower curtains to catch the expected fluids. A crookneck lamp clamped to the edge of the desk threw a circle of light on the sheet. Esther looked away from the machine sitting on the low dresser, from the tray of instruments, the loops of rubber tubing, the metal bucket on the floor.

Once he pocketed Deborah's cash and examined her, the doctor turned on the radio, loud. The first time she made the trip with a pregnant woman, Esther thought he liked to work to music, was inspired by the crashing cymbals and majestic horns. Silly you, Rosa had said afterwards: the symphony was to cover up the noise if a woman screamed or cried.

Deborah didn't make a sound, just clutched Esther's hands against her chest. Esther didn't know where to look. Not into Deborah's eyes, that was too private, and certainly not at the bloody stew being sucked through the tubing and into the bucket at the doctor's feet. What would he do with that? Flush it? A mascara trail snaked from the corner of Deborah's eye and disappeared into her hairline. Esther squeezed her eyes closed, thought about Molly, left with Mama for the afternoon with two bottles of breast milk and a long list of instructions. The orchestra advanced to a softer movement. The bedside clock ticked with a minutely irregular heartbeat. The suction machine whirred, gurgled, and stopped.

Before, Esther and Rosa had always been adamant about after-care. They drove the woman back to Rosa's apartment to rest for a few hours, brewed tea that the clerk at the health food store recommended to contract the uterus after a miscarriage. When the woman was ready, they delivered her home and returned the rental car. They checked in with her twice a day, ticking off the questions Maggie had written down for them.

"You're so good at this," Rosa had told Maggie. "Why don't you come with us?"

"Too risky," Maggie said. If she were busted, she'd never get her nursing license.

This time it was only Esther, which might be just as well. Rosa had always been hypercritical of Deborah with her ironed hair and nose job, said she had the politics of a banana slug. There was no safe apartment to return to, and she couldn't call Maggie to ask whether three pads in an hour was too much bleeding. When the guy was done, Esther helped Deborah get dressed with a tenderness that surprised them both. They drove around for a while, stopped for a milkshake at the rest area on the interstate. Then they had to drop off the rental car and take the bus to their mother's apartment to retrieve their babies. After Deborah and Sarah headed home to Bubba, Esther snuggled on the sofa with Molly while Mama dozed on Pop's recliner. Esther wished she could call Jake and tell him everything went okay, but he'd still be at the hospital. He had been worried the evening before when they talked on the phone.

"Helping someone abort a fetus is a criminal offense," he had said. "You could go to prison."

She didn't answer that part, couldn't think about it. "It's important," she'd answered. "And someone has to do it." I may not be a real activist anymore, she told herself, but I can do this.

When Mama woke up, she looked at Esther. "You girls must have really shopped hard. Deborah looked exhausted. What did you buy?" Mama looked pretty tired herself. Depleted. Could sadness and loss cause those blue rings around her eyes?

Esther shrugged. "Nothing fit right."

Mama pushed herself out of the recliner. "You've been a big help, but I'm okay now. It's time for you to go home to Jake."

Molly released Esther's breast and said, "Dada."

Esther brushed a rusty colored curl from Molly's forehead. "That's right. Daddy. Jake."

"Dada," Molly repeated, then pulled the frayed edge of her baby blanket to her lips.

Esther scrutinized her mother's face, trying to read the family tree in the new wrinkles around her mouth, trying to extract Rosa's news from Mama's crow's-feet.

"Before I leave, can you tell me anything about Rosa? Did she have the baby?"

Mama looked down. "If I say a single word to you, Rosa swears she'll cut off all contact with me, and that's precious little to begin with. She's furious at you. I think she's wrong, but I have to do like she says."

Molly might have a cousin, but Mama refused to say. What if there was no baby? What if she'd had to use someone like the Butcher? Esther hoped Rosa didn't have to go somewhere like that alone, without a sister to hold her hand while the machine droned and the cymbals crashed.

CHAPTER 17

Esther

"Dada work?" Molly asked.

"Yup, Monkey. Dada work." Jake took his jacket from the hook, turned to Esther.

"I'll be home late. Staff meeting. Are you going to finish that application? Today's the deadline, if you want to start with the summer semester."

Jake had been after her to return to college and finish her degree. When she got into bed with her novel the evening before, the course catalog for the nearby state university had been on her pillow, opened to the painting courses. She probably should've finished in Ann Arbor when she had the inspiration, because now the muse had deserted her, gone off into the ozone with Pop and Rosa.

"What about Molly?" Esther asked.

"She's two. She's ready for day care. She'll love it."

"College takes a lot of energy, especially with a baby."

Jake set his backpack on the floor and put his arms around Esther. "Grief can take a long time, but Pop would want you to try to get on with your life."

Esther didn't know what Pop would want. "I'm trying. But every time I think about him, Rosa sticks her nose into my memories and takes them over." Esther took a long drink of coffee, wondering if Rosa still disapproved of caffeine. "I'll do the application today. I promise."

"All done," Molly said, sweeping the remaining goldfish crackers off the tray and onto the floor. "Play truck."

In the living room, Molly filled the yellow metal truck with load after load of alphabet blocks, pushing them around the room and then dumping them into her dolly's cradle. Esther poured a second cup of coffee and switched on the television news.

"Last night, an explosion destroyed a Greenwich Village townhouse in New York City," the reporter announced. The footage jumped from a row of brownstones, front wall gone, exposing the inside to the camera like a child's dollhouse, to smoky clouds, people milling in the street, fire trucks. Was it the filming or her own brain that made the images so incoherent, so hard to understand? There was talk of a Weatherman underground bomb factory, of dynamite and nails, unidentified body parts, all mixed up with shots of movie star neighbors, daughters and sons of famous lawyers and rich men, rubble in the street. A neighbor described two young women running from the blast, naked.

Could Rosa be making bombs? Could that naked woman be her sister, running from a project gone terribly, horribly wrong?

Esther felt Molly's hand patting her cheek. "Mama cry?"

"Mama's fine." She stood up, turned off the television. "Let's play. You want to make pictures?"

After settling Molly with a large piece of newsprint and four fat crayons, Esther located her address book on the kitchen shelf, between *The Joy of Cooking* and Adelle Davis. Would Allen still be living in the same apartment, Rosa's apartment, or should she call him at work? Perhaps without Rosa's fire he had grown tired of tilting at windmills, left Legal Aid, and joined a fancy corporate practice. That thought made Esther smile, but then she remembered the explosion and the smile died.

Allen's hello sounded sleepy. She should have waited. She should have thought more about it before dialing, because what on earth could she say to him? They had not spoken since Rosa left.

"Hello? Who's there?" Now he sounded annoyed, but his voice was the same.

"Hi, Allen. This is Esther. Esther Green."

He didn't answer right away. Maybe she should hang up. She felt nauseous, faint, crazy.

"Esther. Is something wrong?"

"No, it's just . . . have you heard from Rosa? Is she okay?"

"Why?"

"That explosion. The Weathermen? In Greenwich Village?"

"You're worried that Rosa might be involved?" His voice sounded strange, as if he were making fun of her, but also as if he might have had the same worry himself. "No, I very much doubt that Rosa was anywhere near the townhouse."

"Do you hear from her? Is she okay?"

Allen's sigh was audible. "I can't tell you anything concrete. But yes, the last message I got, she was doing all right."

"What about her . . . about your . . . did she have a baby, Allen?" Once she got started, Esther didn't want the conversation to end. She wished she were in Allen's crowded, messy living room with stacks of yellow pads and wax-crusted wine bottles. She wanted to see his face, observe every nuance of expression behind his scruffy beard, capture every possible detail about Rosa.

"We have a daughter. Emma. Born in February. I'm sorry but that's all I can tell you."

Esther heard the click but didn't move the receiver from her ear. "Emma," she said to herself. She turned to Molly. "You have a cousin and her name is Emma. I have a niece and her name is Emma."

"Bye bye?" Molly asked.

Esther hung up the phone, closed the address book, and returned it to the shelf. She brought the college application packet to the table and read what she had already written. In the space for expected field of study, she scratched out "Painting."

Rosa's face appeared in her mind. A face unharmed, not burned from dynamite, skewered by nails, nor crushed by brick walls, eyes still luminous and scornful.

"No art?" Rosa's image mocked. "But you've *always* wanted to be a great artist. You can't give it up now."

"Back off," Esther told the apparition. "I want to do something else, something that's all mine. Besides, it's none of your business anymore, is it?"

She printed "Art Education" on the blank line. She couldn't think of a profession less connected to her sister, less sullied by her. She couldn't imagine a profession Rosa was less likely to respect.

CHAPTER 18

Allen

Allen hung up the phone. It took guts for Esther to call. Did she say where she was? He couldn't remember. He had heard that she and Jake moved out east somewhere after Rosa's aborted trial. In Esther's shoes, he would have probably done the same thing.

He picked a shriveled corn flake from the front of his pajama top. He should shower and get to work. Instead, he sat on the side of the bed, his side of the bed. He opened the drawer of the bedside table and removed the manila envelope, thin with treasures.

The first photograph had arrived a year before, four months after Rosa left. A Polaroid print had appeared on his desk at work, accompanying one of the notes Rosa somehow managed to get to him. An infant faced the camera, her eyes slits against the bright sunshine. An adult hand held a knit hat, as if Rosa had just slipped it off her head, to reveal wispy dark curls. The date was scribbled on the white border: March 17. Rosa had drawn a cartoon bubble above the baby's mouth and printed inside, "Hello, Papa. I'm Emma. I'm four weeks old."

Emma.

More photos and notes were delivered over the next few months. Always with Rosa cut out of the photo, or just her hand visible, steadying a wobbly, almost-sitting baby. Always with a nondescript background of leafy branches or a brick wall, void of distinguishing characteristics like street signs or storefronts. Never a return address or postmark; no way for him to write back. Through the photos, Allen watched Emma smile and crawl and finally stand alone. She balanced on pudgy feet, hands splayed out for balance.

He studied each photo in turn, marveling at the mix of his and Rosa's skin hues, their features. He noted how she held her head tilted to the side and recognized the gesture from his own baby pictures. Sometimes he wondered if the pictures made it better, or worse. If they forged a connection to the severed parts of him, or just mocked the wounds. But still he kissed the tip of his finger and touched each image of Emma's face every night. It was a ritual learned from his mother, who made the same homage for the thirty-nine months his dad spent in prison.

Also like his mother, Allen refused to wash the pillowcase on Rosa's side of the bed. Even so, the scent of the patchouli oil she dabbed between her breasts before lovemaking had faded. He buried his face in her pillow, but there was nothing left—except in his imagination, where Rosa still sparkled, sizzled. She was unlike any girl he'd ever known, from her wild hair to the small red star on her breast.

What would have happened if he had gone with her to the demonstration? Would he have persuaded her not to attack the police? More likely he would have been seduced by her fire into throwing apples at cops, leaving a little girl with two parents who were wanted by the FBI. Still, maybe if he'd been part of it, Rosa would have told him she was pregnant, instead of him hearing the news from a stranger on the phone.

CHAPTER 19

Rosa

The contractions came faster. They clambered one on top of another until there was no space to breathe. Rosa tried to recall her labor with Emma. Had it been this bad, this unrelenting and furious and uncontrollable? She couldn't remember, couldn't concentrate. The pain was so big it filled her up. It left no room for a lungful of air or a cogent thought.

She shouldn't be having this baby at all, and certainly shouldn't have come back to Michigan for the delivery. But from the beginning, she had a deep, scared feeling about this pregnancy and she needed Maggie with her. The midwife kept checking Rosa's cervix, but Rosa watched Maggie's face for clues. And Maggie's face was grim.

Even with Maggie looking so gloomy, Rosa was glad to let someone else be in charge. Being underground had sounded so romantic, but living on the run with a fifteen-month-old child was lonely and hard: temp jobs through a different agency every couple of weeks. Changing apartments and day care centers every few months. Not being able to get deeply involved in any political group—not beyond being a follower, a member of the crowd. Never getting close enough to anyone for them to start asking questions about where she came from or why her baby's skin was dark. Following the rules about what was safe and what was not. Rosa had never done very well with rules. She was breaking a major one right then—never return to your hometown.

Having this baby was breaking another rule. One nobody had bothered to tell her because it was so obvious, so basic. Even if Rosa hadn't understood for sure how risky, how dumb it was to continue the pregnancy, Maggie's response would have made it clear.

A month after Pop's death, Maggie visited Rosa and Emma in their one-room apartment in Ohio. Rosa wore baggy clothes all weekend and waited until Sunday afternoon to make her announcement.

"You're what?" Maggie put her elbows on the Formica kitchen table and leaned close to Rosa.

"You heard me."

"Who's the guy?"

"No one. A mistake."

"Do you want me to arrange things?"

"Nah, I'm going to have this baby."

"Are you crazy? You can't take care of two babies."

"I can't explain it, but I need to do this."

"You're nuts. Listen, I'll go with you. We have better contacts now than the Butcher."

"It's too late."

Maggie raked her fingers through the short stubble of her hair and muttered that she'd never understand straight women.

"One more thing," Rosa said. "I'm coming home for the birth."

"Not Detroit. You know that, Rosie."

"Okay. Compromise. Ann Arbor." And Esther had always claimed that Rosa was missing the gene for compromise.

"That's not much of a concession. I know a great midwife there, but it's awfully risky. You're too well-known in Michigan."

"I'm tired," Rosa said. "I want to go home."

Tired and lonely. Tired of following the rules to avoid getting caught, tired of living a half-life. Some days she just didn't have the energy to take care of herself and Emma. Maggie didn't know any of that because

Rosa hadn't told her, hadn't told anyone. She was just tired of running away. She couldn't do it anymore.

Maggie was worried about it, but she talked to the midwife, borrowed an apartment, and made the arrangements for a home birth.

It was hot for June, and the State Street apartment was steamy and close. Emma sat next to her on the mattress on the floor jangling a set of keys. Rosa smiled at her in between contractions when there was an in-between. She rumpled Emma's dark curls with hands damp from sweat and fear. Sometimes Emma wobbled away to find her stuffed armadillo or the yellow metal truck that dumped crumpled paper rocks onto the floor. Maggie kept an eye on Emma. She bathed Rosa's face and belly with a cool washcloth and conferred in whispers with the midwife.

Rosa spiraled her fingers over the taut skin of her belly and watched Maggie get Emma ready for bed. At sixteen months old, Emma had just two words, "Mama" and "Didi," her name for the armadillo. Rosa knew she had placed her daughter's well-being in danger by returning to Michigan, but she needed to be home. Whatever happened with this birth, with everything, Maggie would take care of things. Maggie would make sure Emma was safe.

Besides, she couldn't stay in Ohio. It wasn't safe after the shootings. Her job at the campus cafeteria was okay, and she helped write anti-war leaflets in the evenings. It wasn't a bad life, and the women in the university day care center were kind to Emma. But when the National Guard troops started shooting at students on the Commons on May 4, Rosa had been on lunch break, sitting on the steps of Taylor Hall, eating her sandwich. "They're blanks," the students near her yelled, but Rosa knew they weren't. She walked back to her cash register early, trying to look uninvolved. She wanted to stay, to help or riot. But her eight-months-pregnant shape made her stand out too much in the crowd of students. And what would happen to Emma if she got arrested, or hurt? She packed up their clothes and they were on a bus out of town within hours.

Rosa turned onto her side. She grimaced, dug the heel of her hand into the sore spot on her back. She wished Mama were there too, fussing and making her *phuff* noise and taking charge. Funny, when just a few years ago, she had felt wondrously free to be finally away from parents and home.

To escape the pain, she made herself remember the autumn when Esther finally joined her in Ann Arbor for college. The four of them worked so well together, the sisters and Allen and Jake. They were finally adults. They helped organize the very first teach-in against the war. That night, drunk on the energy of their success, the four of them renewed their camp vows, this time forming their circle in the center of the Diag in the heart of the Michigan campus. Again, the ring of sparks fused them together. Rosa felt so alive and full of hope.

"Hey, Rosa," Maggie said, her face close. The midwife squatted at the foot of the bed looking grim. "You're bleeding too much. Hemorrhaging. We have to transfer you to a hospital."

"I told you. No hospital." The contractions were less intense, but Rosa's head was caught in a cyclone. Dizzy, from the idea of a hospital, or maybe from the bleeding. She could feel the stickiness under her bottom, the warmth seeping up her back. "Please."

She had broken the rule against returning to Detroit once before, in March when she went to the hospital to visit Mama. Another stupid move. She didn't go home when Pop was buried because she knew the Feds would be staking out the service, but when Mama collapsed a few weeks later, Rosa couldn't stay away. Maggie gave her a set of soiled scrubs and snuck her into the hospital.

Mama had been sprouting monitor wires, tubes in her nose and both arms. Deep pencil-thin creases circled her mouth and nose, tracing the inward collapse of her facial bones. She wanted to ask Maggie if those lines meant anything about how sick Mama was, but she wasn't sure she could bear the answer. Mama was sedated but seemed to listen to Rosa talk about Pop and Emma, and then Rosa slipped out of the hospital without being caught.

Rosa couldn't count on luck like that again, even now when she badly needed it. She looked at Maggie's face and knew there was no choice about the hospital. The pain was still there, but it had retreated far away. Rosa closed her eyes. Maybe she could rest for a minute, though it was hard with all the shadowy images hovering in the mist behind her eyes: National Guard troops on the campus with bayonets. Brown-rumped horses rearing up. A luminous circle with Allen and Esther and Jake on the Diag. Thousands of cranes bursting into the air from a bed of daylilies.

"Wake up." Maggie held a drowsy Emma over her shoulder. "Say goodbye to your mama," Maggie whispered, holding Emma's sleep-flushed cheek to Rosa's sweaty neck for a nuzzle and a kiss, and then against Rosa's bare belly for just a moment. "And to your baby brother or sister." Then Maggie held Rosa's chin in her free hand. "The ambulance is on the way. I'm taking Emma to Allen. I'm so sorry, Rosie."

Rosa kept her eyes open long enough to see Maggie open the door to the back stairs with Emma cradled in one arm, whimpering. Maggie's other hand towed a plastic garbage bag spilling diapers and baby clothes and the stuffed Didi. Rosa could hear the thump of Maggie's shoes and the garbage bag going down the back stairs. The crescendo of Emma's crying. *Maggie knows something she's not telling me*, Rosa thought. She dozed as the distant whine of the ambulance grew louder.

CHAPTER 20

Allen

Enough work for one night, Allen decided, tossing the yellow pad into the squall of files and loose papers on his desk. Rosa used to make fun of his legal pads, laughing at the way the lined pages turned up in odd and unexpected places in their apartment. "I can understand you working on a brief in bed," she complained, "or even on the john. But in the shower?"

He stood in front of the desk, considering a massive organizational effort, then turned away. Why bother. He opened the window to the unseasonably warm June breeze and sank into the cracked leather chair. He shifted his right buttock off the broken spring, moved the coffee cups onto the floor, and positioned his feet on the hassock. Kicking off his huaraches, he leaned over to his desk and grabbed the yellow pad. Maybe he'd just spend a few more minutes on this brief.

It was after midnight when the doorbell rang. Who would visit so late?

Maggie stood in the dark hallway, holding an overstuffed garbage bag and a sleeping baby. She pushed past him into the apartment.

"It's your turn, Daddy." Maggie dropped the bag onto the floor and continued into the living room.

"What happened? Where's Rosa?"

"Don't ask. Better that you don't know anything tonight. If anyone questions you, just say that you answered the doorbell and found the baby there. Alone. Okay?"

"Is she all right?"

"I hope so." Maggie sat on the sofa, turning the baby to face Allen. "Don't you want to meet your daughter?"

Emma slept, clutching a grubby stuffed animal against her neck and sucking her ring and middle fingers.

"Aren't they supposed to suck their thumbs?"

"They find comfort however they can." Maggie looked at him. "Just like the rest of us."

This wasn't how he had imagined meeting his kid. He had pictured Rosa calling him, summoning him to a motel on the outskirts of some dusty Midwestern town, where they could be a family for a weekend or a month or a lifetime, despite the practical concerns of arrest warrants and FBI surveillance and the need to make a living. He squatted and reached for Emma's other hand, sleep-limp on the couch.

Emma closed her fingers around his thumb, opened her eyes, and blinked twice. She stared at him for a long moment. Then she wailed.

Allen pulled his hand away and looked at Maggie. "Do something."

"You're her father. Pick her up."

He couldn't figure out where to put his hands, how to hold her. Emma screamed louder, arching her back and throwing her head away from his grasp. He caught her awkwardly and cradled her head, damp with fury and tears, in his hand. He looked at Maggie. "Help me."

"Walk with her. Talk to her, softly. Doesn't matter what you say. Tell her who you are, tell her stories, tell her legal nonsense. Walk and talk."

Allen started down the hallway, trying to imitate the peculiar bouncing gait he remembered Esther and Jake using when Molly was fussy. Emma's crying sounded angry now. Who was he fooling? He couldn't do this. He had zero experience with babies. His kid was smart. No way could an imposter father fool her. She hurled her head back again, looked at him, and howled louder.

"Please, Maggie. I can't do this."

Maggie walked next to him, her arms around father and child. She spoke into Emma's ear. "Hey, sweet Emma. This furry-faced guy is your papa. He's going to take good care of you until your mama comes back. It's okay. I promise." Maggie accompanied her words with drumbeat pats on Emma's back, a *lubdub* of reassurance.

Emma's cries slowed to whimpers, and she stuck her fingers back into her mouth. Allen felt limp with relief. But this was crazy. There was no room in his life for this. He had work to do, important work, defending the voiceless. How could he be a lawyer and take care of a sixteen-month-old girl?

How could he not? This was Rosa's baby. His daughter. He felt split open and frozen solid at the same time.

Allen whispered into Emma's other ear, mimicking the cadence of Maggie's words. "I promise, too," he said. "I'm going to take very good care of you."

As soon as I learn how, he added to himself.

Maggie turned back to the living room. "My shift starts in an hour. I'll be back in the morning to give you a crash course in toddler care. For tonight, everything you need is here." Maggie pointed to the garbage bag. "Diapers, wipes, clothes. And Didi." Maggie tucked the stuffed armadillo next to Emma's face. "Whatever you do, don't forget Didi."

Allen spent the rest of the night watching Emma. She slept on the sofa; he sat next to her on the floor, protecting her from falling off. Twice she woke up, took stock of her surroundings, and screamed. Twice he walked and talked to her. He tried to arrange her over his shoulder like Maggie had. He told her about his cases; they would put most people to sleep, but not Emma. The second time she cried so hard she vomited over his shoulder and down the back of his sweater. He wanted to drop her. He wanted to cry. He wanted Maggie to come back. No, he wanted Rosa to be here, to comfort their daughter and make it all right. He wanted Rosa to comfort him. He closed his eyes, swayed in the dark hallway, and spoke to his daughter.

"Give me a break here, kiddo. I'm lost. I have no fucking idea what to do with you. I've never changed a diaper in my life. Never fed a baby. Cut me some slack, okay?"

Finally Emma slept and he put her down on the sofa. Even with her face smeared with mucus and vomit, she was beautiful. Even relaxed into dreams, she was a mystery. He searched her face for clues about what had happened to Rosa that night, to bring Emma here. Must be something very bad. He rested his head on the couch cushion, inches from Emma's foot.

When he awoke again, it was just turning light. His back ached. Something smelled bad. He groaned, rotated his stiff neck, and turned to Emma. Her eyes were open and staring at him. He returned her gaze, afraid to move. His heart galloped. How could a grown man, a smart man, often called arrogant or cocky or worse by people who didn't like him much, be so intimidated by a little girl? Pre-verbal. Twenty-five pounds max.

Emma opened her mouth and started fussing. It sounded different, as if she was trying to say something. As if she wanted something. Maybe her toy, that grubby thing Maggie said was so important. "This what you need, kiddo?" he asked, dancing the armadillo in front of her.

"Didi." She grabbed it from him with both hands and closed her eyes.

That wasn't so hard. Maybe he could do this. He stretched, then went to make coffee.

The phone rang just after sunrise. Allen lunged for it on the first ring.

"Yeah?"

"Hi, Allen. Grenwich here."

Tom Grenwich was the morning paper's crime beat reporter. It had to be about Rosa. About whatever Maggie didn't want to tell him the night before. Allen stretched the phone cord so he could check on Emma sleeping in the living room. "Morning, Tom. What's up?"

"Rosa. An ambulance brought her into an ER in Ann Arbor around 1:00 a.m. She was in labor. Having a baby."

"A baby?" How could that be?

"Or trying to, but she hemorrhaged. Something tore loose inside." Grenwich spoke quickly, too fast for Allen to catch the jagged words, the shards of sentences. "A doc in the ER recognized Rosa from the newspaper and called the cops. She was busted."

"Is she okay?"

"They saved her. Lost the baby."

"Where is she?" How could there be another baby?

"They transferred her to Detroit City General. Under heavy guard. As soon as she can be moved, they'll take her downtown."

"Thanks, man. I appreciate the call."

"No problem. Just one question, Allen?"

Uh oh. "What's that?"

"No one seems to know how Rosa got to the hospital, who called the ambulance. She was alone and unconscious. Any ideas? Off the record, of course."

"Not a clue. I haven't seen her since she went under." That much was certainly true.

When Emma woke up, Allen managed to change her diaper and fill her bottle with milk from his fridge. "Do you need it warmed up?" he asked her.

She grabbed the bottle and drank.

"Guess not." This kid knew what she wanted. Just like her mama.

When Maggie returned, Allen and Emma were sitting on the kitchen floor, tossing utensils into a constellation of pots and pans. Maggie taught him to change diapers and bathe the squirming, slippery child in the kitchen sink. She explained what foods to feed her. They found a crib and rocking chair at Goodwill, and a woman in the building to babysit while Allen worked.

"Okay," Maggie said. "You're ready to be a daddy and I'm ready to sleep."

"Wait," Allen begged. "I don't know anything about babies. Couldn't you . . . you know." He stopped, already ashamed of himself.

Maggie stood still for a moment. Allen recognized something like longing flicker across her face, then vanish.

"Don't even think it." She walked to the front door. "It won't be long before the cops or social services figure out Rosa has a kid. They'll see Emma as a way to make Rosa cooperate. Emma will need your protection. And, if there's a custody battle for this kid, who's likely to have clout? The biological father who's a lawyer, even if he's black? Or a dyke friend who's a nurse working rotating shifts? What do you think, Counselor?"

He nodded and closed the door behind her. Emma was starting to drift off, so he sat with her in the new rocking chair. He sang folk songs, then Loon Lake songs. They were all embedded with images of Rosa: Rosa as a teenager, Rosa in custody, Rosa bleeding, Rosa pregnant again. She had always insisted that monogamy was part of the system they were fighting, people owning other people, restricting their freedom. That one-and-only stuff is fine for Mama and Pop, she used to say. Allen went along with her; it was easier than arguing. Now, he felt like a fool. Why had he kept himself alone for her all these months? She obviously hadn't done the same. And now here he was, stuck with her baby.

Allen buried his nose in the soft curls of Emma's hair, sniffed the tangy fragrance of her scalp.

No. Their baby.

CHAPTER 21

Rosa

Rosa wasn't worried about facing Allen. He wouldn't yell or rant, wouldn't blame or guilt her. He didn't need to. In the three days since her arrest in the Emergency Room, she'd done nothing but reproach herself.

Allen stood silhouetted in the visiting room doorway at the city jail. Behind him, the June sunlight blazed in the courtyard. It transformed his Afro and full beard into a soft explosion, melting away the excuses she had rehearsed. When she stood to greet him, the room spun. She grabbed the table edge. Blood loss, she told herself. The hospital wanted to keep her another day, but the DA said she could recuperate in jail. The guard closed the door behind Allen, and they were alone. She opened her arms.

"Rosa," he whispered.

"I'm so sorry."

"Shush. It's okay."

How could it be okay? She had screwed up big time and he had to pick up the pieces. Not that Emma was a burden, but Allen didn't exactly choose fatherhood. Esther used to say that Allen would want a kid in a second if Rosa agreed, that he turned into instant mush whenever he saw Molly. Back then, Rosa hadn't paid much attention to

Esther's claims or Allen's wishes. Now it was important. She loosened her embrace, leaned back so she could see his face.

"How are you doing with Emma?"

Allen grinned. "I'm learning. She's a great kid." He paused. "How are you doing without her?"

Rosa rested her face on his shoulder. She had promised herself not to lose control. She had to stay strong to face the new trial, to fight the new charges. The new lies.

"I miss her terribly." The waves of dizziness came back, or maybe this was sorrow.

"Listen, Rosa. I'm so sorry about what happened in the hospital." He paused. "Tell me about the baby."

Rosa burrowed her face deeper into the cave of his beard. "Later. Not now." She let herself rest there for another few moments, then pushed away. "Let's talk about my defense. I want a better lawyer this time. Not Dwayne."

A pained expression flickered across Allen's face. Disappointment, maybe, or sadness. Didn't he want to fight anymore?

The crash of broken glass burst from the corridor outside the visiting room. Shouting followed, then heavy thuds moving from left to right. When the last echo faded, Allen let his arms drop to his side and sat down at the wooden table. Rosa looked at the dark hollows under his eyes, at his untrimmed beard. She wanted to take his left hand, run her finger along the hard writing callus on the index finger. She imagined him touching her breast. She squeezed her eyes closed and sat down across the table from him.

"You know about the new charges, right?" Allen rubbed his hand over his beard. "The Lansing bombing?"

"That's bullshit. I never bombed anything."

"I know that, but they claim to have witnesses. It's a whole new ball game."

"Their witnesses are lying. I've been out of state, except two days in March to visit Mama in the hospital." Her mind wandered from the stew of lies and charges, truths and deceptions. Mama would be worried, too, and probably really angry. No use dwelling on that. She focused on Allen's face. "How can they pin a bombing on me?"

"Can you prove where you were on February 12?"

"Even if I could remember, if I gave you names of witnesses, that would get the people who helped me underground in trouble, right?"

"Maybe. But these charges, this trial, they're different."

"DA Turner must be salivating." Rosa grinned. "He lost his election, and now he gets another chance to nail Red Rosa. Maybe this time it will propel him into Congress."

Allen's sour look was fleeting, but she noticed it. He disliked the nickname, one the local newspaper coined when she went underground. "Get serious here. We're talking real prison time. Ten years, fifteen maybe."

"I am serious."

Allen looked away.

"What?"

"It is possible Turner is involved in more than just prosecuting this case."

"What do you mean?"

Allen waved his hand in front of his face. "Forget I said that. They're just rumors and rumors won't help us here."

"Tell me the rumors."

"I'll explain later. First, tell me how you're doing."

"Tell me how we can win this case." Rosa pushed back from the table, scraping the chair on the floor. "Who's the best criminal defense attorney in town? Can we get Goodman? We *have* to fight. The war is still going strong."

"Maybe that's not the point. Not the most critical issue right now. What about you? What about Emma?"

Rosa stood up, wobbled, and grabbed the table. A strong wave of dizziness and dread battered her, then dragged her down. What *was* the point? Putting up a good fight? Even if you knew you couldn't win? What was that Brecht poem Pop used to recite, about continuing to struggle even when you knew it was futile? About how—if nothing else—you could really put the screws to the rulers. Esther had never liked the poem. Stop being so melodramatic and self-important, she'd say.

And what about Esther? Had anyone heard from her? Mama wouldn't say a word, of course, but maybe Allen had heard something. The air in the small room thickened and pulsed, a cloud of heavy regret. She fell forward onto her hands, fingers gripping the tabletop.

"What's wrong?" Allen was steadying her, guiding her back into the chair. "You're so pale."

"I'll be all right. Just help me fight this, Allen. Get Goodman, someone top notch. Hit the books, the law library. You're good at this."

"We're going to lose. You know that?"

"Maybe. But we'll remind citizens that they don't have to go along with genocide."

"Could you please drop the fucking polemic? It's different now. We have to think about Emma."

Rosa couldn't hold it in any longer. The sorrow cloud enveloped her. It stung her eyes and torched her throat. She let the tears come.

On a rainy October morning four months later, Rosa was escorted into the courtroom. She tried to look confident despite the uniformed guard at each elbow. It was a new trial, but loud echoes from the past ricocheted off the wood panel walls. A different courtroom, but it was the mirror image of the first, with the same light wood benches, the same deep red drapes. She rubbed her finger along the curved grain of the oak table, tracing the spiral eddy. Only two years had passed, but Rosa's limbs felt twenty years heavier as she was escorted to a seat at the defense table.

Time had warped and stretched and folded in on itself. She could barely remember the nightmare last June. Bleeding and almost dying. Losing her little boy. Losing Emma, too, in a way. The memories were ghosts—broken images, dizzying strobe lights, flashes of thundering pain and sirens. The nurse at the hospital said people usually didn't get those memories back. Not enough blood to the brain. At least she was home now, in Detroit. Even though Pop was gone. Mama was slowly getting her strength back after being so sick; she and Maggie were helping with Emma. Allen came to visit every day. Sitting in the windowless jail conference room, he filled in the missing hours bit by bit.

Allen never talked about Esther, except once to mention that she and Jake had moved east. And that she was staying with Mama during the trial. Mama wouldn't say anything. "You told me never to mention her name to you," Mama said, pursing her lips and shaking her head at Rosa's questions. "I know better than to get between you girls."

Rosa scratched at a dark splotch on the oak table with her fingernail. It looked like tar. Probably a petrified drop of coffee from the pot in the prisoners' waiting room. Allen reached over and covered her scraping fingers, quieting them. He couldn't calm her brain, though, couldn't soften the waves of panic when she thought about the people determined to send her to prison.

"Don't give up," Allen said the day before Esther was scheduled to testify. "You will have to serve time, but I think we can keep it short. Especially if you show some remorse."

"No remorse," she insisted. She didn't *feel* sorry, not about her reaction to the brutality of the cops, not about trying to make a difference. Mostly she felt angry that the war was still going strong. Furious that Turner was trying to frame her for a bombing she didn't do. She felt pride, too, that she had to be brought in the back door of the court building because of the warring picket lines out front. Off-duty police officers carried signs: THIRTY YEARS FOR RED ROSA. Anti-war demonstrators chanted, "One injured cop; two million dead Vietnamese civilians."

She did try harder to hold her tongue in court, saving her indictments of the war for the moments of maximal effect. She had not yet been removed from the courtroom and exiled to the little room for unruly defendants.

The bailiff called the next witness. "Esther Green."

Rosa watched from the defense table as her sister was sworn in. Allen said she was subpoenaed as an unfriendly witness for the prosecution this time. Maybe she had a change of heart? Esther looked thin. Her voice quivered slightly as she described the injured protester. Why did she go into all that detail about the way the blood bubbled from his scalp wound? What difference did it make if someone bled on a white T-shirt, obliterating the peace sign? Who cared if the tear gas was so thick it turned a sparkling summer afternoon into a hazy green dusk? Esther was thinking like a painter, not an activist. But Esther had always been easily distracted. That's why she never won the olive game.

"What were you thinking about, Mrs. Green? What did you hope to accomplish?" DA Turner leaned close to Esther, resting his elbow on the edge of the witness box.

Rosa frowned. She hated it when the bad guys acted sympathetic. Hopefully it wouldn't fool Esther. Rosa leaned forward also, to not miss a word of her sister's testimony. Esther was staring toward the back of the courtroom.

"Mrs. Green, please answer the question."

"I'm sorry?" Esther looked at Turner.

"Why did you do it? What did you and Rosa hope to achieve?"

"We wanted to end the war," Esther said.

Rosa cringed. It sounded so lame. Why didn't Esther show some spunk?

"You wanted to end the war in Vietnam, so you threw rocks at mounted police trying to enforce the city ordinance requiring permits for street rallies?" The DA looked at the jury and raised his open palms in an I-don't-get-it gesture.

"Apples," Esther said.

"Yes. Apples." The DA sighed loud enough to reach the back of the courtroom. "Mrs. Green, your sister Rosa is a committed activist, a self-proclaimed revolutionary leader. Have you ever been afraid of her?"

"No."

"But you usually followed her lead?"

"I admired her. But I can think for myself."

"On August 17, wasn't it Rosa Levin who suggested throwing apples at the horses and officers?"

Esther sat motionless, like a heron stalking a fish in shallow water. What did she want? Rosa wondered. What was she thinking?

The DA's voice was insistent. "If you had been alone on Grand River Avenue that day, Mrs. Green, would you have thrown the apples?"

"I don't know. Probably not."

"One last question, Mrs. Green." Turner leaned even closer. "If your sister Rosa asked you to do something risky, like jump off a bridge, would you do it? Even though you knew it was dangerous?"

"Objection." Goodman was on his feet. "Irrelevant."

"I'm trying to establish the defendant's character, Your Honor. Mrs. Green's relationship to her sister is crucially relevant to these proceedings."

"Objection overruled."

Thirty feet separated the sisters—from defense table to witness box—but Rosa could see right into Esther's brain. Jump off a bridge, Esther was thinking. How about jumping off a fire escape? How about a late summer day when they were little girls, just old enough to be trusted outside in the backyard without an adult? That day came back so clearly. Heat shimmering on the street. How bored Rosa was. She beat Esther in the olive game, was tired of playing cat's cradle—that was for babies—and was pissed off that she had to stay in the yard with her little sister. Where did the idea come from? I double dare you, Esther, to climb the fire escape ladder to the second floor and jump. Rosa knew how much it would hurt to land on the hard-packed dirt, their scraggly lawn of weeds crowned with spent dandelions. Esther climbed up and kneeled balanced on the edge of the fire escape railing.

Rosa had watched Esther climb, the metallic taste of fear in her mouth. Then Esther jumped. In the long moment of her falling, Rosa wanted her sister to fly. Would she die? Or be paralyzed, like the boy in her second grade class who was harnessed into a wheelchair and drooled into a bib like a baby, even though he could spell with a communication board and was plenty smart?

DA Turner leaned closer. "Answer the question, Mrs. Green. Would you jump off a bridge if your sister told you to?"

All these years, Esther had never tattled. Waiting for the ambulance, Rosa had raised her index finger to her lips and whispered, "Sister secret. Don't rat." And Esther didn't, not even in the hospital when the morphine made her eyes look funny, when their parents asked her over and over why she did something so stupid. Esther insisted she was clumsy and lost her balance.

Please. Rosa stared at Esther. Don't rat.

Esther turned then, to finally look at Rosa. Her eyes held a question. Rosa heard it as clearly as if Esther had shouted across the courtroom. Will you forgive me? Esther wanted to know. Give me a sign we're okay, her eyes implored. If you forgive me, I'll lie for you. All Rosa had to do was nod or smile, and Esther wouldn't talk.

For an instant, Rosa was tempted. But that would be giving in, wouldn't it? Going back on everything she'd said and done. And Rosa wouldn't—couldn't—betray her principles. And anyway, maybe she just imagined the meaning of Esther's glance.

"Mrs. Green." The judge's voice was sharp. "Answer the question."

"I'm sorry, Your Honor," Esther replied, then turned to the jury. "The answer is yes. At that time in my life I would have jumped off a bridge for my sister."

CHAPTER 22

Allen

"Dada!"

Allen groaned quietly and rubbed both hands over the roughness of his beard, although honestly he loved this nocturnal ritual. He picked Emma up from the crib in the darkened bedroom. She didn't need a nighttime bottle anymore but often woke at about midnight for a cuddle, just as Maggie had predicted.

With one hand, he dumped the ragged stack of files and books from the seat of the rocking chair and retrieved the corduroy pillow hanging by one tie. He switched on the lavender nightlight made from a sea urchin shell, another offering from Maggie.

"It's okay, little woman," he murmured, settling into the rocker with Emma sprawled over his chest and shoulder. Her blanket sleeper was twisted around one leg, and Allen straightened it without disturbing his daughter. After four months, he felt pretty competent at this father stuff. He could feed her and dress her and get her to the babysitter in the morning. He could comfort her and read her favorite books in the right order at bedtime. His right foot kept the motion of the rocker while his left hand rubbed Emma's back, fingering the perfect row of bumps along her spine through the fabric. Even in the muted light,

Emma's skin was a rich mix of her parents' hues, her brown curls untamed and fierce like her mother's.

He didn't mind the interruption. There was no way he could sleep, not with Rosa's sentencing the next morning. This time around, the prosecution had been unstoppable. There was the original testimony from the cop and the neurosurgeon, plus the damning evidence of Rosa skipping town and disappearing. There was Esther's bizarre but somehow damning admission about jumping off a bridge if her sister told her to. And then there were the false charges, the bombing of a military research facility in Lansing. Three agents from the Lansing FBI office testified that Rosa was at the scene. No physical evidence, just their say-so, but they didn't budge on cross-examination. The vague rumors that Turner was crooked, that he was somehow involved with their testimony, were unconfirmed and inadmissible. And Rosa had no alibi for the night the building blew up. She refused to utter a single word about her time underground, unwilling to endanger the people who helped her. Nobody had been surprised when the jury found her guilty on all counts.

Emma fidgeted on Allen's chest, half-woke with a whimper, and then quieted. Allen felt the warmth spread through his flannel shirt to his skin. He shifted Emma in his arms and unfastened the diagonal zipper on the blanket sleeper. Damn. Forgot the rubber pants again. He repositioned her damp weight over his heart.

Maybe he should have tried harder to persuade Rosa to plea bargain. What if he had dug deeper during those late nights at the law library, with Emma sleeping on a blanket under the table? Why hadn't he been able to unearth an obscure precedent, imagine a brilliant defense, anything to help Goodman save Rosa? Why hadn't he been smarter?

Allen tried to rub the sting from his eyes. He knew it would have taken a miracle to change the outcome. Even the best team of defense lawyers in the country couldn't beat the case DA Turner and his federal buddies manufactured against Rosa. No one could have gotten a different verdict given the way the cards were stacked. Not now, with the Charles Manson trial making headlines in Los Angeles, and Turner referencing Manson in his closing statement.

His Rosa was going to prison.

He buried his nose in the warm crevasse of Emma's neck and inhaled the lingering scent of baby shampoo mixed with the tangy fragrance all her own. *Eau de Emma*, he liked to call it, wondering if Rosa had taken as much pleasure in the aroma of their daughter's skin as he did.

His face burned to remember how during Rosa's first trial, before he had any clue what he was talking about, he had minimized the power of Esther's attachment to her baby, had seen it as a mere excuse, an impediment that interfered with her commitment to activism. That was before Emma. He could probably never admit it to Rosa, but snuggling his daughter on his chest, he understood Esther's decision. That didn't mean he agreed with it or would make the same decision, but he got it.

Stop thinking like that, he scolded himself. What's the big deal about going to prison? Doing time is a real possibility for anyone who wants to change the world. Kids survive. Emma has her father. She'll see her mother every week, even if it has to be in a prison visiting room. Allen knew that drill. He'd visited his dad at Angola Prison every Sunday for three plus years. His dad was innocent of breaking and entering, but he did organize his union and he was good at it, so a trumped-up charge and railroaded conviction must have seemed like the simplest way to stop him. Allen always felt a little embarrassed that the only jail he knew from inside was in Mississippi, and that was just overnight to throw a scare into the northern college kids doing voter registration on spring break.

Allen stood up carefully and managed to change Emma's diaper and put her, still sleeping, back into her crib. Trying to relax his shoulders, he rolled his head 360 degrees like Rosa taught him years ago at camp. The taut muscles screamed on the first circle, whimpered on the second, and finally gave up and stretched a little on the third. Rosa always said he was too wound up, too tense. Look who's talking. That woman was coiled so tight that even he got nervous when the spring inside her threatened to let loose.

He looked down at their daughter. "Your mama's going to prison," he whispered.

But what was he supposed to do with the feelings that crept into his head in the dark, when he cuddled Emma before putting her to bed? What about the despair, when he thought about Rosa locked away for the next decade? Or the jealousy, when he imagined Rosa with another guy, conceiving that dead infant boy? And how could he keep himself steadfast for the movement, when he picked Emma up at the babysitter's apartment after work and delight cracked the girl's face and his own heart, and he'd do anything for her?

CHAPTER 23

Esther

Esther settled Oliver in the wicker bassinet next to her rocking chair, watching his mouth continue to suck off the breast: pucker and relax, pucker and relax. The little guy was mellow, nursing and napping with admirable regularity for six days old. Had Molly ever been so easy?

With a fluttery snore, Mama shifted her position on the cushioned bay window seat. Esther eased herself up from the rocking chair, grunting at the tug on her episiotomy stitches, and tucked the quilt back around Mama's shoulders. Her finger stroked the starburst pattern, then jerked away from the peak of Mama's collarbone, sharp through the thin cardigan.

"You're still too skinny," she whispered.

"I heard that." Mama opened one eye. "Let me nap. I'm exhausted."

"Fine." Esther picked up the mug of cold tea and started toward the kitchen. "But you do need to gain weight."

"Rosa's even thinner," Mama said, her voice slipping back into doze.

Esther turned back. "Have you seen her?"

"Of course. And it's time for you girls to stop your nonsense. Talk to each other. If not for your sake, think about your children. Molly and Oliver should know their family."

"I thought you refused to play mediator?"

"It's crazy to get between you two." Mama shook her head. "But enough already. It's way past time you girls make things right."

"Rosa will never forgive me." Esther sat down, still holding the mug.

"It goes both ways," Mama said. "Do you forgive her?"

"For what?"

"Well, for one thing, for daring you to jump off the fire escape, breaking your leg."

"You knew about that?"

Mama made her *How stupid do you think I am* face and then closed her eyes.

Esther touched her shoulder. "Mama? You knew?"

Mama didn't answer. And when she didn't want to talk, nothing could make her. Her doctor said nothing was wrong, but Mama still wasn't her old self. Jake said it was depression, the cumulative effect of two trials, Pop's death, and Rosa going to prison. But after three years she should be back to normal. Mama had insisted on coming from Detroit to help with the new baby. That was a laugh—it was more like Esther having *three* children to take care of. Mama needed a cup of tea or half a banana more often than Oliver wanted to nurse.

Esther set the mug in the sink, then leaned against the doorjamb between the kitchen and the living room, looking out the oversized bay window. After an early April snowfall, the meadow was weeks behind the usual greening. A marsh hawk skimmed above the field, then swooped low, harassed by a pair of crows.

She had twenty minutes max before Jake would bring Molly home from art class. Esther knew she should nap. Jake reminded her every morning before heading to the hospital: Every time the baby sleeps, the mother should sleep too. Esther glanced at Mama and Oliver, both asleep, then shuffled to the upright desk in the alcove off the kitchen. She ripped a page from the notebook tucked into one of the desk slots, picked off each small ragged torn edge, and started to write.

Dear Rosa,

I'm not sure why I'm writing you this letter, except that Mama let slip just now that she had seen you. Thinking about it logically, it makes perfect sense that she would visit you in prison. But I had never considered the possibility and it surprised me. Normally she refuses to talk about you at all, claiming she'd have to be crazy to get between the two of us. I guess she has a point there.

I wrote you a letter once before, right after you went underground. I never mailed it, but I still think about you every day. Now that I know where you are, I could probably actually send this one, if I thought you would read it, which I don't. Maybe I'm writing this as much for me as for you, but believe it or not, I still miss you enormously.

Don't get the wrong impression. I'm not pathetic without you. I'm building a good life here with Jake and Molly and Oliver, without anything or anyone left over from Michigan. Has Mama told you about Oliver? Molly has a brother. Your daughter—Emma is such a pretty name—has another cousin. That's why Mama is here, helping me—can you see me roll my eyes on that last sentence? Molly is five, already reading by herself. She's a solemn little girl, as if all the pain of our family settled in her chest like pleurisy—does anyone get that anymore? Oliver is only six days old, so maybe it's hard to tell, but he was born smiling and hasn't stopped. Jake says he's too young to smile, and Mama insists it's gas, but I'm his mother and I know. He's too young to distinguish any family resemblance, but he does have the bushiest eyebrows I've ever seen on an infant. Like Uncle Max.

I'm sorry about your baby boy, the one you lost. When I read about your arrest in the newspaper, I felt so sad for you, and for Allen and Emma. I felt sad for me, too, that I couldn't tell you that in person, with a sister hug.

Which reminds me, who does Emma look like? I wish I had a picture.

Esther put down her pen and rummaged in the top drawer for the photograph she had found buried in a box of Molly's outgrown baby clothes. It was from camp. She and Rosa stood in front of the Peace Monument, backlit, with their faces in shadow and the sunlight igniting their hair. Their wild curls morphed into the cloud of metal cranes winging into the sky.

Jake is happy here. He finished his residency and joined a group practice with a patient mix of middle-class kids and Medicaid. His special interest is children with cerebral palsy, and he's been working with a neurosurgeon on a new treatment. He loves the work. And you'd never believe it, but he has become a fanatic bird-watcher. Jake, who used to say that except for all that nature, camp was perfect. Now he gets orgasmic finding a nuthatch at the suet log. He put a picture window in the living room, one in the kitchen, even one in front of the tub in the upstairs bathroom. All three have southern exposures with views across the field to the mountain. The kitchen table looks out at the bird feeders and we eat side by side, with Jake's running commentary: Here come the grackles. Now, why did the female cardinal fly off? Gee, haven't seen the bluebirds today.

I'm content too. Mostly. I've been taking classes at the state college for my art teaching certification. Those studio classes in Ann Arbor didn't count for much toward this degree and it's taking me a long time. It's not the kind of dream I once had for myself, but I guess I'm not going to be an avant-garde political artist. You're probably not going to be an intrepid Amazon Basin explorer or save the world from American corporate greed either. Don't bother commenting; I can well imagine what you think of my career choice. But I like it, even though life will be even busier trying to juggle classes with a baby.

I've started making art again too. Just for myself, not because I think I'm an artist anymore, or ever could be one again.

So, Rosa, is it rude to complain to you about being too busy, with you being in prison? If so, I'm not sorry. Do you remember what you said to me at the march, before it all happened? I was agonizing about leaving Molly at home and you said it was all about priorities. Your priority was ending the war, and mine was my baby. We both made our choices, sister, and I guess we're both stuck with the consequences.

Mama said that you've lost weight. Are you okay?

I'm finally getting used to Massachusetts, to New England. I know we promised each other, you and I, that we'd move to Greenwich Village when we grew up. But let's face it, that's not the only broken promise between us.

Somewhere in the back of her brain, Esther heard the car door slam, but it didn't register, not really, and she kept writing until she looked up to see Jake standing next to the desk. With a quick intake of breath, she spread her left hand over the notebook page, covering her words. He picked up the photograph leaning against the base of the lamp.

"You're writing to her?" Jake's voice got quiet and precise when he was upset. "And mooning over her picture? I can't believe it."

Esther tried to explain. "With the sun behind us, our faces are in shadow and you can't tell our hair color is different. We look like twins."

"Why on Earth would you *want* to look like her?"

Esther closed the notebook and pressed it against her chest. "She's my sister."

"Yeah, and she tried to ruin your life."

"That's not true. She just tried to live hers. And anyway, I want Molly and Oliver to know they have an aunt and a cousin."

"That's self-destructive, sweetheart. That chapter of our lives is over. Besides," Jake said as he turned away, "you promised." He put his arms around Molly, who stood alone in the middle of the kitchen. "Let's check out Mr. Rogers."

Did she ever actually promise? And even if she had, how could Jake be right about this, about never telling their kids about Rosa, when it felt so wrong?

She stashed the notebook in the back of the bottom desk drawer and stared out at the meadow. The old glass was wavy, distorting the view, making the marsh hawk waver in flight. She had caught something, a mouse or a vole, most likely. The crows, three of them now, were dive-bombing her luncheon.

"Esther?" Mama called from the living room, her voice faltering. "Would you make me a cup of tea?"

CHAPTER 24

Rosa

Rosa barely touched her lunch. She wanted to be first in line at the visiting room door to claim her favorite table. It wobbled unless the folded cardboard was wedged tight under the short leg, but the location in the far corner next to the window was more important than stability. It was sheltered from the bank of vending machines where families congregated. That table was as private as it got in this place.

She stared at the cement sidewalk leading from the parking lot guard post to the visitor entrance door. It had snowed last week and a crust remained, a bone-white sheen in the thin northern Michigan sunlight. That steel-barred window framed her mental photo album of Emma's childhood. She was only allowed two photographs in her cell, but in her mind Rosa had a thick and luscious file of images taken on the sidewalk outside: Baby Emma in Allen's arms, sucking two fingers. Toddler Emma, swinging on the sidewalk between Allen and Maggie. Emma at two and a half, chasing dandelion seeds across the sparse prison yard. Three-year-old Emma last winter, scarlet-faced and screaming, mittens and boots beating on the snow, because Allen had said no time for a snowman, your mommy is waiting.

"Who's coming today, Rosa?" Patty called from the next table. Her lisp was always more noticeable on visiting days.

Rosa tore her gaze from the empty sidewalk. "Emma and Allen. You?"

Patty shrugged. "My mom said she'd bring the kids if she could. No promises."

"Your sister still making trouble?"

Patty nodded, pointed out the window.

The first visitors had appeared on the sidewalk inside the guard gate. No Emma yet. Emma usually led the pack of visitors, skipping ahead of Allen. Most days she was the first person to be checked into the visiting room by the guards, the first child to jump into an inmate's open arms. Running was forbidden, but the guards responded to Emma's open face and her knock-knock jokes. They rarely yelled at her to slow down.

There she was now, tugging at Allen's arm to make him walk faster. Her jacket flapped open in the November wind. Why didn't Allen make sure it was zipped up? When they got alongside the window, Emma turned and waved with both arms, jumping up and down. Allen waved too, then he took Emma's hand and led her toward the door. Emma kept waving, walking backwards.

Rosa swallowed hard and turned to the doorway where her family would appear. First they'd give their names at the main gate to make sure they were on the approved list. Then, a second name check, bag inspection, and interrogation at the inner gate. Finally, the guards at the visiting room door. Mac was on duty, Emma's favorite. The girl jiggled with impatience while he checked their names off on his clipboard.

"I've got one," she told Mac. "Knock, knock."

"Who's there?"

"Police."

"Police who?"

"Police let me in. It's cold out here." Emma giggled.

"Good one," Mac said with a laugh. "My turn. Knock, knock."

"Who's there?"

"Dewey."

"Dewey who?"

"Dewey have to keep telling these awful knock knock jokes?" Mac grinned at her, nodded to Allen, and passed them both into the visiting room.

Emma ran from the entrance to the red line painted on the floor. The line barricaded prisoners from the door, from the visitors' bathrooms, from the vending machines. She launched herself into the air and into Rosa's arms.

If Rosa could get through the first hug, she usually did okay. But some days she couldn't bear the heaviness in her arms, so profoundly missing from her days. On some visits, that weight evoked a half-moan, a small sob, despite her best efforts at self-control. Any little exhalation of joy and loss could be a trigger. Visits could be excruciating in their sweetness. Allen claimed he could tell by the first minutes how difficult it would be. "Be strong for Emma," he whispered as he hugged Rosa on those precarious Sundays.

Each visitor was allowed one embrace at the beginning of the visit, and another to say goodbye. That was the rule, although some guards were more lenient with kids. When Mac was on duty, Emma was allowed to snuggle on Rosa's lap for the whole two hours. King George enforced regulations to the letter. Stan the Man went out of his way to hassle Rosa. One time he cut her visit short for "excessive physical contact," and his sharp whisper of "commie bitch" pursued her down the hallway to her unit.

Patty had done time in California prisons and swore things were so lax there that the visiting rooms stank of semen. But in northern Michigan, a prisoner never touched flesh or money. Never crossed the red line. Never used the vending machine. Never peed in the visitor's bathroom. Never, ever left the line of sight of the guards. Not even Mac. Rosa could live with the rules. But sometimes it was almost more than she could endure to cuddle with Emma, to lean for a moment against Allen's bulk, shoulders speaking everything that tongues and breasts yearned to say.

Allen touched her hand briefly under the table. "How're you doing?"

"The same. Not too bad. You?"

"Okay."

"Anything new?" Rosa rested her cheek lightly on Emma's head.

"Good news today," Allen said. "Maggie took a job as camp nurse at Loon Lake for the summer. She can bring Emma."

Rosa stared at Allen. "They'll let her do that, even though Emma's not her kid?"

"An exception. Because it's you."

"Play with me, Mama." Emma put both hands on Rosa's cheeks, pulling her mother's face close to her own.

Rosa blew a raspberry into Emma's neck, making her laugh. "Cat's Cradle?"

"Me first." Emma pulled a long string from the front pocket of her pink backpack and looped it around her hands. Her stubby fingers fumbled as she constructed the Cradle.

Rosa's throat swelled and ached. Emma at camp—that was amazing. She turned to Allen. "But camp pays peanuts. How can Maggie swing it?"

Emma squirmed sideways on Rosa's lap, held the Cradle out for her mother. "Your turn."

Rosa grasped the two crossed strings between thumbs and pointer fingers, and pulled them apart, under and up through the middle of the Cradle.

"Soldier's Bed," Emma announced. "Why's it called that?"

"Because it looks like a cross on a coffin." Allen turned to Rosa. "Maggie's been working graveyard shift and saving the differential. I'll make up the difference in salary. It's worth every penny. Emma will love it."

"I love it. Maggie's so great. Your turn, Emma."

Rosa watched Emma fumble with the narrow crisscrossed string triangles. The next figure was tricky. With a flourish the girl lifted the crossed strings, pulled them up and away from the center, and scooped under the side strings to make the Candles.

"Maggie says she'll do this until Emma's old enough to be a regular camper," Allen said. "Then she plans to move south to work in an abortion clinic. She says that's the frontline of women's health."

"Thank her for me. A big hug, okay?" Rosa quickly configured the Manger, then held her hands out to Emma.

"Yeah. Listen, there's other news." Allen lowered his voice to a whisper. "Nothing concrete, but there've been rumors about COINTELPRO being involved with your case."

"The Feds? Involved how?"

"Seems that in addition to the Black Panthers, they targeted new left groups in the late sixties," Allen said.

"Like us."

"Yeah. Like I said, the rumors have been around for a while. But apparently now there's evidence in some files liberated from the FBI field office in Pennsylvania. And I hear they're pretty damning."

"I can't do this," Emma whined. "It's too hard." She shook her hands, tangled up in the string, and her bottom lip started to quiver.

Allen leaned over and unwound the string from Emma's fingers. He scrunched it into a ball and unzipped her backpack. "It's okay. Let's play something else. Magic markers?"

"Let's try this again." Rosa pried open his fist and took the string, then re-made the opening moves and extended the Cradle toward Emma. "You can do it."

Emma looked at the string cradle, then at the markers on the table. She leaned back against Rosa's chest and stuck her fingers in her mouth.

Rocking forward and back in the metal chair, Rosa buried her face in Emma's hair, sniffed the spicy scent of her daughter's scalp.

"Anyway," Allen said. "Seems like Hoover's FBI henchmen did more than spying and disrupting meetings of left-wing groups. There's evidence they manipulated the justice system to get activists off the street. False charges, perjured testimony, wrongful imprisonment. Sound familiar?"

"The Lansing bombing?"

Allen grinned. "Could be. Don't hold your breath though. This could take years to sort out. Senator Church is talking about a Congressional investigation, with subpoena power."

She shouldn't get her hopes up, Rosa knew that, but it would be hard not to. And damn those bastards. Their trumped-up lies about the Lansing bombing on top of the legitimate charges—well, they weren't legitimate, but they *were* her actions—bought her a fifteen-year sentence. And of course she made it worse, running out on her first trial. She'd probably have to serve ten or eleven, maybe more if the parole board was right-wing. Emma would be halfway grown when she got out. Every night she chewed on the hard crust of her decisions.

The sound of sobbing from Patty's table drew Rosa's attention. No kids today. Patty's weeping overpowered her mother's consoling tones.

"I have some news of my own." Rosa stroked Emma's hair, wrapped a curl around her finger. "I got assigned a new job. You'll never guess."

"I give up," Allen said.

"The prison laundry. Can you believe it?"

In their old life, eons ago, laundry had been an ongoing battleground. Rosa had first urged Allen to help, then demanded it. She knew he believed in his heart that they should share the chores, but with his long work hours, he rarely found the time to cook or clean. When she did persuade him to go with her to the Laundromat, he would sit on one of the metal chairs lined up along the front window, scribbling notes on a legal pad with the edges curling up in the muggy air. One winter day six months before her arrest, folding blue jeans and T-shirts at the Formica table, Rosa told him that the Laundromat visit was really a Women's Liberation organizing project. She made up slogans and chanted them until Allen finally put down the yellow pad and helped her fold.

Allen smiled at her across the visiting room table. "Seize the Tide," he whispered.

"Fuck the detergent; become an insurgent," she answered.

"Put down the basinet; pick up the bayonet," they chanted together.

CHAPTER 25

Rosa

Rosa surveyed the prison classroom: scarred wooden desks bolted to the floor. Fourteen women bent over their books and papers, relieved that the reading aloud portion of the class was over. Her students' reading levels ranged from not-at-all to almost-ready-for-the-GED. She straightened the stack of books on her desk, mulling over the right book assignment for each student. She switched two scrap paper bookmarks labeled with students' names. Saralynn needed the larger print more than Adina.

It had taken years of work to make the class happen. Even after the prison warden agreed in principle, Rosa had to swear she wouldn't talk politics, just basic reading skills. Then the warden had refused to allow inmates to take any books to their cells. That policy took months to reverse. The next hurdle was the prison library, barely adequate for basic reference, and totally unprepared to meet these women's need for books with grade-school language and adult content. Allen's office spearheaded a book collection, and his secretary hit the jackpot with a series of comic books written for teenage girls.

Her students' attitudes varied too, from belligerent to fearful to simply ashamed, their emotions written in their body language. Lorraine's feet were contorted, twisted around the metal desk legs.

Saralynn's nose almost touched the brightly-colored page of her comic book, but she refused to wear her glasses. Fitzy hunched over, making herself as small as possible while she chewed on her pencil and looked out the barred window at the winter sky.

Patty raised her hand and Rosa walked to her front row seat. Patty pointed to the page. "I don't know this word."

"Conscience."

Patty frowned and turned the book face down on the desk. "I'm so stupid. I have to look up half the words I read."

"You're anything but stupid, Patty. *To Kill a Mockingbird* isn't an easy book. Give yourself a break."

Lorraine made a derisive snort, loud in the cement-walled classroom. "What? Teacher's pet doesn't know a word?" She untangled her legs from the desk supports and stood to face the class.

"That's enough, Lorraine," Rosa said. "We respect each other in this room."

"Do we, Teach? Or do you respect some more than others? And the word is 'conscience'—how ironic is that? Professor More-Ethical-Than-Anyone-Else has failed in her attempt to rescue the masses from our ignorance and wrong-thinking."

Rosa never knew how to handle student attacks. Before prison, she would have immediately struck back, but in this place even she could read the potential for danger in that kind of response. The last time a student lashed out at her for her politics, she mentioned it to Allen. He recommended ignoring the behavior. Everyone's stressed and angry, he'd said. It's not really about you.

But it *was* about her. Rosa knew that some of the students resented her and disrespected her politics. They said she brought her conviction on herself like some kind of martyr. And in this place, without her community of friends, it was hard not to wonder sometimes if they were right.

But how to answer Lorraine? Gently. "If you'd like to talk with me about this in private, I'd be happy to do that."

Lorraine sneered and sauntered to the door, leaving her book spread open on the desk.

Saralynn pointed to the caged clock on the wall. "Time's up, Teach."

"Okay." Rosa walked back to her desk. "Before you leave, come pick up your book for next week."

Twenty minutes later, Rosa slid her tray down the metal table and sat next to Patty. The dining hall was buzzing with arguments about which of the two prisoners caught fighting in the shower room that morning had more reason to be pissed off. Most inmates thought Sister Star was justified, and besides, her arm was broken and in a cast. But no one wanted Crazy Nan angry at them, and she'd be even meaner after two weeks of solitary.

Patty grimaced. "The stew is particularly tasty tonight."

"Another Julia Child recipe?" Rosa poked the turgid gray liquid with her fork. "I see two carrots, half a celery stalk, a sliver of onion, and chunks of unidentifiable dead flesh." She glanced at Patty. "By the way, your reading aloud was great in class today."

Patty looked down. "Thanks," she mumbled.

"I mean it," Rosa said. "You're smart and you learn fast."

Patty stirred her stew. "Smart? I barely finished fifth grade. Couldn't even figure out that the word was 'conscience.' That's pathetic."

"From fifth grade to *Mockingbird* in six weeks, Patty? That's amazing. You're my star pupil."

Patty didn't answer. Rosa dipped her spoon into the broth. Over-thickened with flour again. Maybe it filled the belly, but it tasted like paste.

"You *are* smart. You can get your GED, maybe even go to college." Rosa glanced at Patty again. Perhaps she had better back off. Sometimes Patty got so embarrassed by praise that she avoided Rosa for days.

But today Patty looked pleased. "I love reading. I love class. I only wish it could be every day instead of once a week."

"Me too," Rosa said. "Except I'm not sure I could take Lorraine every day."

"She's a miserable bitch. Just trying to make trouble. Ignore her." Patty smiled.

Rosa couldn't completely forget about Lorraine, but when Patty smiled, she looked so much like Maggie. The way the tip of her tongue peeked out between the top and bottom rows of teeth. "Sometimes you remind me of my best friend at home," Rosa said.

"What's her name?"

"Maggie. She's a nurse."

"She smart like you?"

"Much smarter. She moved down to Georgia a couple of years ago to work in a women's health clinic. There's only one doctor in the whole state who will do abortions, and he can only give them two days a month. So Maggie plans to go back to school to become a PA and learn to perform abortions."

Patty stared into her lap. "I don't believe in abortion. My kids keep me going."

Rosa chewed. Most likely beef, based more on the gristle than the flavor. Even though she and Patty disagreed about most issues, it didn't tarnish their friendship. Like the war—Patty refused to talk about it, saying that her brother had never been the same since returning from Vietnam. Patty blamed his misery on the anti-war movement.

"What's happening with your kids?" Rosa asked.

"My mom still has them, but my bitch of a sister has filed for custody. Claims she'll be a better mother. I'll kill her before I let her have my babies. She'd raise them to look down on me." Patty dipped her bread into the thick broth, bit off the soppy end. "Mom says she'll bring the kids this weekend. Tommy's having trouble with math and Mom says he misses me awful bad." She bit her lip.

"I'm sorry."

"Are Allen and Emma coming?"

Rosa shook her head. "They're spending the weekend in New York. Emma has a reunion for her summer camp. Allen is talking about moving to Manhattan." What would that mean for her stuck in northern

Michigan, Rosa wondered, then pushed the thought away. "Maggie said she'd come, though, so I won't be lonely."

Maggie opened her arms and Rosa fell into her friend's hug. Suddenly it was okay that Emma chose her camp friends over her mom this one time. The girl was almost ten. It was *good* she had friends and fun things to do. Maggie and Rosa sat close together at Rosa's favorite table in the back corner of the visiting room.

"Get up." Sister Star loomed over their table, flanked by her two buddies, rumored to be the meanest women inside. The plaster cast on Star's right arm was thick with scrawled signatures and drawings. "I want this table."

Rosa hesitated.

"Didn't you hear the sister, commie girl?" Wolf-woman took a step toward the table. "Unless you want trouble, you and your butch girlfriend better move now."

Maggie stood up, took Rosa's arm. "We're leaving."

There were no empty tables left, so Rosa and Maggie leaned against the far wall.

"Hey," Maggie said. "I've missed you."

"Hey yourself." Rosa rubbed the stubble on Maggie's head. "Those thugs—thugesses?—are right. You look more dyke every time I see you."

"Enjoy it while you can," Maggie said. "I'll have to grow my hair out for school. I hear Alabama might be even more homophobic than Georgia."

"When do you start?"

"May 1. It's two full years, including summers." Maggie leaned down to scoop up a baseball cap that frisbeed across the room, followed by a small boy.

"Hiya, Tommy." Rosa took the cap from Maggie and put it on the boy's head, pulling the visor down over his eyes. Tommy quickly turned it backwards. A tuft of black hair stuck out over the Velcro strap.

"Thanks, Miz Levin." He raced back to Patty.

Rosa waved at Patty. She pointed to Maggie and mouthed her name across the noisy room. Patty waved back and hugged Tommy.

"It means missing camp this summer," Maggie said. "But Emma doesn't need me anymore. She's totally comfortable there."

"Allen said she was so psyched about this reunion that she's ignoring the fact that he'll be job hunting."

"What about you?" Maggie asked. "Are you ignoring it too?"

"Kind of. We always dreamed of moving to New York City. But I thought I'd be going too."

"It'll be hard for them to visit so often."

"I'm definitely ignoring that part."

"That reminds me," Maggie said, pulling a photo from her pocket. "Emma asked me to give you this. Our team is five and zero and Emma is a pretty good third baseman."

In the photo, Emma and Maggie stood arm in arm in front of a scoreboard and wire cage in their matching team uniforms.

"Thanks." Rosa took the picture. She couldn't think of anything clever to say, something appreciative and funny.

Maggie leaned closer, lowered her voice. "Allen has some news too, that he can't put in a letter. Has he mentioned the investigation into COINTELPRO violations in Michigan?"

Rosa nodded. "Years ago. But every time I ask him what's going on, he changes the subject. What's the story?"

"The Church Committee reports included a reference to the federal agents who testified against you. When they were subpoenaed for the state hearings, they admitted they lied."

"We knew that," Rosa said.

"Now everyone knows it. And there's more. Seems like DA Turner orchestrated the perjury, along with his pal on the Detroit Red Squad."

"Slimy bastard. I'm glad it's out in the open now, but what good does it do me?"

Maggie grinned. "You might get out of here sooner."

"I wouldn't argue with that."

"One more thing." Maggie turned her head slightly away.

"What's that?" Rosa asked. Why was Maggie uncomfortable?

"The agents? They testified that the reason they lied about you and the bombing was . . . well, it was because of Allen."

"Allen?"

"Yeah, their target was actually the National Lawyers Guild."

"What?"

"Remember, Allen was chapter president that year. The meetings were held in your apartment." Maggie put her arm around Rosa's shoulders. "If you believe those turkeys, they framed you to discredit Allen. They've been gunning for the Guild for years, trying to prove they're commies. It wasn't personal."

Not personal? Her cell felt particularly cold and lonely that evening, with only rumors and suspicions for company. Ignoring the ache in her hips, Rosa paced back and forth, then around in circles. She refused to let herself get hopeful about the possibility of early release. And what did it mean that the Feds had been going after Allen? She was just some kind of collateral damage? Why didn't Allen come and tell her the COINTELPRO news himself? Well, she could answer that. He felt responsible, guilty that she was paying for his activism.

She wasn't going to think about that. Or let herself prematurely mourn Allen and Emma's possible move to New York. Maybe none of it would happen. Instead she'd think about how good Maggie was, how lucky she was to have a friend like her. Soon even those thoughts turned sour, as she pictured Maggie and Emma on the mother-daughter softball team. It wasn't fair that Maggie got to mother *her* daughter.

Rosa groaned and collapsed onto the thin mattress. This place was toxic, poisoning everything that was good in her life. Had been good. Things used to be good, when she was little, and her parents knew everything, and Esther looked up to her. Esther had always been quick to see the absurdity in any situation, and Rosa often had to remind her to get serious. Like the story of how Grandma Leah converted the family outhouse into a clandestine print shop and published anti-government pamphlets there. Esther loved that part and would ask Grandma Leah, "Did it stink in there? Wasn't it convenient, when you had to go?" Rosa loved the story too, even though it ended with Leah beaten and ex-iled before escaping to America. Even without the drama of her escape, Rosa had always felt a strong connection with her grandmother. Partly it was because Leah so often tempered Mama's exasperation with her older daughter.

"No, she's *not* stubborn," Leah would correct Mama's complaints af-ter observing one of their frequent mother-daughter battles. "Rosa is resolute, independent." Rosa's earliest memories were of Mama yank-ing the knots from her red curls while lamenting that Leah's flaming snarls were reincarnated in Rosa.

"Who needs hair like this?" Mama would complain. "It goes with the personality. Heaven help us." Rosa was never sure if Mama was more upset about the hair or the temperament. She couldn't help wish-ing that her Emma had inherited the unruly red curls along with the determination. Of course, some might argue that Leah's temperament in Rosa's body had been disastrous. Look where she ended up. Even Lorraine, a total loser serving her third sentence for possession and dis-tribution, saw right through her. Professor More-Ethical-Than-Any-one-Else. Maybe she wasn't cut out for teaching.

Rosa leaned back against the damp wall. Maybe she could finally write to Esther. She opened her notebook.

I've been writing you this letter in my head for years. I know I said some awful things to you. I doubt that you've forgotten what I wrote after my first trial, more than ten years ago. I know I haven't.

Don't think I've forgiven you. No way. What you did was unforgivable. But I think about you a lot. I'm not really sure why I'm writing you. Of course there's the obvious reason. I will get out of here some day, maybe sooner rather than later. I suppose at some point I have to decide if I want to ever see you again.

Sometimes I feel like there's not much left in me. I have arthritis. On days like

*today it's pretty crippling. The prison doc tells me it's an autoimmune disease.
That for some reason my body is attacking itself. That's bull. It's from living in a
damp cell.*

*The other thing is that I'm scared. I don't know what I'll do outside. For work.
For politics. What happens if Allen and Emma move to New York and leave me
behind?*

*Then there's you. I don't know what to do about you . . . I can feel my anger
softening. Melting away. But who would I be without my anger?*

One thing I do know: I'll never mail this letter.

Rosa put down the pen and closed her eyes. She remembered the evening she and Esther promised to grow old together. Rosa had been
brushing their grandmother's long hair. It was pewter gray, still thick.
Leah kept saying, "Enough, enough, you spoil an old woman," but she
leaned her head back and closed her eyes into slits like a cat, and rocked
with the force of the brushing. Rosa told Leah this was payback, for all
the times Leah had brushed her hair.

Esther had leaned close and swished the wispy silver ends of Leah's
hair back and forth against her lips. She made Rosa promise that when
they got old, they would both have long gray braids down their backs.
They would move to New York City and live in the Village, a couple
of blocks apart, each with a succession of passionate lovers who were
revolutionaries and artists and they would each have a bunch of love
babies. They would see each other every day.

The corridor lights flickered off and on, off and on. Ten minutes
until lights out. The day's final roll call would soon begin. Rosa closed
the notebook and slipped it under the student papers ready to return
at the next class. She lay on the thin mattress.

Really? New York City? Without her?

CHAPTER 26

Esther

At the squeal of the school bus brakes, Esther closed her notebook. She'd find time after dinner to finish her lesson plans. Teaching was more challenging than she expected, especially helping her students to make artistic connections between their academic subjects and the natural world. By the time she opened the front door, Oliver was flying down the driveway, unzipped jacket flapping like the gawky wings of a fledgling, backpack dragging, and gravel spraying behind his sneakers.

"Stop kicking rocks at me." Molly trailed behind her brother.

"Careful," Esther called to him. "And watch your pack."

Oliver hugged the backpack to his chest, making his running gait even more ungainly. Esther knew how much he treasured the steel gray pack, new in September for kindergarten. Like the big kids'; no more Cookie Monster or Flintstones.

Esther caught the backpack he tossed at her as he darted into the house.

"I've got something so cool to show you, Esther," Molly said.

Esther still felt a tingle of joy every time Molly or Oliver called her by her given name. She and Jake had always encouraged it, hoping it would breed respect for each person in the family as an individual, not just a role. Her women's group back in Detroit had argued the issue for weeks without coming to a conclusion, but it felt right, even though whenever her children were upset or unhappy the names Mommy and Daddy magically reappeared. Esther stood in the doorway for a moment, looking at the front yard. Thanksgiving was still two weeks away, but already the leaves were brown crisps blowing across the front yard. Following her children into the kitchen, she wondered how Rosa's daughter addressed her mom.

Oliver teetered on a kitchen chair pulled up to the counter, grabbing peanut butter and graham crackers from the cupboard. Esther helped him climb down, took two glasses from the dish drainer, and poured milk. When she turned back to the table, Oliver was licking peanut butter off his fingers.

Molly stood at the table holding an origami crane in each hand. "Look what I made today for our unit on Japan. Mrs. Sullivan showed us a movie about Sadako. She was this girl my age who got leukemia from the bomb we dropped on her city."

Esther caught her breath. Her head spun and her vision blurred. She managed to put the glasses on the table and sit down without spilling the milk.

Molly flew the sparkly green crane in front of Esther's face. "There was a legend that if she folded a thousand origami cranes, she'd get better."

"Mommy?" Oliver's voice sounded far away.

"But she died before she could finish. It really happened. Mrs. Sullivan said there's even a book about it. Could we go to the library right now and get the book? Please?"

Oliver climbed into Esther's lap and captured her face between his hands, sticky with peanut butter. "Mommy?"

"I'm okay, sweetie." Esther turned to Molly. "You surprised me, that's all. I heard about Sadako when I was your age. At summer camp. There was no book yet, but my counselor told us the story."

Oliver sucked peanut butter from his pinkie. "You went to camp?"

"Can we get the book today?" Molly asked. "I want to do a book report on it. And some origami paper too, okay?"

Esther leaned back against the hard kitchen chair. Could Molly possibly remember the origami cranes mobile that once hung over her crib, the mobile that somehow got lost in the move to Massachusetts? It made Esther dizzy to think that Molly had inherited Esther's fascination for Sadako's story, along with her DNA and artistic talent.

Oliver's voice dragged her back to the kitchen. "I want to go to camp."

"You're too young," Esther said. What about Molly, though? Might be more exciting than hanging around this backwater every summer. "Maybe you'd like to go to sleep-away camp this summer, Mol?"

"I'd rather take horseback riding lessons. Rachel's mom found a place and we could go together."

"You know what Jake says. It's—"

Oliver finished her sentence, "—too dangerous."

"Jake thinks everything's too dangerous. Rachel's parents let *her* ride." Molly rubbed her fingernail along the crane's wing fold. "Can we go to the library now? I want to keep this book forever."

"Homework first," Esther said. "Then we'll think about it."

"It's Friday. I've got all weekend for homework." Molly put her arms around Esther's neck. "Can we please go now?"

Late Sunday afternoon, Esther sat at her desk in the alcove off the kitchen. Jake insisted on a late season meal of chicken grilled on the patio, and was trying to convince the charcoal. She reached into the bottom drawer for the red box. She liked to display Rosa's photo when she wrote, but there wasn't enough privacy. Mustard scratched at the chair and meowed, so Esther scooped up the yellow cat, unable to jump lap-high anymore. She stroked the silkiness of his abundant belly and opened her notebook to a fresh page. *Dear Rosa*, she began.

The strangest thing happened on Friday with Molly. She came home from school with origami cranes. I almost fainted. Her teacher told the class the story of Sadako and taught them how to fold them. Molly made cranes all weekend. She used

up the package of origami paper, and kept going—using scraps of wrapping paper,
newspaper, even tried to make one out of toilet paper.

She looks so much like you with that red hair, springy curls with energy to spare.
She loves to paint, but insists she's no good. Of course, who am I to talk? I haven't
made art in years. It's too mixed up in the arrest and what happened to us after-
wards. Still, I felt bad a few weeks ago when Molly quit her painting class.

The night after Molly made that announcement, Jake and Esther were
lying in bed, talking over the day's dribs and drabs. Esther mentioned
Molly's decision.

"I really wish she'd keep painting. She's talented."

"Maybe she'd just rather do something else for a while," Jake said.

"No," Esther said. "She's scared she won't be good enough. I know
that feeling. But I wish Molly had more gumption. I wish Molly were
more like my sister."

That ended the conversation.

I can't stop thinking about Molly and Sadako. Do you suppose it could be that mo-
bile I hung over her crib? I was pretty obsessed with cranes too. Remember how I
tried to convince you that our tattoos should be cranes? Remember our argument?
Remember the concert?

Until that trip, Esther had always listened to Mama's gloom and doom
stories and had never *ever* hitchhiked before—not even in the Mid-
west, much less all the way to Berkeley. She felt a fierce liberation in
lying to Mama, saying they were leaving the driving to Greyhound and
then cashing in the tickets and sticking out their thumbs. It was 1967
and the three of them—Rosa and Maggie and Esther—felt free and
invincible. Esther was already pregnant with Molly but didn't know it
yet. She did know that something unusual was happening because her
body hummed and glowed from the inside out, even though no one else
could see it.

The high point of the California trip was the concert. They almost
didn't go. They weren't into the new rock group called the Grateful

Dead. But a guy selling tickets in People's Park convinced them that the concert would be incredible. So they took the standing room only bus up the hill to the university stadium in ninety-degree heat that everyone kept saying never happened in the Bay Area in the summer.

Esther never forgot how the lyrics of the songs blazed through her bloodstream that day, detonating every cell. Maybe it didn't seem like much all these years later, but that summer, they thought the music was utterly profound. With 20,000 other people in the stadium, they were part of something momentous. Right after the concert, they got their tattoos.

Maggie thought we were crazy! She said it was that splendid Mexican weed making the decision and kept fretting about blood poisoning or some bizarre infection. But you and I knew what we wanted—to be branded as sisters in the revolution with our twin red stars, one each on our left breasts. I'm glad we did the stars, instead of peace cranes like I wanted. It was perfection.

I'll never forget that trip. I don't think I've ever had that much fun, before or since. That was before Danny died, before the demonstration, before it all fell apart. I'm so glad I had that trip and that I didn't know what was coming.

"Esther, you'd better come look at this," Jake called from the living room. "On the news."

She carried the notebook with her, a finger marking the place.

Jake stood in the doorway holding the platter of chicken just off the grill and pointed the barbecue fork to the television. A black and white photograph, *the* photograph, filled the screen.

"In a rare gubernatorial pardon," the announcer said, "radical anti-war activist and convicted bomber Rosa Levin was released from a Michigan prison today, seven years before the completion of her sentence." The camera zoomed in on Rosa, on her oval face and high voltage hair.

The camera cut to the reporter. "Ms. Levin's early release was based on information in the Church Committee report about the federal Counter Intelligence Program, known as COINTELPRO. FBI targeting of Ms. Levin and perjured testimony by federal agents at her trial were the basis for the pardon. The Governor's statement alluded to collusion between FBI agents, elected officials, and Detroit Red Squad personnel."

Esther reminded herself to breathe as she watched Rosa walk down a long concrete sidewalk, flanked by Allen on one side and a girl about Molly's age on the other. Emma. A crowd of reporters and photographers surrounded them as they reached a car parked at the end of the walkway.

Emma looked smaller than Molly, but her hair was the same tangled mess. The color on their television was lousy, but Emma's hair didn't look red like her mother's.

"Ms. Levin made a short statement to reporters," the anchorman continued. Rosa's face again filled the television screen and she spoke directly to the camera.

"I was entirely innocent of the bombing charges. But in 1970, the government found it easier to lock me away than listen to my accusations about the genocide in Vietnam. Now citizens know the truth. We know about Watergate and about COINTELPRO. We know what the government has been doing in our names. We have no excuse. We have a lot of work to do."

Rosa turned her back on the camera and edged into the car, awkward, less agile than Esther remembered. Rosa thrust her fist into the spotlight of the slanted November sun. Her face ducked away from the camera, toward the girl and the man next to her in the front seat.

The camera panned the concrete towers and barbed wire crowned prison walls, then cut to a thin man, identified as the warden. "Ms. Levin is outspoken," he read from a paper on his desk, "but she made significant contributions to the prison community through her literacy work. She earned the respect of both prisoners and Department of Corrections personnel."

Esther's throat ached. Would that comment make Rosa proud or pissed off?

Back in the newsroom, the camera returned to Rosa's half of the old photo while the reporter wrapped up. "Ms. Levin plans to relocate to New York City, where she will live with her boyfriend, civil liberties attorney Allen Jefferson, and their ten-year-old daughter."

New York. Rosa in Manhattan, three hours to the south. Living the life they had imagined together as young women. Esther pictured a third-floor walkup in the Village. On the windowsill, a droopy geranium with curling brown leaves, forgotten in a life overflowing with activism and friends, meetings and art films and coffeehouses.

And what about the daughter? What had Rosa told Emma about their history? Did Emma know she had an aunt, a cousin? Did Emma go to Loon Lake Camp, just four hours north of the relatives she had never met?

Esther felt Jake's arms around her, felt his kiss on her forehead. "It's okay, Essie. No one here will ever suspect she's your sister. It'll be all right."

Esther shook her head, wordless. Sometimes Jake just didn't get it.

"Chicken's ready," he said.

Esther rested her hand on his arm. "Start without me. I need a couple minutes."

At her desk, trying to ignore the conversation around the kitchen table, Esther opened the notebook and returned to the letter.

I just watched your prison release on television.

Do you ever think about seeing me? It would be legal now; my probation ended long ago. Did you know I had to sign an agreement that I wouldn't participate in any demonstrations, organizing, or political meetings? And I had to agree to swear I wouldn't hang out with any known felons. Even my sister. Especially my sister.

Believe it or not, Rosa, I went to a demonstration last month.

Esther wasn't proud of how well that court-ordered proscription against activism worked; it was eleven years after August 17, 1968 before she attended another demonstration. She read about the pro-choice rally at the high school in Northampton and decided to go. It seemed pretty low-key, but Jake hated the idea.

"But *why?*" he had asked. "You're not active in abortion rights work anymore."

"*That's* why," Esther said. "Because I'm not active in any political work anymore."

"Sure you are. What do you call all those environmental groups you work with?"

Esther shook her head, imagining Rosa's opinion of her local Save the Earth committee. "That's different. I want our kids to develop good politics about big issues—racism and feminism and the environment. How can they do that if we don't set an example?"

"That was some example you set," Jake said quietly, then touched her arm. "Sorry. It's just that I'm worried. Rallies can be dangerous."

Esther shook her head. "Not this one. It'll be okay. Anyway, I'm going and taking the kids. You can come with us if you like."

It hadn't been okay. Esther had wandered by all the tables, read literature without really seeing a single word, listened to the speeches from the very back of the auditorium. She'd grasped Jake's hand the whole time, hardly able to breathe.

> It was awful. I was so scared. I kept thinking about all those women we helped in Detroit. I kept looking around for the cops, expecting them to spot me, point me out to each other, arrest me, shoot me, worse, I don't know. Jake was great. He kept the kids involved, although explaining abortion to Molly wasn't easy.
>
> The odd thing is, I don't know if I was so uptight, so uncomfortable, because I was afraid I would be identified. Or maybe afraid I wouldn't be.
>
> Damn, I miss you, Rosa.
>
> But I'm not going to send this letter. You're the one who called me a traitor, said I wasn't your sister anymore. You have to make the first move. And I'm sick and tired of not living my life until that happens. So I'm not waiting anymore. You're out of prison and starting a new life. And I'm going to forgive myself and start living fully, too. I'm going to make art again. Seriously.

Esther tore the pages from her notebook, folded them, and opened the bottom desk drawer. The stack of letters to Rosa had overflowed the

Japanese box and now filled a brown envelope with one prong of the metal fastener missing.

CHAPTER 27

Jake

Jake pulled the car into the driveway, slowing down over the icy bump left by the snowplow. He hadn't been looking forward to the weekend, but a winter camping trip was the only thing Oliver wanted for his seventh birthday, and it was more fun than Jake expected. He and Esther even managed a starry walk together, after Oliver's friend Kenny finally stopped crying for his mother and the boys fell asleep. The snow in the woods was clean and sparkling. Too bad Molly refused to come, but no big surprise there. To a twelve-year-old girl, a weekend at her best friend's house won out every time over listening to two days of nonstop fart jokes.

After they delivered Kenny home, Oliver fell asleep in the back seat, surrounded by the smell of stale campfire and wet sleeping bags. Jake carried him up to bed, removing only his boots and snowsuit.

"Would you pick Molly up?" Esther asked. "I'm going to soak in the bathtub."

Driving to Rachel's house, Jake pictured Esther in the upstairs bath. The bay window, reaching from floor to ceiling, looked out into the heart of a swamp maple tree whose blazing red leaves heralded autumn every October. In lucky years, May brought a robin's nest with startlingly blue eggs. They had searched for the right tub, finally found an antique cast iron clawfoot that was big enough to fit both kids and the necessary fleet of plastic tugboats and yellow duckies. Big enough for Esther to soak her whole body, up to her chin, one hand holding her book safe above the water, while the pages curled in the humid air.

Molly was waiting and slid into the back seat.

"Have a good weekend?" Jake asked.

"Yeah. You guys have fun?"

Jake heard the slight derision in Molly's voice but decided to ignore it. She was still pretty reasonable for almost a teenager. Not that he was under any illusion that he had much control over the situation. At the office, he watched kids who had once listened with delight to their own heartbeat with his stethoscope become sullen strangers, unwilling to look him in the eyes or answer a simple question.

"It was great," he said. "What's the homework situation?"

"All done."

"Good," he said. Sometimes he wished Molly weren't quite so serious and conscientious. "After I check in with work, you want to play some cards?"

"I guess," Molly said. She leaned forward to rest her chin on the back of the front seat. "If I get to choose the games."

His answering service reported no urgent messages, so he knocked on the door of Molly's bedroom, tucked under the eaves. He smiled at the handwritten sign in curlicue letters with flower decorations. *Do not enter without permission. This is Molly Green's private abode.*

"Who is it?"

"Sting. I'm looking for a female vocalist for my next album."

"*Right*, Jake. Come in."

Esther had always insisted that their kids call them by their first names. Jake hadn't argued with her, but sometimes he longed to be called Dad. "Where's the TV table?" he asked. "And what do you want to play?"

"Why call it a TV table when we're not allowed to have TVs in our bedrooms, or watch TV when we eat?" She always asked that question, as if someday Jake would answer differently, but didn't wait for his answer. "Steal the Old Man's Bundle," she said.

Jake shook his head. "It's all luck. How about Gin?"

"No way. You always win. Casino or nothing."

"You drive a hard bargain." Jake shuffled the cards.

Halfway through the first game, Esther called from the bathroom, her voice muffled. "Jake, I need you."

"Be right back," he told Molly. Esther probably needed help getting out of the tub. She had low blood pressure and often felt faint after soaking in a hot bath.

Jake stopped just inside the bathroom door. Esther's face was pale, not flushed pink from a hot bath. Both hands covered her left breast. He kneeled at the tub.

"What's wrong?"

"I found a lump."

Jake got Esther settled in bed, promising to call Ira after dinner. His med school friend specialized in breast oncology. He returned to Molly, sprawled on her bed with her worn copy of *Rose in Bloom*.

"Your mother isn't feeling well. Come help me make tuna casserole for dinner?"

"I'll be there in a minute. I'm at the best part. Charlie is dying and Rose is trying to be brave."

Jake twisted the stiff metal opener around the cans of tuna fish. Most breast lumps were benign; this one was probably just a cyst. Nothing to agonize about. By ancient habit, he squeezed the water with little flecks of tuna into a bowl for the cat. But Mustard had died last summer. The memory undid him and his eyes flooded with worry.

Molly walked into the kitchen. "What's wrong?"

"Mustard," Jake said. "I poured the tuna water for him."

Molly put her arms around Jake, hugging him without saying anything. The top of her head reached his chin, and he rested his cheek against her hair. Molly had gone with him to the vet that last day. Mustard couldn't eat or drink or even lift his head, and his breaths came slow and jerky. He was so light his bones seemed empty. The vet asked Molly if she wanted to hold the cat and she said yes, even though Jake could tell she was scared. She cradled him and Jake stroked the pale yellow fur. The vet shaved a little rectangle of fur from his front leg and slipped the needle into his vein. She pushed in the clear fluid and then Mustard didn't breathe at all. Molly's cheeks were flooded and Jake realized that his were, too. The vet gave Molly an old towel, and she cradled Mustard's body on the drive home. They buried him in the corner of the backyard, behind the black-eyed Susies, covered by a heavy piece of slate to remember the spot.

Jake poured the tuna water into the sink. He hadn't thought of Mustard in months.

Six weeks after the mastectomy, Esther raised the issue of Loon Lake Camp. She had been moving food around her dinner plate, even though Jake had served her a tiny portion.

"Molly," she said, "how would you like to go to camp this summer? Loon Lake Camp, it's in New Hampshire."

Jake stared at her, but Esther's eyes remained fixed on the lopsided slab plate Oliver made her for Chanukah, holding salt and pepper shakers and extra napkins.

Molly frowned. "I won't know anyone there. I want to—"

"Stay home. We know." Oliver bounced from his seat. "But I want to go to camp. Why can't I go?"

"You're too young, Ollie," Jake replied automatically. "In a few years."

Esther's red bandana had slipped on her smooth head and she tugged it down over her ear. "I told you about Loon Lake, Molly, remember? It's where I heard about Sadako?"

Molly had been crazy obsessed the year before about Sadako and the cranes. Jake figured it was probably the contemporary version of girls and horses. But really, Sadako was just what they needed in this family, another tear-jerker. They might as well rent the *Love Story* video and give up. Jake reached for the bowl of veggies and ginger stir fry. "Anyone want more?"

"It's the third time this week," Molly groaned. "Can't we have burgers?"

"Ginger helps the chemo nausea," Esther said. "What about camp?"

"I'd rather stay home this summer. Ride my bike and—"

"And hang out with Rachel," Oliver said.

"Think about it." Esther pulled a folded brochure from her pocket and placed it on the table, next to the brown rice. "Take a look at this."

Molly ignored the brochure and slapped her brother. "Stop finishing my sentences. You talk too much."

Oliver balled up his napkin and threw it at Molly. "Do not."

Jake intercepted the napkin without comment and stared at the Loon Lake photo on the front of the brochure. When did Esther get that? Why hadn't she mentioned it to him? Because she knew what he'd say, that's why.

He looked at Molly and grinned. "Did I ever tell you about the time I was an intern and a mom in the pediatric ICU climbed into the crib to comfort her sick baby? When she had to go to the bathroom, she couldn't figure out how to get the side rail down. She pushed the code blue button instead of the nurse call button. You wouldn't believe the confusion." Jake knew he'd told that story far too many times before, and his family couldn't care less about confusion in an ICU. A desperate measure, but it worked. They stopped talking about Loon Lake.

After the kids went up to bed, Jake brought Esther a cup of chamomile tea. The kitchen window was cracked open and the murmur of the peepers was loud in the dark room.

Jake cleared his throat. His voice had become a foreigner to him these past few weeks, breaking and cracking without warning like a boy in puberty.

"For crying out loud, it's a crazy summer to send Molly away, with you sick. But even if she does want to go to camp, let's send her somewhere else. Any place but Loon Lake."

"It's our history, Jake. Her legacy. I want Molly to know where she comes from."

"Why tear open old wounds? You need to concentrate on getting well."

Esther took a sip of tea. "Maybe I know what I need better than you. Maybe it's time to reconnect with my old life. I've got to make my peace with her, in case I die." She put her hand on his. "This is the first step."

"You're not going to die."

He didn't mean to shout, but his voice betrayed him again. Esther murmured calm words, but he felt no calm. He let his head fall into the cradle of his hands.

CHAPTER 28

Rosa

Rosa watched her mother taste the chicken salad.

"Needs salt," Mama said, then quickly added, "But it's delicious."

Rosa shrugged. "My domestic skills are a little rusty."

Emma patted Rosa's hand. "I love your cooking. I'll miss it at camp."

Rosa laughed. "That's not saying much—camp food is terrible."

Emma's face got serious. "Are you sure it's okay if I go this summer, Mom? You won't miss me too much?"

Rosa loved being called Mom. Turned out the women's collective didn't know everything, back when they made pronouncements about the politics of family language.

Allen stood up. "Anyone want more iced tea?"

Mama held out her glass.

"I'll see you on visiting day," Rosa said. How odd to be the one visiting, after almost a decade of being visited in prison. She shook off those thoughts. "Are you packed, Emma? The bus leaves early."

Emma shrugged. "No problem. I never unpacked last summer. That's how Dad and I do it."

Rosa felt her jaw drop and recognized the same expression on Mama's face.

Emma looked from her mom to her grandmother, then turned to Allen and grinned. They slapped four hands together in a high five and spoke in one voice, "Gotcha!"

The next morning, Rosa found a free table at an outdoor café near the Port Authority and sank into the molded plastic chair. It was only 10:00 a.m., but she'd been up since four. Mama had insisted on taking the seven o'clock bus back to Detroit. "A week is long enough," she'd said, "even to celebrate my sixtieth. Besides, you people need to say your goodbyes without me in the way." Rosa and Allen helped Mama onto her bus, then lugged Emma's two duffle bags to the Loon Lake charter on the other side of the bus station.

Saying goodbye to Emma had been bizarre, the way so many situations felt warped since her release from prison. She was a mother sending her only child off to summer camp, armed with bug spray and Kotex—just in case—and wishing the bus would never leave. But the air shimmered with ghosts of her own self at eleven saying goodbye to Mama and Pop, impatient for her Loon Lake summer to begin. Esther's image was there too, a specter hanging on her arm.

Emma had been teary. "Are you *absolutely* sure you'll be okay?"

"She'll be fine." Allen's hand nudged Emma up the stairs. "Time to go."

Turning away from Allen's hovering, Rosa walked along the bus, her fingers marking wavy lines in the dust, until she saw Emma's face in the window, sitting with her friend Poose. Rosa blew a kiss.

Allen brushed Rosa's hair away from her face. "Just three weeks to visiting day."

"I know. It's okay." Rosa blew her nose. "You want to get some breakfast?"

Allen checked his watch. "Can't. I have a client at eleven and a brief due Thursday. You'll be all right?"

Rosa sighed and closed the menu. Nine months since she got out, and ordinary tasks still felt monumental. Every simple decision was immense. Pancakes or an omelet? French toast, or maybe granola with yogurt and fruit? It was more than being indecisive. She was not in control. She had cried all the way to New York from prison, with Allen murmuring comforting phrases on one side, and Emma leaning forward from the back seat, asking over and over why she was crying, wasn't she happy to be free?

"Ma'am?" The waitress stood next to the table, pad in hand.

"Pancakes, I guess," Rosa said. "And coffee, please. Black."

Of course she was happy, but her brain refused to cooperate. Liberated from the constrictions of prison, it had also freed itself from the confines of the here and now. Pictures from the past—not precisely random ones, she had to admit—elbowed aside the concrete objects in front of her eyes. Horses' rumps and swinging billy clubs. Puking into the rose bush. Esther's face in the photograph on the television screen, her eyes closed as if to deny their act. Emma and Didi draped over Maggie's shoulder, right before the ambulance came. Those images were slippery, sneaky, elusive, then blossoming into full color when she tried to read a novel or write a press release or cook pasta.

The persistence of the images had finally been the clincher, the reason why she told Emma that yes, she *should* go to camp this summer. Maybe, with a little space from suddenly being a mother to a girl she hardly knew, Rosa could pull herself together. She kept making stupid mistakes as a mother, things she should have known. Allen kept telling her to give herself a break. Nine years in prison. A new city. It all takes time, he said. But she had already lost so much time.

The waitress brought her food and Rosa took a bite of pancake. Should've had the granola. She didn't really like pancakes, but they never had pancakes in prison, so that was in their favor. As a child, the only time she liked them was in the woods, cooked on the grungy old Coleman stove. Pop would drop fat blueberries one by one into the skillet-sized pancakes. Every summer, Mama and Pop would pick them up at camp and they'd have an East Coast family vacation. Camping in the early years, then renting a cottage on the Maine coast or the

Cape, so quiet and lazy after the frenetic fun of camp. She would read. Esther would draw. Pop would fish. Mama would nap and write letters to Miriam.

Scraping away the excess syrup and butter, Rosa took another bite. She slipped the yellow pad from her bag and dug for a pen.

> Dear Esther,
>
> I sent my daughter away to camp this morning, even though I just got her back a few months ago. Poor Emma. Poor me. I missed out on most of her childhood. Allen toilet trained her, perching on the edge of the bathtub and singing to her on the potty. Would you believe he couldn't bear to throw out the plastic yellow potty chair—it's still in the back of the bedroom closet. He taught her to ride the subway and quizzed her for spelling tests. I'm lucky Emma doesn't hate me, even though our only mother-daughter bonding for nine years was in prison visiting rooms.
>
> Emma's at Loon Lake. She's been going to camp for years with Maggie, keeping up the family tradition. Sometimes I wonder how Emma sees the events that shaped her life—our action, our arrest, my life underground and all the rest of it. I wonder how she sees activism, how she'll choose to act, or not, as an adult. It wouldn't surprise me if our family history ends up haunting her too. A few moments on a shimmering city street in 1968 and none of us have ever been the same.

"Anything else?" the waitress asked before tucking the check under the edge of Rosa's plate.

Rosa shook her head and kept writing.

> Even with everything that's happened, I don't think I would do anything differently, if I had the chance. Except maybe—if I could do it over again—I wouldn't have banished you so completely from my life.

Rosa put down the pen and looked around at the café, now mostly empty. The butter and syrup congealed on her pancakes. She finger-combed her hair away from her face and captured it clumsily with the wooden barrette clipped to her blue jeans. She shoved the pad and pen into her bag.

Was that true, what she just wrote about Esther? She had no idea.

CHAPTER 29

Esther

Esther went to bed early, but she couldn't fall asleep. The next morning Jake would drive Molly to Loon Lake, the place where she and Jake found each other and connected so deeply with Rosa and Allen they believed that nothing could break them apart.

Jake's and Molly's voices drifted up from the porch. Molly was unhappy about camp and Esther knew she should go downstairs. But it was day eleven of her chemo cycle, the day she always felt worst. Her oncology nurse said the dip in white blood cells was the reason she felt so easily overwhelmed, so quick to tears, as if her heart were scraped raw and every touch started it bleeding.

The slam of a door startled her, then footsteps running up the stairs and down the hall to Molly's room. Maybe Molly wasn't ready for camp. Maybe she should stay home this summer. Jake had been against the plan from the beginning. In fact, he was horrified. Kept asking Esther what good it would possibly do. She didn't have an answer for that, not really, except that Molly was growing up without her history, knowing nothing about the values that motivated generations of her family. Nothing about their sad legacy and buried secrets.

Last week, Jake had asked Esther outright if she wanted Molly to learn about Rosa, the demonstration, all *that*. He demanded to know if Rosa's daughter went to Loon Lake. Esther didn't know. She didn't tell him she had asked Mama that exact question on the telephone, but Mama refused to answer, said she was pleading the Fifth. "I know better than to get between you two," she said. "Talk to your sister."

No way could she fall asleep now. Esther rearranged her pillows so she could sit up, and reached into the drawer of her desk for the red fabric box. She removed the cover, stroked the graceful arc of the embroidered bridge above the blue stream now faded almost to white. Then she turned it over, looked at the photograph taped inside. The two girls stared at her, frozen in black and white childhood.

It had been a long time since Esther had allowed herself the ritual of the four small inner boxes. From the first box she lifted the tri-colored braid of hair and brought it to her lips. She breathed deeply, but there were no longer any smells clinging to the hair, and she coiled the braid carefully back in its box. From the second and third boxes she emptied a collection of tiny teeth into the palm of her hand. When Molly and Oliver asked what the tooth fairy did with their teeth in exchange for a quarter, she never told them that their baby teeth were disintegrating near the photo of their lost aunt.

The final box held Rosa's circle pin. The day after Rosa left town during her first trial, Esther had used her emergency key to enter the apartment Rosa shared with Allen. With Molly sleeping warm against her chest, Esther stood in the bedroom looking at the detritus of her sister's discarded life. There was nothing left of her Rosa in that place, except the small gold circle on the dresser, which Esther had slipped into her pocket.

Esther replaced the red fabric box into the drawer and reached for her notebook.

Rosa, why haven't you contacted me? Can't you just apologize, and then I will too and we can be sisters again? I've spent a lot of time over the past twelve years thinking about my guilt, and yours, Rosie, and measured it against those mounted cops busting heads. And now it's possible that we might not have a lot of time left.

The hardest part of having breast cancer wasn't losing my breast. It wasn't losing my hair or the nausea either, though all those things are awful. The hardest part was losing my tattoo. Maybe I don't deserve that tattoo anymore.

No, that's not quite true. The absolute hardest part is realizing that I could die without ever seeing you again. Without our daughters ever meeting, without us ever reconciling. That's why I'm doing this thing, this risky, scary, bad-mother thing. I'm sending Molly to Loon Lake tomorrow morning, without telling her anything, trusting her to somehow figure it out and make things right. I know it's an awful burden to place on a twelve-year-old, but Jake won't help and I'm simply too sick to figure out another way to do it.

The irony is that I'm doing it for Molly and Oliver, but it could be another very bad decision.

I think this disease is my punishment for everything that happened. After all, you can't get cancer of the heart. My left breast is the next closest thing.

PART TWO

1980

CHAPTER 30

Molly

The whole four-hour drive to camp, I willed myself not to cry. My father seemed to sense my misery, because even though he was usually very strict about kids in the back seat, he let me sit up front. So I could enjoy the White Mountains, he said. He didn't talk much, just a half-hearted description of camp traditions and what a good time I'd have.

Usually on long drives I liked to peer into the passing cars, to try to glimpse something private, like a woman stroking the neck of the man driving, her fingers burrowing inside his shirt collar, or a baby sleeping in a car seat with drool glistening on his chin, or a teenage boy squeezing a zit. But driving up Route 16 that early July morning, I stared into the side view mirror, where the clouds froze sharp in the sky and the trees slipped backwards, retreating from the car's forward motion.

The Harriet Tubman bunk was a dump. Initials and names and drawings carved or scrawled with magic marker on every inch of the walls. Wooden cubbies wedged two-by-two between the beds. Striped mattresses with yellow-brown stains heaped with duffel bags and stuffed animals, inside-out sweatshirts and baseball caps.

A counselor with even more freckles than me introduced herself as Crystal and pointed to the empty cot near the far wall. My name was printed on masking tape stuck to the metal headboard. I let my backpack slide off my arm, scratching the mosquito bites on the way down, onto the trunk of folded blankets and sheets, each with a "Molly Green" label that Esther and I had ironed on.

Jake wandered off while Crystal showed me around the bunk. The worst part was the bathroom. Toilet cubicles without doors, just shower curtains hung on rusty rings, and an outhouse smell. "Remember me?" I wanted to yell at Jake. "I'm the kid who refused to use those stink-a-poo places on family camping trips." Instead I listened to Crystal tell me about the orientation session coming up and about how everyone got a special shampoo. I told her I had to go find my dad.

"Come back after you say goodbye," Crystal said. "I'll introduce you to your bunkmates."

I found Jake sitting on the grass in the center of the camp buildings, staring at the peace monument. It was even more amazing than the photograph on the camp brochure. Hundreds of shiny metal birds shaped like origami cranes on toothpick-thin steel stakes perched at different heights, exploding out of a thick patch of day lilies. The cranes swayed in the breeze, dark against the summer sky. After a while he stood up and announced he had to leave.

"Just three weeks to visiting day," he said. "You'll have a great time."

He hugged me longer than usual and for a minute it seemed like he wanted to say something more, but he just kissed my nose and walked away. I watched the Subaru jostle down the rutted road until it disappeared behind a cloud of gray dust. Walking slowly back to Harriet Tubman, I kicked gravel and wished I was home with Rachel and our friends. I wasn't sure how I ended up at camp when Jake didn't want me to go and I certainly wasn't interested. Why did it matter so much to Esther?

The night last spring when Esther announced I should go to camp, after Oliver and I had been sent up to bed, I couldn't sleep. I had walked back downstairs to tell my parents I really didn't want to go. Their voices seeped out from under the closed kitchen door, so I sat on the dark stairway landing, hugging my knees and trying to follow the argument. I could hear the peepers from the pond, but it was hard to make out the words from the kitchen. I scooted down a few steps on my bum to get closer.

"*Anywhere* but Loon Lake," I heard Jake say.

What was so special about Loon Lake? I know my parents met there, but what did that have to do with me? I slipped down to the bottom step, right behind the kitchen door that could swing open at any minute if someone had to go to pee or Esther had to throw up.

"I need to make my peace with her," Esther said. "In case I die."

"You're not going to die," Jake shouted. Then Esther's voice got soft and smooth and covered up his yelling. It made no sense. Who was "her"?

I tiptoed back up to my room and re-read the brochure Esther gave me. About how these two Italian guys in Boston were framed for murder a long time ago. After they were executed, some people who had tried to save them bought land at the base of Crooked Mountain in New Hampshire and started a camp to teach kids about justice. On the front cover of the brochure was a photograph of the peace monument, the one I found Jake staring at. For two months I had studied that brochure every night, until the paper crumbled at the fold and I had to tape it together. I liked that a girl my age designed the peace monument, based on the story of Sadako, the Japanese girl with leukemia whose friends folded a thousand origami cranes.

When I was young, like fourth grade, I was seriously obsessed with Sadako. My first research paper was about the belief in Japan that cranes live a thousand years and represent happiness and hope. If you're really sick and you fold a thousand paper cranes, they will save your life.

Seeing the photo of the cranes monument in the camp brochure when I had been so into paper cranes was a creepy coincidence, but it also made me comfortable. Like Loon Lake Camp and I already had something in common. I was twelve, and the girl who designed the sculpture had been twelve, and Sadako was twelve when she died. The week before camp, I found my old Sadako story on the bookshelf and re-read it a couple of times. But when I packed, I left it at home, and I tucked the brochure back into the frame of the mirror over my dresser.

After that one dinner, there was no more discussion about my going to camp. In my family, we talked about all the things you'd expect from a pediatrician father and a schoolteacher mom. About how masturbation wouldn't hurt you but smoking would. About the importance of being truthful and contributing to your community. No one argued much in my family, or talked very much about feelings. I always figured we were a pretty regular family, except that my parents insisted that Oliver and I call them by their first names, which my friends thought was way cool. Anyway, it wasn't a huge surprise when Esther called me into her bedroom a few weeks later.

"I really want you to go to camp this summer," she said. "Is that okay with you?"

It wasn't, really, but Esther was so sick and seemed to want this so badly. So I agreed. It was only for a month. How bad could it be?

Back in the bunk, I sat on my cot waiting for Crystal. Three girls came in, elbowing each other and goofing around, their hair wrapped up in towels.

"Can you believe the stink of that stuff?" the chubby one said.

"Why do they have to shampoo all of us? *I* certainly don't have lice." That was the blonde girl. Right away I didn't like her.

"Do too, I can see them jump," the tall one said.

"You live in Brooklyn—*you* probably have lice." That was blondie.

The tall girl, the one who lived in Brooklyn, plopped herself on the cot next to me, her wide smile showing a gap in her teeth. She introduced herself as Carrie and started drying her hair.

"They're Sharon and Poose." Carrie pointed to blondie and her friend.

"I'm Molly. What about lice?"

"On the first day they treat everyone, whether or not you've got the buggers. So no one feels bad."

"Treat how?"

"Don't worry. Nothing toxic at this place. They've got organic shampoo that smells like rotten broccoli. It makes the lice run away, holding their noses." Carrie laughed, demonstrating. Then she dropped the towel on the floor and tugged gray sweatpants and a fluorescent green T-shirt over her bathing suit.

The other girls jostled each other in front of the narrow wall mirror, spraying water squirts combed from wet hair. They gathered their clothes and towels in their arms and started toward the door.

The blonde, Sharon, glanced at me and spoke to Poose in a loud whisper. "Can you believe the new girl's a Twelver?" They tried to squeeze through the cabin door at the same time. "She doesn't look older than ten to me."

Carrie ignored the comment and waited for me while I got my dead broccoli shampoo. Then we joined the rest of the bunk for orientation. Crystal talked about the awesome spirit of Harriet Tubman bunk and All-Camp Share and the Charlie King concert planned for Sunday and how we should start thinking about our skits for visiting day.

One girl caught my eye right away. She sat cross-legged in the crabgrass, straight across our circle of campers. Her skin was super tan, halfway between Carrie's brown and my redhead paleness.

"Returning campers, please pair up with the new folks for the skits," Crystal said. I wasn't really paying attention because I kept peeking at that girl, whose hair tangled around her head like a halo run wild. When the girl glanced up and saw me looking at her, she grinned. She wasn't exactly pretty, but there was something about her.

"Who's the girl over there, with the curly hair?" I whispered to Carrie.

"That's Emma." Carrie's voice sounded different. Impressed maybe. "She lives in Greenwich Village. She's been coming here for years. Her mom is so famous they named a bunk for her."

The girl named Emma intertwined long stalks of clover in and out around her bare toes, leaving the lavender flowers sticking up like dollar store rings. The two girls flanking her wove her wet curls into a dozen tiny braids. Watching her, I understood what Esther meant when she said a person should be comfortable inside her own skin.

While the counselors talked, I sprawled on my stomach in the grass, my chin heavy in the V of my hands. Carrie chewed on the sweet white part of shoots of grass she eased from their roots, making a pile of the discarded stalks limp with tooth marks. Maybe it was because her skin was dark, but Carrie had the whitest teeth I had ever seen, which made the gap between her top front teeth extra noticeable. She stuck a bunch of the stalks into the extra space and that made me laugh.

"OK, new campers," Crystal said. "We have a camp tour before Free Swim. Returning campers, you're welcome to join us."

Six of us set off with Crystal: four newbies plus Carrie and Emma. "I'll come along in case you forget something," Emma told Crystal with a grin.

"This is the center of camp." Crystal opened her arms to embrace the egg-shaped field with the peace memorial. "It's called the Heart." She pointed out the Sacco & Vanzetti dining hall and the Lillian Hellman Theater and the Jackie Robinson ball field. We followed the packed dirt path past bunks named Anne Frank and Elizabeth Gurley Someone toward the infirmary. Walking along, we met two other groups of campers. Everyone seemed to know Emma, so we kept stopping to talk.

"These are the three Rosas." Crystal pointed to a cluster of buildings in a clearing of white pine and purple lupine. Back home, lupine grew lush along the back fence in Esther's garden. "Rosa Parks, Rosa Luxemburg and Red Rosa."

There was so much to remember. Except for Anne Frank, who I'd read about, and Rosa Parks, who I studied in fifth grade social studies, I had no clue who those other people were. At least the infirmary didn't have a fancy name and the nurse was a regular person named Sue.

Crystal pointed to a building set in a grove of white pines. "That's the CIT bunk, Emma Lazarus," she said. "She wrote the poem about the Statue of Liberty. You know: Give me your poor, tired masses yearning to be free."

"Were you named for her?" Carrie asked Emma.

"No, for Emma Goldman. She was an anarchist who believed in free love. My dad used to tell me stories about her when I was little."

Anarchist? This camp was a foreign country and I didn't speak the language. I kicked a stone along the path, trying to keep it from rolling out-of-bounds into the grass.

An hour later, I sat alone on the shady end of the dock, a leafy tent of willow branches shielding me from the noisy chaos of Free Swim. The branches skipped across the water with each puff of breeze. I watched a group of girls from my bunk—Carrie and Poose and Emma and Sharon—splashing in the roped-off swimming area with some boys. They went all blurry until I wiped a lake splatter off my glasses with a dry corner of the towel Esther had labeled so it wouldn't get lost.

"The camp laundry is terrible," Esther had warned while she packed my stuff. "And the food isn't wonderful. But everything else about camp is great. You'll love it there."

I hated it. Camp was weird and a dump.

Then Emma yelled, "Hey, Molly," from the shallow water. She half-swam, half-splashed her way to the dock. She heaved herself up, coughing and snorting and trying to wipe her face with her wet arm.

I offered my towel.

"Thanks." Emma wiped her face and then her hair, which still smelled a little putrid. "One of these days I'll learn how to swim."

"But Carrie said you've been coming here for years." I shifted my position on the splintery dock. My bare feet bobbled to the rhythm of the waves.

Emma nodded. "Forever. You want advice on surviving Loon Lake?"

"Sure."

"First lesson: ignore the rules about the toilets. Camp can't afford the composting ones, so they tell us to conserve water by flushing less often: If it's yellow, let it mellow; if it's brown, flush it down."

"Gross."

"Yeah. The second major danger is the dining hall. Say you're a vegetarian so you never have to eat Mystery Meat. The pasta's not bad."

"Got it," I said. My best friend Rachel tried not eating meat for a few weeks because she loved animals and wanted to be a vet, but it didn't work out because she hated vegetables and tofu made her gag.

"Come on, Emma!" Poose and Sharon called from the swimming area, where they were splashing a boy and laughing.

Emma waved at them.

"Everyone here knows you, don't they?" I asked.

"Yeah. My parents came here ages ago. My aunt was camp nurse until a couple years ago and I came with her when I was a baby."

"Is that how come you know who all those people are, the ones the buildings are named after?" My face burned as I remembered how stupid I felt on the orientation tour. I picked at the scabs on my thigh. The mosquito bites looked like the big dipper with an extra star in the handle. My parents came to this camp too, but I doubted they would have known important people like Emma's mom.

Sharon swam over to our shady spot. "Come on, Emma," she said, splashing Emma and ignoring me. "We have to plan our skit for visiting day."

"Just a sec," Emma told her, then turned back to me. "Most kids here come from left-wing families. We grow up knowing this stuff."

I watched my hair weep drops of lake water onto the big dipper.

"Aren't your parents political?" Emma asked.

"What do you mean, political?"

Emma tilted her head and looked at me. "You know, activists. Demonstrations and stuff?"

The only time I remembered ever going to a demonstration with my family was a pro-choice rally a year or so before. Esther seemed petrified, even though it was dinky and not scary at all. Nothing like the stuff we saw on the news. One time, when Rachel's parents invited me to go with them to New York to protest against Three Mile Island, my parents wouldn't let me go.

"No," I said. "They're not."

Emma slid off the dock into the water toward her friends. "So why are you here?"

My parents wanted to know all my secrets but they didn't tell me anything. Like why they sent me away to a weird camp four hours from home, even though Esther was sick, even though I didn't want to come.

"I have no idea," I admitted.

CHAPTER 31

Molly

Friday after dinner was All-Camp-Circle. Camp director Eva wept as she introduced the Independence Day speaker, a guy with dreadlocks and a soft voice. She didn't seem at all embarrassed about crying in public.

"What's wrong with her?" I asked Carrie.

"Nothing. Eva feels things strongly."

The speaker described how his father came to America from Jamaica looking for farm work but ended up on death row in Texas, framed for the murder of a cop. After the father was executed, his sons—the speaker and his twin brother—traveled all around the country trying to convince people to abolish the death penalty. The speaker quoted a line from Gandhi: "An eye for an eye only ends up making the whole world blind," then he turned the quote into a song he taught us, with a reggae beat but a mournful harmony.

As we sang it over and over in a round, my throat ached with sadness. Maybe my parents had liked coming to camp and being depressed all the time, but it wasn't my idea of fun. After our voices faded into the evening quiet, I walked with Crystal and Emma and Carrie to the dining hall for the weekly square dance. I wished I were home with Rachel. She always made me feel better when I felt gloomy.

"You okay?" Carrie asked.

"I guess," I said. "That was so sad."

Carrie put her arm around my shoulders. "Which is exactly why we do square dancing after All-Camp-Circle."

"The campfire programs make us think about important stuff," Crystal added. "So then we dance and everyone feels better."

Emma laughed. "Yeah. That way campers don't have nightmares and interrupt their counselor's evening off duty."

"Nothing disturbs *my* beauty sleep," Sharon said.

I still didn't like her.

I knew about square dancing from when it was too stormy to go outside for school recess. But square dancing at Loon Lake was *nothing* like that. The caller was Zander, a skinny staff guy with white hair and skin so pale his veins showed blue.

"Most camps do folk dancing or contra dancing." Zander introduced us new campers to the weekly dance. "But in square dancing, the eight people in each square have to work together to make the figures come out right. It's socialist dancing," he said, leaning his long face to the side.

The campers groaned in unison.

"He says that every year," Emma said.

"Anyone can be partners in Loon Lake squares," Zander said. "We don't say *ladies* or *gents* here. We say *skirts* and *pants*. So grab a costume from the costume box on the table at the back of the room and pick your partner. Pants on the left, skirts on the right."

It made me laugh to watch the Tenner boys dash for wrap-around flowered skirts and curtsy to their girl partners in overalls. Emma rolled her eyes at Poose, who stuffed herself into a low-cut peasant blouse that was too tight and flirted with the pimply boys from Malcolm X bunk. I stayed in my cut-offs, but Emma pulled a lavender tutu over her tie-dyed shorts and stood on my right side. That made her my partner, the *skirt*. To my left, Carrie wore an orange paisley skirt rolled up at the waist and a cowboy hat.

"I'm your corner, partner," Carrie drawled as she bowed to me, then laughed. "Mighty hard to keep this stuff straight."

I did feel better when we started dancing. I concentrated hard on *square through* and *shoot the star* and *wheel and deal*, and slowly the images of the sad Jamaican guy and the long death row corridor of prison cells colored gray with loneliness started to fade. But when we rested between dances, fanning our red and sweating faces with folded paper fans, the final words of the song spiraled around and around in my ears. *An eye for an eye until we all are blind.*

The next day, the five of us argued about the campfire program as we walked back from the lake, towels slung around our shoulders. Emma and Poose agreed with the speaker, that the death penalty was wrong. Carrie said sometimes it was justified. I just kicked at last year's leaves, already fractured into small brown pieces, covering the dirt path like a skin disease. I wasn't sure what I thought.

"What about a guy who rapes and murders a little girl?" Carrie asked.

"And what about the Nazis?" I added. "Didn't they deserve the death penalty?"

"Don't you know anything?" Sharon made a nasty face at me. "Most people on death row aren't Hitler."

"Most of them are poor and black," Emma said. "And they can't get a good lawyer or a fair trial. Anyone who's not white and rich is screwed in the courts."

"There goes Emma again," Carrie said with a laugh. "Race you back." She took off down the dirt trail with Poose and Sharon close behind.

I stayed back with Emma. "But if someone kills a person, shouldn't they pay for the crime?" I asked.

"Sure, they should pay for it, in prison. But if killing is wrong, why is it right for the government to do it?" Emma asked with a triumphant tone.

I sucked in a deep breath of the spicy forest air, tasting the tangy flavor on my tongue. I wished I had a smart answer for Emma. A gust of wind turned the leaves over with flashes of silver and I grabbed a branch. "My dad says when the leaves expose their bare bottoms like this, they're flirting with the wind."

"Don't change the subject." Emma's green eyes skewered me. "Didn't you learn any history in your school? Innocent people get executed all the time. Like Sacco and Vanzetti. They lived in Boston too."

"I live in western Massachusetts, not Boston. Didn't you learn geography in *your* school?" I walked tall, facing straight ahead. Emma was such a know-it-all.

I tripped on a twisty root in the trail and fell hard. The root was gnarled and tortuous like the hard veins in the crook of Esther's arms. *Sclerotic* was what the oncology nurse called them. The chemo made her veins thick and dense, like petrified wood. Thinking about chemo made my eyes fill and spill over. I sat in the middle of the path rubbing my knees and trying not to bawl.

"You okay?" Emma asked.

I didn't mean to tell her. I didn't mean to say anything about Esther, but I just blurted it out. "My mother has cancer and I'm afraid she's going to die."

Emma squatted next to me in the broken leaves. "Is she getting, you know, treatment?"

"She had an operation. Now she gets chemo."

"I'm sorry. I couldn't stand it if my mom was sick."

I wiped my eyes. "What am I doing here? I should be home."

Emma put her arm around me and steered me toward our bunk. "Listen. Tonight, after everyone is asleep, I want to show you something. It's how come I know about the courts and how crooked they are." She paused and then added quietly, "It's about *my* mother."

After lights out, Emma and I pretended to sleep. Finally the whispers and giggles around us faded into the moth-wing breathing of a dozen sleeping campers. We slipped out of the bunk and I followed Emma past the organic vegetable gardens, breaking off a few velvet-skinned string beans. We stopped in front of a squat building, tacked like an afterthought behind the camp office.

"This is the archive. It's supposed to be off-limits to campers, but they never lock the door." Emma eased the rusty padlock from its perch and creaked open the heavy door, then fumbled along the wall until she found the light switch.

Three walls were crowded with floor-to-ceiling shelves. The fourth was covered with camp photos, labeled with dates in clumsy calligraphy and grouped by decades. A panoramic photo represented each year, the fingernail-sized faces mostly shaded by baseball caps or squinting against the sun. I stepped forward to examine the smaller bunk groupings labeled TENNER BOYS—JOE HILL or CIT GIRLS—ROSA PARKS surrounding each large photograph.

"Maggie used to bring me here a lot, while she looked at old stuff. It was boring and the dust made me sneeze."

I turned back to Emma. "Who's Maggie?"

"My mom's best friend. I call her my aunt. She was camp nurse before Sue. Starting when I was really little, I came to camp with her as a counselor's brat." Emma looked right at me then. "My mom was in prison."

Prison?

"That's how I know about the court system," Emma said. "They railroaded my mom and sent her to prison for nine years."

"What did she do?"

"I'll show you." Emma pulled an oversized book off the shelf, releasing a fine shower of dust. "You know Sasha, the Yiddish teacher? She cuts out newspaper articles and pictures about camp and campers and pastes them into albums. This book is 1968 to 1970."

We perched on stools next to each other, carefully turning the stiff pages spread-eagled on the pine table. A musty smell rose from the paper. Emma read a headline aloud in a mock-pompous television news voice: "DA Considers Attempted Murder Charge in Anti-War Assault Case."

"Assault?"

"That's what my mom did," Emma said. "There was this humongous anti-war demonstration about Vietnam. In Detroit. My mom went with her sister and Maggie. These mounted police were beating up protestors and Mom threw apples at them."

"How can apples hurt anyone?"

"They were hard apples, little green ones. One hit a horse and it freaked and a cop fell off. That's assault. He was paralyzed or something. Listen to this one: 'Jewish Radical Cop-Attacker Comes From Union Family.' See, they didn't like her because of her background."

"What happened to her?"

"There was a trial." Emma leaned her face close to mine. "Mom tried to talk about the war being wrong, but the judge wouldn't let her. So she went underground."

"Huh?"

"Into hiding. A few months later, I was born and she hid me with her. But later someone recognized her and she was arrested again. In the second trial they framed her for a bombing she didn't do and she went to prison."

"If she didn't do anything, why did the jury convict her?"

"The FBI lied. My dad said it was to scare other people, so they wouldn't protest. They went after my mom because she was Jewish and socialist."

Socialist? Socialists were frowning young men in black and white photos in my social studies book. They wore heavy dark clothes and wanted everyone to be poor.

"What happened to you?" I asked.

"My dad took care of me. When I grow up I want to be a people's lawyer, just like him." Emma's voice was soft, but I could hear the pride. "We visited my mom in prison almost every week. I spent summers here, with Maggie." Emma smiled. "When I was little, I felt closest to my mom at camp. My parents came here as kids. They met here."

"That's so neat," I said. "My parents met here too."

"Cool." Emma turned back to the album. "Look, here's the very first story: 'Sisters Arrested for Injury to Officer.'"

I studied the large black and white photograph under the headline. Two young women with pale oval faces and frizzy hair were caught with their arms flung out, fingers extended, as if they had just thrown something. Emma's finger pointed to the woman on the left. "That's my mom, Rosa."

But I stared at the other woman, the one on the right whose eyes were closed. The air in the room went all stale and dead and so heavy my lungs couldn't suck it in.

"What's wrong?" Emma asked.

"I don't understand." I pointed. "That looks like *my* mother."

Emma stared at me. "That's impossible. That's Esther Levin, my mom's sister. She's the person who finked on my mom and sent her to prison."

"Esther Levin Green." I pictured the gold letters on the diploma Jake framed when Esther graduated college. It hung on the wall over my mother's desk in the alcove off the kitchen. A smoldering started deep inside my throat and spread like a fiery sunburn over my neck and face. Know-it-all Emma was dead wrong about this. There was no way that Esther could have a sister and never visit her or talk on the phone. That would be like me never seeing Oliver again. He was totally annoying now and I hated that he finished my sentences, but when he was little he loved to cuddle and twirl my curls around his finger as he sucked his thumb. He was my *brother.*

"My mother doesn't have a sister," I said. "I would know. She would've told me."

Emma looked at me, then at the photograph, then back at me. Like she was trying to see if I resembled my mother. Or maybe if I was somehow responsible.

"What did you mean," I asked, "that Esther finked on her sister?"

"Esther made a deal. She testified against my mom and sent her to prison." Emma spoke like they were cuss words. "So she could avoid prison and could take care of her baby." She jabbed her finger in my face. "That must be you."

Right then, everything in the world divided in half, ripped right down the middle into two different universes, like Superman and Bizarro in the musty comics Jake lugged along on camping trips. In Emma's half, people were socialists and anarchists. They attacked policemen and went to prison. In my world, people were regular and their kids hung out with their friends and had fun. How could we be in the same family?

A moth bumped its frantic dance against the window.

Emma wouldn't stop talking. "My grandparents—well, I guess *our* grandparents—had to sell their Detroit shoe store to pay the fines."

I covered my ears with my hands so I wouldn't have to hear her lies. *My* grandmother lived in Detroit and collected porcelain cocker spaniels. We visited her every year at Passover. She had promised to leave me her china doggies in her will. Would she leave half to Emma? How come my grandmother never mentioned Emma, or Rosa?

"No." I crossed my arms and frowned at Emma. "I don't believe any of this."

So Emma repeated the whole story again, about cops beating people and throwing apples and the horse rearing up and the cop falling down. Except this time she told it with two sisters, Rosa and Esther. This time it was worse because I knew what was coming, and her sentences punched holes in my lungs, up one side and down the other.

Finally, she finished and the room was quiet except for the dull lament of a lone cricket. I thought about how before chemo, Esther's dark hair coiled down the back of her denim jumper, caught with a thick blue rubber band from the grocery store broccoli. I tried to picture my mother standing on a dusty city street throwing things at policemen.

"No way," I whispered when I had breath again.

Emma touched the two faces on the photograph. First Rosa, then Esther. "They look so much alike. Except that you can't tell how red Rosa's hair is. Just like yours. Is Esther's hair red?"

"Brown," I said. "Like yours."

"Your mom got off easy. She never spent a single day in prison."

The Superman and Bizarro worlds came crashing together and that was just as impossible. I pushed off the stool and walked to the wall of photographs, turning away from Emma.

"I'm going back to the bunk. I don't want to hear any more. I love my mom."

"I know," Emma said softly. "I love mine too." She slid off her stool too and joined me at the wall. She pointed to the 1958 group photo, where four teenagers stood slightly apart from the crowd. The two boys leaned against the white oak tree at the edge of the field, their tanned arms around two frizzy-haired girls. "They're all together here. Rosa and Allen. Jake and Esther."

Jake and Esther. My parents. I turned away from the photo and looked down at the burning in my right fist. I rubbed at the row of curved marks my fingernails had gouged in the soft part of my palm. I squeezed my lips together thin and tight, and pointed at her face, like she did to me, before.

"I don't believe a word of this," I said. "You made this stuff up."

CHAPTER 32

Molly

The next morning I pulled a stool close to the steel kitchen counter, daunted by the Mount Everest of creamy white garlic heads on the cutting board. Daunted and hungry and sad. At breakfast, Emma sat huddled with Poose and the Malcolm X boys. Their laughter mocked me across the dining room. Carrie invited me to join her and Wynona and Willow, the twins from Queens, but I told her I wasn't hungry and sat alone.

The camp cook, Skinny Myrna, showed me how to press down firmly with both hands on the side of the heavy cleaver to crack the crisp skin of each garlic clove so it peeled off easily.

"You're not one of those garlic press girlies, are you?" Myrna's top lip curled up on the right side of her mouth, revealing one brown front tooth.

"Oh, no," I said quickly. "My mother and I always chop by hand."

"Good." Myrna turned away to get the celery and onion choppers started. My head felt light and whirly and for a second I wished I were an onion chopper, so I would have an excuse for tears. But my fingers knew the work, and my mind flew home to the marsh hawk that lived in the fields behind my house. One day when I was little and walking in the field, I startled the bird and we stared at each other for a long moment until it flew off. I ran back to the house and looked through the New England field guide until I found the right picture. That weekend Jake pointed out the marsh hawks' nest. I named them Sadie and Hawkins.

Sadie was my particular friend and I often spotted her perched in the big oak between our field and our neighbor's. She let me borrow her wings and eyes when I wanted to fly. While my hands chopped garlic that morning at camp, my mind swooped and soared in spiraling circles, catching small breezes off Mount Tom. The field down the end of the road was our favorite flying place. It was much bigger than my family's field, and the grasses moved like ocean swells in the wind. From the sky, my house looked small and secrets didn't matter.

I brought my fingers to my nose, inhaling the pungent tang of the garlic, and rubbed the stickiness between my fingers. I reached for another head to break into cloves.

Then I was back in the air, swooping low over Rogers Drive where the poor white trash lived. Esther said it was disrespectful to call them that, but the kids at school did. All the Rogers lived along one road in misshapen family combinations amidst rusting cars without tires, and straggly sunflowers at odd spots instead of in neat gardens. I flew over the five Rogers boys riding the row of oversized metal mailboxes like cowboys on their rodeo horses, then circled back above the abandoned tobacco barn.

With the edge of the cleaver, I shaped the mound of minced garlic on the cutting board into the double hump shape of the mountain at home. The lines started to waver and float and my head felt light and spinning. The heavy knife slipped from my hand and clunked onto the table, the tip gouging into the mountainside.

Myrna glanced at me over her bony shoulder. "You look awful," she said. "Go see the nurse."

I didn't feel well but I certainly didn't need a nurse. So I wandered back to the empty bunk, stopping at the narrow mirror hanging between Sharon and Carrie's cots. I tugged a corkscrew curl to twice its usual earlobe length, then let it spring back.

I didn't belong at this camp. I didn't know the people the buildings were named for, and anyway, I was scrawny for twelve and I needed braces. Esther joked that I was "dentally retarded" and the orthodontist said my teeth weren't ready yet, even though most of the kids in my seventh grade class had braces by the time school ended in June. Chest bumps like Hershey's kisses tented my T-shirt. When I rounded my shoulders, the tents disappeared in folds of cotton. Esther said I was a late bloomer and breasts would come, but I didn't want them because cancer could grow there. The hurt in my throat expanded, sending aching down my chest and into my arms. The floaty feeling came back stronger and there were sparkles in the air, and I grabbed for the edge of Carrie's cubby but I missed and fell.

I woke to a loud buzzing and thumping, the persistent drone of a June bug bumping against a screen. My head throbbed at the sides, near my eyes. I was in a bed, not my cot. Not at home and not in Harriet Tub-man. There was a row of beds and the nurse was there. Sue. She sat on a folding chair next to my bed.

"What happened?" I asked her.

"You fainted. How do you feel now?"

"Okay." Fainting didn't sound as serious when the nurse wore a tank top.

"Has it ever happened before?"

I shook my head, but that made it hurt more. "No."

"Any idea why?" Sue asked.

My eyes filled.

Sue's voice was quiet. "Tell me about it?"

About what? About Esther having cancer? About people being sent to prison or even executed for crimes they didn't do? About not know-ing anymore who were the good guys and who were the bad guys and how to tell them apart? About Emma's lies? Or maybe worse than lies? About Emma not wanting to be my friend? Sue probably wouldn't un-derstand any of that.

"I just want to go home."

Sue nodded. "It's hard to be away from home when you're sick. Did you have breakfast today?"

I shook my head, just a little.

"Well, that's probably why you fainted." Sue stood up. "We'll start with some crackers, then a little chicken soup."

Sue sat with me while I ate.

"This is good," I said.

"I'm going to keep you here in the infirmary overnight. Just to be sure you're okay."

"Can I call my parents?" Phone calls were discouraged. They said it made campers more homesick. But maybe they'd allow it because I fainted.

"Wait and see how you feel tomorrow."

"I know how I feel. I don't like it here. I want to call my mother."

"Why don't you like camp?"

"I don't belong here. I'm too skinny and no one likes me and my family is all wrong and I don't fit in."

Sue rubbed my shoulder. "Did something happen today, besides not eating?"

"Do you know about Red Rosa? Emma's mother?"

Sue nodded. "I've heard the story."

Maybe I could talk to Sue. She seemed like an ordinary person, someone who wouldn't hate a person for something her mother did when the person was just a baby. Something her mother *maybe* did.

"Rosa had a sister."

Sue nodded. "I remember. They both came to this camp."

Maybe I didn't have to tell Sue *everything*. "Emma says the sister betrayed Rosa, sent her to prison."

Sue hesitated. "That's what people say. I don't know what actually happened."

"Emma said her mother hasn't spoken to her sister in all these years. Rosa hates her sister. Just because Esther made a mistake."

Sue wiped my cheeks with a napkin that smelled like chicken soup. "Maybe both sisters made mistakes."

Sleepy, relieved, I let my eyes close.

When I woke up again the room was shadowy, as if the infirmary had been sketched in charcoal. Stripes of moonlight fell across the blanket. I scooted up in bed, propped my pillow against the pine wall. My finger traced the moon stripes as they crashed into the checks of my pajamas.

"Hey, sleepyhead." Emma's voice came from the next bed.

I turned to look at her. "Are you sick too?"

Even in the dim light, I could see Emma roll her eyes. "Duh. I'm here to visit you." She slipped off her bed and onto mine. We sat cross-legged, kneecaps just touching. "I'm really sorry that I made you sad. And that your mother's sick."

"I don't know if I believe you. What you said."

That wasn't totally true, I realized. I did believe it. Mostly. But I didn't know what to *feel* about Emma's story. I didn't know what it meant about my family or what it meant about me.

"Anyway, it's no fair that I never knew. How come you knew all about it and I didn't?"

"It's no secret in my family." Her voice got that proud edge again, like she was making a speech even though she was whispering.

My throat went tight and achy all the way down to my chest. "I hate this place. I'm going to go home as soon as Jake can come pick me up."

Emma shook her head. "Please don't. Lots of kids are homesick, especially at first, but you'll like it here when you get used to it."

"I hate it here."

"Stay. We can do a skit together for visiting day."

Visiting day? Esther and Jake and Oliver here, in the same place as Rosa?

Emma seemed to take the silence for yes. "We don't have to talk about our mothers."

But there wasn't room in my brain for much else. I'd been thinking about our mothers constantly—what they did, what happened. How did they feel about each other now? How did Esther feel, being sick without her sister even knowing about it? And what did it have to do with their daughters? With us.

"Could *you* do something like that?" I asked Emma. "Throw things at policemen?"

"Maybe. If I felt strongly enough. Could you?"

I didn't have an answer. I wondered about the horse. And the policeman. "Do you ever think about the cop?" I asked. "Like if he ever walked again. Or if he had little kids?"

Emma hesitated. "Rosa would say we should think about all the Vietnamese who were killed, and *their* kids."

"I guess. That seems kind of far away."

"Yeah."

The sound of a door closing silenced us. "Probably just Sue going to the bathroom," Emma whispered.

But I had more questions. "Weren't you ashamed that your mother was in prison?"

Emma looked surprised. "Rosa's a hero. I'm proud of her. Esther's the person to be ashamed of, after what she said in court."

I wasn't sure what a hero was, except people in history like Joan of Arc or Madame Curie. And what could Esther have said at the trial that was so wrong? Did she tell the truth? Was she supposed to lie? I couldn't bring myself to ask. "I just can't believe my parents never told me," I said. "I'm really pissed off about that. But then I think about Esther being so sick, and I can't be angry with her. It's so not fair that I never knew I had an aunt and uncle and everything."

We stared at each other across the dark inches of nighttime. We both seemed to have the same thought at the same moment, but I said it first.

"We're cousins, aren't we?"

CHAPTER 33

Molly

"Stop it, Molly. You're going to tip us over."

I knew I should take it easy, but I *liked* Emma being the one caught off-balance. I jabbed the paddle deep into the water and with five jerky strokes propelled the canoe out of the boat cove toward the middle of the lake, leaving the other canoes bunched near the shore.

Emma's fingers clenched the metal rim, her stiff arms trying to balance the wobbling boat. "I mean it. Slow down. I told you I can't swim."

I lifted my paddle from the water. Poking through the afternoon haze, the peak of Crooked Mountain looked like a circus clown's head, tilting to the side as if posing a silent question to the lake.

"Okay. Let's drift for a while." I rested the paddle across the canoe and sat tall, like the illustration in a book I loved as a kid, about an Indian boy paddling his canoe all the way to the ocean. Naturally I was always the Indian princess, with long braids hanging down the front of my fringed buckskin shirt. Even though the fringed shirt would look pretty silly under the bright orange life jacket. Even though I knew I was too old for that sort of fantasy.

"Thank you." Emma bowed at the waist with exaggerated politeness, her hands waving in imitation of courtly respect.

I returned the gesture, flourishing my new camp cap stitched with the logo of an origami crane. The canoe wobbled and Emma grabbed both sides. "Stop it," she yelled. "You're awful."

"Be nice to me. Remember who knows how to paddle and who's afraid of the water." Being with Emma reminded me of my arguments with Oliver: fierce on the outside and tender inside.

She pointed at a small wooded island. "If you paddle over there, slowly, I'll show you the blueberries."

Five minutes later, our canoe drifted alongside the thick berry bushes overhanging the water.

"They're so tiny. Nothing like the blueberries we get at home." I picked a leaf out of my mouth. "Tell me about your mom." I swirled my fingers in the water. In the days since we visited the archives, I'd been curious about Rosa. "She sounds so, I don't know, ferocious."

"She is, kind of. But when we walk around the city, she keeps folded-up dollar bills in her pocket for the homeless. They remind her of people in prison. The discards, she calls them."

"Is it strange having your mom be famous?" I splashed at a water bug floating on spindly crooked legs on the surface of the lake.

"Sometimes. People come up to her in restaurants, even on the street. They recognize her and want to talk."

"What about all those years in prison? She went away and left you alone."

"Not on purpose. Besides, I wasn't alone. I had my dad, and Aunt Maggie."

"Why do you call her Aunt?" I wished I had the courage to point out that Esther was *really* Emma's aunt, but I didn't.

"Maggie was like a second mom. She watched me after school and when Dad came home, we'd eat together."

"Didn't you worry that Maggie and your Dad would, you know, fall in love?"

Emma looked at me funny, then giggled. "Maggie likes girls." After a moment, she grabbed the paddle and dipped it into the water. "Let's go back to camp."

I showed her how to push away the water with the flat side of the paddle, then turn it to slip through the air. We zigzagged toward shore.

"How come you know so much about canoes?" Emma asked, once she got the rhythm.

"There's a pond near our house. How come you know so little?"

"If you don't know how to swim, you don't choose canoeing for Free Choice, do you?"

"Why didn't you learn to swim?"

"When I was little, I was a counselor's brat. I spent all summer on people's laps. Everyone thought that since I was here all those years, I must've learned how to swim. But I never did. Besides, I'm terrified of the water."

"I can't believe you grew up without a mother. What's it like now, having her home?"

Emma peeled a long translucent curl of dead skin from her sunburned thigh. "Sometimes it's hard. Like she wanted me to spend Saturdays doing childcare at the battered women's shelter. I wanted to audition for a teen theater group—they write plays and produce them. When I chose acting, she didn't say anything, but I knew she was disappointed in me."

"She expects a lot of you, doesn't she?" I appreciated Esther letting me decide stuff for myself. "And does she really give money to beggars? Esther would help them find a job and a place to live."

"What's *she* like? Your mom."

"She likes vegetable gardens and painting. Every summer she volunteers with Jake at CP Camp, doing art workshops with the kids."

Emma hooted. "CP! Your parents volunteer for the Communist Party?"

"CP means cerebral palsy."

We looked at each other and burst into laughter, wobbling the canoe. Emma stiffened and grabbed both sides.

"But it's not funny." I remembered what was happening at home. "Esther's really sick."

"So why did you come here?"

"She wanted me to."

We dragged the canoe halfway onto the soggy shore, turned it over, and tied it up under the low branches of a blue spruce. Straddling the canoe's rounded belly, we dangled our bare feet in the water. Our silence hung like a low cloud over the lake.

"I guess I don't exactly hate camp," I said after a while. My big toe painted a figure eight in the murky shallows, sending eddies in all directions. "I hate feeling different."

Emma slapped her foot hard on the water surface, starting ripples that collided with my toe eddies. "I know. I used to go to a private school with lots of leftie kids. Last year my dad transferred me to public school. The kids there don't like me." She paused. "Or maybe I don't like them. Anyway, I don't fit in. If I couldn't hang out with my camp friends on weekends, I'd go crazy."

I couldn't imagine Emma feeling out of place anywhere.

"One time in first grade," Emma continued, "I was invited to a birthday party for a new kid in the building. When my dad came to pick me up, I asked him if we could buy some of those little round green things because they were *good*. Everyone laughed at me. How was I supposed to know? We supported the Farm Workers. We boycotted grapes. We didn't *eat* them."

I couldn't imagine my family not eating grapes because of a farm worker we didn't even know. It seemed like such a faraway kind of reason. But there were different rules at Loon Lake. What mattered here was that Emma's mom was a hero, and that rubbed off on Emma. "Here everyone loves you."

"I belong here. There are other kids like me. Luisa—she's a CIT—her mom is a political prisoner, and Jamal's dad was the tenant rights organizer those landlords in Brooklyn murdered."

"Well, I don't belong and I want to go home."

"I think I'm supposed to hate you." Emma tossed a pebble into the water. The expanding circles spun outwards and slapped the lily pads. "Because of what your mother did to mine."

"But our mothers' fight has nothing to do with us."

"Maybe not. But if I told people here about who your mother is, what she did, how do you think they'd treat you?"

CHAPTER 34

Molly

The next morning, the out-of-tune bugle reveille sounded as discouraged as I felt. I wasn't hungry but I'd promised Sue not to skip meals. Gray clouds hung heavy on the treetops, suffocating the morning. After breakfast was co-op and my job was weeding. Rows of alternating Big Red tomatoes and basil plants stretched forever. I wiped sweat off my forehead with the back of my wrist and watched the dirt dribble onto my thigh. When I tried to brush it off, the dots smeared into dark streaks.

Weeding made me think about Esther. Even on chemo, she planted vegetables and herbs and flowers every spring. A few weeks before camp, we spent the morning cutting the bottoms off paper cups to make collars for the fragile tomato plants. We pushed the collars two inches into the soil surface, to protect the tender stems from cutworms. "So many dangers," Esther had muttered under her breath, patting the soil firmly around the collars. I wasn't sure if she was still talking about the garden.

I sat cross-legged in the dirt and pulled Esther's most recent letter out of my pocket.

Are you having fun, Mol? Have you made any good friends? I hope you're not too homesick. Oliver's soccer camp is fine. He's so tired at the end of the day he doesn't even argue. He misses you—not that he'd admit it, of course. Jake is working hard, as usual. My chemo isn't too bad. Only two more treatments. All of us are looking forward to visiting day—less than two weeks! Remember to write and tell me what foods I should bring for the picnic, okay?

Emma appeared at the end of the row. "You daydreaming?"

"I'm taking a break," I said. Was she still mad at me? Was I still angry about what she said to me?

"It's time to quit," Emma said. "Co-op's over."

Leaning against the shady trunk of the great oak tree, we fanned our sweaty bellies by stretching out the hems of our T-shirts and whipping them up and down. We kicked off our sneakers and dug bare toes into the faint coolness of long grass.

"About yesterday," I started.

Emma held up her hand. "I'm sorry for what I said, about telling people about your mother. I'd never do that."

I didn't think she would. Emma wasn't that mean. Still, I paused before asking, "I was wondering, have you written your family about meeting me?"

"No way."

"Me neither." Actually I had been thinking about nothing else since last night. Should I tell my parents I met Emma?

A redwing blackbird swooped and landed on the grass, shoulders aflame with orange. The redwings flocked around Jake's bird feeders at home. Were he and Esther watching them right this minute? Were they arguing about sending me to camp? Why did Esther insist I come here, even though Jake said, "Anywhere but Loon Lake"?

Then I got it. I mean, I figured it out. Rosa was the *her* Esther needed to make peace with, in case she died. Esther wanted me to come to this camp and find out for myself about Rosa, so I could fix things. What did she think I could do, when the adults couldn't get it right? Jake didn't think it was a good idea, because he was scared. I was scared too. And pissed off. And a little intrigued too, to be totally honest.

"What is it, Molly?"

"I'm just thinking. On visiting day, maybe we should try to get Rosa and Esther together."

Emma shook her head. "Bad idea. My mom wants nothing to do with Esther. Let's just worry about our skit."

"But Esther's sick."

"I don't think that would matter to Rosa."

"Well, it should matter. My mom could die." I got up and brushed the garden dirt from my shorts. "We have to do something. Our mothers screwed up and they don't know how to fix it."

"*Your* mother screwed up," Emma said.

"No," I insisted, hearing Sue's voice in my head. "*Both* of them."

I looked at Emma's face, waiting for her answer but she didn't say anything. I guess she didn't agree with Sue and me.

Three days later, Emma and I stood barefoot in the grass near the edge of the Heart. We stared at each other, our noses less than six inches apart. We did not speak. Dressed in black shorts and black tank tops, our bare feet were planted shoulder-width apart with knees slightly bent. Our hair, still wet from Free Swim, was tucked under black baseball caps worn backwards. Our four hands hung down at our sides, palms facing palms, pinky fingers not quite touching thighs. We concentrated on imagining ourselves standing on either side of a piece of glass, six feet square.

I slowly elevated my right hand to the height of my shoulder. Emma followed with her left, a mere split second behind, precisely maintaining the crucial six inches of space between corresponding body parts. Then my left hand and Emma's right. Trunk shift to one side, and then to the other; four times this exaggerated motion. Always those few inches, always together. Then, subtly, Emma took over the lead. We balanced on one foot, the other in stylized slow motion kick to the side, our big toes almost touching, but never quite. Hands high above our heads with fingers spread. We mirrored each other perfectly, as if we had known each other from birth. As if our families had rented cottages next door for the same week every summer at the Cape, and we folk-danced together every Wednesday night on the Wellfleet pier.

Then Emma stuck out her right hip, letting a sultry pout break the blank expression painted on her face. I erupted into laughter and collapsed onto the grass. "No fair. How can I copy that?"

"Tell me again, what do you call this thing we're doing?"

"Mirror movements. One of Jake's patients couldn't move one arm—even to eat or write—without the other one doing the same thing."

"Like we're doing, only there are two of us."

"Yeah. His patient couldn't help it, but my friend Rachel and I thought it was a neat idea, like a dance. We used to practice a lot."

"This doesn't look much like a dance to me," Emma said. "We have five days to get good enough so we're not laughed out of camp on visiting day."

"What are we going to do, speaking of visiting day?"

Emma frowned. "You mean about getting our mothers together? It's a bad idea. We should be plotting how to keep them apart."

"Maybe." I nestled my face into the cool grass. The earthy smell reminded me of home. What I really wanted was to forget everything Emma told me about Esther. To be a regular kid at camp, even if I didn't love the place.

Emma started to talk about *her* mother, about how mixed up she felt when Rosa made speeches—proud and scared and hopeful. Then she asked about my parents, so I cupped my hands around my lips like Esther taught me and crooned the forlorn call of the coyotes in the fields and the yips of the pups. I showed Emma how Jake extended his neck and flapped his arms to imitate the adolescent birds who followed their parents around our yard begging for food.

Emma laughed. "I've never seen my dad impersonate a bird. What about religion?"

"In my family? Not much."

"Whenever religion comes up, mom quotes that 'opium of the people' line. Except for one holiday."

"Passover, right?" I grinned.

"We always do a Seder," Emma said. "No God, but lots of folk songs."

"Us too. Do you guys have Miriam's cup and a new set of plagues?"

"Toxic pesticides and nuclear weapons and homophobia and poverty."

"Yeah, no more locusts."

Emma grimaced. "This is like that stupid Disney movie where twins found each other at summer camp and switched identities to get their parents back together."

"This isn't Disneyland," I said, hugging my knees. "And I bet this is way harder to fix than divorce. Maybe we should forget about visiting day."

"I'm starting to think maybe we should try to get them together," Emma said. "Although you'd think that being flesh and blood sisters, even having the same tattoo, they'd be able to figure this out for themselves."

"Same what?"

"The tattoos, you know, on their boobs? The little red star?" Emma looked less certain. "Doesn't Esther have one too?"

Ew. I had no idea. Which breast was it? The one she still had, or the one that was cut off and buried, or whatever they did with sick body parts? I bit my lip. Esther must have worked hard to hide the tattoo from me, during all those beach vacations and campground showers. I covered my face with both hands. It was bad enough that Emma knew secrets about her family. It was unbearable that she knew personal things about my own mother that I didn't know.

Emma stood and pulled me to my feet. "Come on. I want to show you something."

At the peace monument in the center of the field, Emma kneeled at the edge of the day lilies. She pointed to the grass next to her and I sat down. From our low vantage point, the metal birds burst upwards from their flowery home, catching and tossing dazzles of sunlight.

"I love the cranes," Emma said. "Don't you?"

I nodded. Then Emma started crawling, right into the middle of the lily patch. So I followed her. At the base of the steel sculpture she brushed grass and dead leaves from the foundation, then licked her finger and rubbed the dirt from a small rectangular plaque. She rocked back on her heels to give me room to see.

I examined the tiny letters: "Peace Cranes. Esther Tovah Levin, 1958."

"I don't get it," I said.

"Your mother was the artist," Emma said. "Esther designed the peace memorial."

The evening before visiting day, as two hundred voices swelled on the chorus of "Two Good Arms," I admired Esther's peace cranes flying in the flickering light of the campfire and thought how amazing it was, that until two weeks earlier when Charlie King visited camp with his song, I had barely heard of Sacco and Vanzetti. The last harmonies evaporated into the New Hampshire dusk and I shifted my position against the rough bark of the massive oak.

Maybe I was imagining it, but I felt the rhythm of sap flowing up and down its trunk. The old white oak was huge and its gnarly roots had pushed up the ground around it. You could stand on one side of the tree and its root-bound hill, and not see a group of people on the other side. That's why Emma and I chose that tree as the site for our big plan. The next day, my family would picnic on one side, and Emma's on the other. We would keep them apart until the perfect moment for the big reunion.

The flames ignited the evening, making my vision crackle and shimmer. I still wasn't sure about our plan. The sisters' reunion might be a bad, bad idea.

CHAPTER 35

Molly

On visiting day, we Tubman bunk campers woke up spectacularly early. The breezy mountain air felt clean and new, blowing away the cobwebs of sleep. Tingly with anticipation, we all waited on the bunk steps after breakfast for the buses and cars to start arriving. Sharon had scrubbed the sparkly green polish from her fingernails and toenails the evening before, while everyone else cleaned the bunk.

"The best thing about visiting day," Poose said, "is that your family brings all your favorite foods." The other girls laughed and joked about fried chicken and homemade brownies, but Emma and I were pretty quiet. Our excitement was mixed up with worry.

We had carefully choreographed where we would each greet our families, and how we would escort them across the grassy field to our staked-out picnic spots on opposite sides of the giant oak. So neither family would catch sight or sound of the other until the perfect time.

Then there was Oliver sprinting across the field, his arms outstretched, banking into a turn and swooping at me for an exuberant hug. We marched arm in arm, grinning and trying to trip each other, back toward our parents, waiting just a few feet away on the path at the edge of the grass. Esther was so thin. It was hard to look at her. Her head was wrapped in a turquoise scarf, with a fancy knot at her neck. I closed my eyes when I kissed her, then hugged her gingerly, wondering if she was still nauseous and tired all the time.

"I missed you." Esther's voice sounded exactly the same. She smelled the same too, like rain.

"Me too," I said. "I've been thinking about you a lot." That was certainly true.

"I want to hear all about camp. Your friends, everything." Esther stroked my hair and I wondered if the red made her think of Rosa. Did that make her hate my hair or love it?

"You didn't get too old for a Molly sandwich, did you?" Jake asked.

"No way," I said, but I wondered if maybe I had. Jake hugged my back—that made me the sandwich meat in our childhood game.

"Enough mushy stuff," Oliver said. "Let's eat."

I picked up the beach quilt and started walking. "I've got the best spot picked out—my favorite place in camp." I led the family parade to the far side of the white oak, facing the woods and the path down to the lake. Esther pulled paper plates and paisley napkins from the canvas bag, pausing and smiling at me between every handful.

I wasn't ready for this. Rachel had always complained a lot about her mom, but I usually liked mine okay. Now I had no clue who Esther really was: my sweet mama, who made paper dolls from scratch? Who was sick and could die? Or a radical rabble-rouser who kept a secret so big it grew into a lie? I didn't know which, and maybe I wasn't ready to find out for sure. But it was hard to be around her.

So I turned to Jake. "Come take a walk with me?"

"Now?"

"Just to the lake and back. I want to talk to you."

Esther looked hurt but she nodded. "Go ahead, but be back in fifteen minutes or Oliver and I will eat your brownies."

CHAPTER 36

Jake

A walk to the lake? Uh oh. Molly must have something important to tell him to willingly give up a minute with her mother after being separated for three weeks. Besides, she had that look on her face, that narrowing of her lips they all recognized. Translation: she meant business. Molly had had that expression all her life—as a sleepless infant, a stubborn toddler, a serious child. He could only imagine what was in store when puberty hit full force. He wanted to ask her what was so important but knew his girl well enough to wait for her to speak.

Their feet crunched on the gravel path, punctuating the silence. Molly swallowed audibly and spoke, not looking at Jake. "I met someone special this summer."

"Yeah?" A boy? Wouldn't Molly be more likely to confide a romance to her mother? He had a bad feeling about this.

"Her name is Emma Levin."

Memories walloped him. Jake concentrated on his feet, inspecting each step as if the pebbles on the path were sharp stilettos over a raging river. Right foot, then left, then right. When he spoke, his own voice sounded as if gravel filled his mouth and his throat. "How did you and . . . Emma figure it out?"

"There are all these old newspapers in the archive. I was so surprised, so freaked out. Why did I have to hear from Emma? Why didn't *you guys* tell me?"

"I'm not sure I can explain it so you'll understand."

"I'm not a baby."

He stared down at his feet. Every step was treacherous. "I know you're not. But your mother and I have tried to forget. It was a very painful time."

"But doesn't Esther miss Rosa? Why didn't Mom visit her sister in prison? And what about Emma—were you *ever* going to tell me I have a cousin? I don't get it."

The path opened out to the lake. Molly walked to the water and sat on the sandy beach. He stood next to her. The wavelets caught the sunlight and tossed it back to the sky.

"Esther was young." Jake wanted to explain even though he knew it was futile. Sometimes he wasn't sure he understood anymore. "She felt strongly about the war. When she saw cops beating people, she reacted. She used bad judgment. It was wrong and she told the truth in court. She paid for her mistake." His voice cracked.

Molly reached out and almost touched him. Then she pulled her hand back and stuck it in her pocket.

He teetered on the precipice of a place he did not want to go. He crossed his arms over his chest, felt his own substance, his weight, the thumping of his heart.

Jake looked at his daughter. "She paid, and the biggest price was her sister's contempt. Esther was devastated."

He couldn't possibly tell Molly how distraught her mother had been. How sometimes he barely recognized the girl he fell in love with, the one who wanted to experience everything in life and paint every emotion. How much he missed that other Esther. How even her body had changed, become denser. Not just the weight of twenty years; this transformation was on the molecular level. He used to imagine that their cells were best buddies, wordlessly passing adoration back and forth like sodium and potassium through semi-permeable membranes. He blinked a few times, cleared his throat.

"We moved to Massachusetts to make a new life for ourselves. For you and Oliver. That's all."

"It's not enough. Not *near* enough. You should have told me."

His arms and legs felt impossibly heavy. He had carried this for so long.

Molly stood up, turned her back on the lake. "You don't have anything else to say?"

"Just that I'm sorry. We probably *should* have told you, but we don't talk about this. Some old things are better left in the dark." He looked past Molly's shoulder to the surface of the lake.

"Germs fester in the dark, don't they? Microbes grow and multiply and make you sick. Isn't that what you always tell us? Keeping this kind of secret is like lying. You should tell the truth. That's what you always tell us to do."

Maybe she was right. Maybe it was time to let go. Jake closed his eyes. The promise had been there for so long, interwoven in his neurons with the smell of sour milk, with the photograph Esther tried to hide from him in her desk. Maybe he was hiding behind his children.

"Maybe," he whispered.

"You guys sent me here. You set me up." Molly turned back toward the path. "Now it's my turn. I'm taking it from here."

Jake followed her. What did she mean by that?

CHAPTER 37

Molly

As Jake and I rejoined Esther and Oliver on the picnic quilt, I was unsatisfied, pissed off, and even more determined to make this thing happen.

Cold cuke soup, curry-fried chicken, potato chips, and freshly sliced tomatoes sprinkled with basil from Esther's garden were set out in the center of the blanket. All my favorite foods. I reached for a slice of tomato, dripping red splotches of juice across my sneaker. I moved to rub off the stain with the heel of my hand just as Oliver poured a paper cup of lemonade. My elbow hit his hand and made him spill on his T-shirt, so he tossed the rest of the cup on me. At home, that would mean war, but that day I didn't care, just mopped it up with the paper towel Esther handed me.

I tried to eat, but the celery stick and cream cheese gummed up my mouth. Dill and worry flavored the soup. If I stood up and turned around, I might be able to see the other side of the tree, where Emma was supposed to be sitting with her family. I didn't look.

Jake handed me a bowl of cucumber soup for Esther.

"Cukes from your garden?" I asked her.

"We picked the first ones yesterday. Oliver helped me make the soup."

Oliver grinned, opening his mouth to reveal a clump of half-chewed potato chips.

"Ugh. Where did you find him?"

Esther patted the blanket next to her and I scooted over. "Tell me about your bunk," she said. "Your friends."

"They're great." I rested my head against Esther's shoulder and looked down at the quilt. I traced the sunburst pattern, my finger wandering from yellow to ochre to sienna to rust, silently echoing the names of the colors in the watercolor set Esther gave me for my tenth birthday. What if Esther was too sick to handle our plan?

Esther looked up from her soup. "What's wrong, Mol?"

I wasn't ready but I had to say something. So I said the first thing that popped into my head. "I discovered something about you this summer."

Esther's spoon froze midway between bowl and mouth. Her eyes were deep as midnight and I couldn't read them.

"I learned that you're an artist. That you designed the cranes. I love them and I'm so proud of you."

Esther smiled and I relaxed. The chatter continued as we ate. Everyone had questions about camp, about friends, about swimming. Esther touched me a lot, patting my arm or lifting the damp hair off the back of my neck and blowing a soft wind onto my skin. I let her, even though I wanted to say, "Stop treating me like a baby." Even though I wanted to blurt out the truth. When Oliver went to play soccer with some boys from the next blanket, I almost stopped him, so he could meet Rosa too. But I changed my mind and let him go.

When there was a lull in the conversation, I scooted up the hill between my family and Emma's. I stood up and stretched against the tree trunk, pretending to do some oddball yoga pose but really spying on Emma's family on the other side. It was pretty easy to figure out who was who. Emma was cuddled up next to a dark-skinned man whose frizzy hair seemed to meander off his head into his beard. That must be her father, Allen. Emma had never said he was black, but now her super-tan skin made sense. Her dad was talking and poking the air with his finger in a serious way. A woman with reddish curls—Red

Rosa, of course—was mimicking his gesture and laughing, with her mouth open so you could see all her teeth.

Emma saw me and raised her eyebrows.

"I'm not sure about this." I mouthed the words in exaggerated silent diction.

"What?" Emma mouthed back, her face scrunched up and perplexed.

I scooted closer and whispered, "I'm scared."

At the sound, Rosa glanced up from her conversation. She looked at me, then at Emma. Squinted at me again for a long moment. I imagined she was trying to bring twelve years into focus. She turned to Emma, mouth open, wordless. Then back to me.

I crossed the pinky and ring fingers of my left hand in the secret ritual Rachel and I made up when we were little and trying to be brave. I kissed the tip of my pinky finger four times and blew the last kiss to the sky for good luck. I wanted to cry, or run away, but I didn't. I stood up.

Rosa got up too. Her hair flared out, an explosion of rusty red. Behind her on the Heart, the cranes shimmered in the sunshine.

Rosa and I faced each other. I opened my arms to her.

"Hi, Aunt Rosa," I said. "I'm Molly."

It felt like a long time before she responded. Like a breath held underwater across the length of the pond and back. Then Rosa's long legs covered the distance between us in two giant steps.

Rosa gathered a handful of my curls in each hand. "You've got my hair."

"Yeah," I said. I paused to gather my courage before continuing. "And Esther's here. She's sick."

Rosa stood motionless, then turned to Esther, who stood behind me, one hand covering her mouth and the other braced against the tree trunk. The sisters stood motionless for a long moment, staring at each other, and then both held out their arms and embraced. Esther buried her face in Rosa's hair. Rosa pushed back the bandana and touched Esther's bare scalp. Allen and Jake shook hands and then they hugged too. The four of them stood together in a tight circle.

"I wrote you letters," Esther said. "So many letters. I never mailed them."

"Me too." Rosa smiled. "I did the same thing."

"I kept them in my pen pal box, hidden away."

"I used to be so envious of that box."

"I was so afraid I'd never see you again."

"Same here." Rosa brushed a tear from her cheek.

"I've gone over those days, over and over, in my head. Agonized about what was right. Maybe I shouldn't have testified."

Rosa nodded. "I've agonized too. I didn't understand how torn you felt about Molly until after Emma was born."

"I wanted to get in touch with you. But I felt so bad, so guilty. I couldn't do anything." Esther squeezed her eyes closed. "I was paralyzed."

"But you did something about it. You sent Molly here."

Esther nodded. "Jake didn't want me to, and I was scared. But yes, I hoped."

"I can't believe it took a couple of kids . . ." Rosa buried the rest of her words in Esther's neck.

I realized I was trembling. I grabbed Emma's hand and squeezed so hard it must have hurt, but she squeezed back, just as hard. We couldn't believe our crazy plan was working. We pulled Emma's family blanket over the hill next to ours and gathered all the food in the middle. Emma and I sat close together at the edge of the blankets. I passed her some of Jake's special chicken. "Taste this."

Emma took a tiny bite and offered me a piece of bread stuffed with cheese. We grinned at each other, but neither of us could eat. We leaned against each other, our bare shoulders finally connecting our families.

"Great soup," Rosa said to Esther.

"From my garden."

Rosa shook her head. "I can't believe you grow veggies."

"I live in the country," Esther said. "I can't believe you live in New York."

Rosa smiled. "Me neither."

Jake sat next to Emma's dad and pointed out Oliver running across the soccer field. "That's my son," Jake said. "Oliver."

Allen smiled. "My nephew. He's pretty fast."

"We watched your release on television," Esther said. "I hoped you'd contact me."

"I was so disoriented," Rosa said. "Nine years inside is a long time."

Esther hugged her sister. "Oh, Rosa. Too long."

"It gave me time to think about things."

"You didn't need *that* much time," Allen said.

"Still," Jake said, "I guess nine years isn't too bad. Considering."

"Considering?" Allen bristled. He looked like the porcupine that had chewed the rotting wood of our back porch until it sagged and buckled. "What does *that* mean?"

"You know, the bombing charges." Jake moved closer to Esther on the blanket.

"Those charges were lies," Allen said. "Rosa didn't bomb anything."

"We know that." Esther touched Rosa's arm.

"Why didn't you defend yourself against them?" Jake asked.

Allen shook his head. "How do you defend yourself when the FBI manufactures evidence?"

Rosa's neck turned red and blotchy. "My only choice would have been to betray my friends, the people who helped me. I couldn't do that." Allen moved close to her side.

Esther's face collapsed. "Like I did, you mean?"

Jake put his arm around Esther's shoulder and whispered into her bandana.

Rosa waved Allen back and took Esther's face between her hands. "You know, you broke my heart."

"If you had forgiven me, I wouldn't have said that stuff at the second trial." A tear snaked down Esther's cheek, plummeting into a dark circle on her T-shirt.

Emma and I just sat there, next to each other, our arms pressed together. Watching and listening. Silent. Whatever made us think we could fix this adult-sized mess? I should have known better. My head and limbs and chest felt like stone, sinking in the thick mud at the edge of the pond, the quicksand of the grown-ups' words. I wished I could turn into Sadie and soar into the sky and leave the sorrow below, but I had no wings.

Jake stepped between the sisters, facing Rosa. "You broke Esther's heart, too, those things you said. And your choice—so principled—meant you went to prison and abandoned your daughter."

"Finking on your sister is better?" Allen jabbed his finger at Jake.

"Allen's right," Rosa said quietly. "What kind of example does that set for your kids?" Rosa paused for a moment while she looked at me. "Or did you ever tell them?"

Esther stepped out from behind Jake. She was silent.

"I thought so," Rosa said.

I couldn't look at Emma. Couldn't reach out to touch my mother. Couldn't think about anything except the piece of cheese bread on the paper plate in front of me. Then Rosa and Allen pulled away their blanket, spilling the lemonade.

Emma got up then, ungluing her arm from mine. She helped pack up their picnic basket and the three of them walked toward the parking lot. Emma turned back once to look at me, her face frozen.

When they left, I suddenly became conscious of the hush around us, of all the stares of other campers and their families. My face burned with shame but my parents didn't appear to notice. Esther's head fell into her hands; she didn't readjust the scarf that slipped off her naked scalp, even when it fell onto the grass. Jake snatched up the fabric, stuffed the picnic leftovers into the bag, and gathered Oliver from the soccer field. He kissed me goodbye and guided Esther with her bald head to the car.

Emma and I never performed our mirror movement skit.

The final week of camp went by in a slow, gray blur. We must have been kept busy with the Peace Olympics. No letters came from Esther that week but Jake wrote, telling me he'd pick me up at 10:00 a.m. sharp on Saturday morning. He didn't mention visiting day. Neither Emma nor I knew how to act with each other. Emma decided to go home at the end of the week too, instead of staying for the second half of the summer.

As we packed up the last morning, I carefully wrote my phone number and address on the dachshund autograph hound Emma bought at the camp store, trying not to rip the muslin with my pen. When Emma and I hugged goodbye, our bodies rocked back and forth as we swayed from one foot to the other. I didn't want to let go, but what could I say to her?

I didn't see Emma get on the bus back to New York City, and she wasn't around to say goodbye when Jake came to take me home.

During August, I often thought about Emma. I fantasized calling her on the pink princess phone Esther had installed in my bedroom as a welcome home present, but I never did. Before school started, I packed away the paper doll collection Esther had made, each figure individually wrapped in a tissue and entombed in a shoebox in the closet. By fall, I realized that some of my old dreams had slipped away too, of becoming a pediatrician like my father or an art teacher like my mother. I refused to sign up for more painting classes, even though Esther insisted I had talent. I started keeping a journal and thought maybe I'd be a writer instead. But I never wrote a single word about what happened at Loon Lake. By the time school started, life was back to normal. Esther's chemo was over and she returned to her classroom too.

After Loon Lake, I stopped calling my mother by her first name. I knew it made her sad, but I didn't care. Maybe that was the point. Sometimes I used Mama. Esther hated that—Mama was what she called her own mother. I called her Mother or Mom. Anything but Esther. Esther was a young woman who once, a long time ago, did something with her sister that I didn't entirely understand and couldn't quite forgive.

PART THREE

2003

CHAPTER 38

Molly

I silenced the television and tossed the remote into the basket on the bedside table. I couldn't stomach the pundits' barely-suppressed glee about weapons of mass destruction. War was coming. And the domestic news wasn't any better. The new treatments for breast cancer showcased on the health segment might be too late. My mother's recurrence wasn't responding to the new chemo. To ward off another crying jag, I grabbed my cell phone from the basket and punched speed dial 2.

Evan's pottery studio was next door to my apartment, on the third floor of a renovated factory building not far from my parents' house in western Massachusetts. The cavernous space where cleaning supplies and brushes were once manufactured now housed photographers and rug importers, nonprofits and land trusts. I felt comfortable with the eclectic mix of artists and borderline businesses. I ran a freelance writing and editing business from my studio apartment, teaching writing as an adjunct to pay the rent. Evan constructed large slab clay sculptures whenever he could carve a few free hours from his job teaching art at the community college. Over the past three years, we had sort of drifted into each other's lives. Well, I drifted. Evan was clear from the beginning that he wanted to exchange more than greetings as we both ordered coffee at the deli downstairs.

Evan answered on the second ring. "Can you believe it?" he fumed. "No smoking guns. No illegal weapons, but those turkeys are going to invade Iraq anyway." He paused. "Molly, what are you thinking about February 15?"

Evan wasn't one to push. So it was curious that he hadn't stopped mentioning the anti-war demonstration in New York, even when faced with my repeated non-answers.

"It's going to be huge," he continued. "International. Even the Art Department agreed to help rent student buses, and you know what *they're* like. Hardly radical." He chuckled and I could picture his goofy expression.

Evan must have noticed my silence. "You don't have to decide now. No pressure. I'll bring a picnic after work tomorrow and we'll start the weekend early."

That's how it was with us: Evan asking. Me waffling. Evan waiting. No pressure: those two words epitomized our entire relationship.

I had first noticed Evan one afternoon at the college. It was an April-tease kind of day; the bright sunshine promised warm weather, but the wind had teeth. After a few minutes, I abandoned the picnic area and moved inside with my tuna sandwich to a corner table in the cafeteria. I graded essays from my Comp 101 classes, despairing that the students would master the concept of an introductory paragraph by May. A lanky man in clay-splattered overalls walked by my table carrying a tray. He looked at me oddly, making me wonder if I had spoken my derogatory opinion of the students aloud. I watched his ponytail swing across his back before returning to wandering thesis statements and split infinitives.

A few days later, I was paying for a decaf latte at the deli on the ground floor of my apartment building when someone tapped me on the shoulder. I turned around to the bib of those clay-streaked overalls.

"Are you following me?" he asked.

"I got here first, so you must be following me." I *never* said things like that, not to men. My mother often observed—accurately and ruefully— that I was missing the gene for flirting.

He laughed. "I'm Evan."

"Molly."

"I teach art." He brushed at dried clay stuck to his overalls. "Mostly ceramics."

"Freshman comp," I countered. "Creative writing when I'm lucky."

He grinned. "Since we seem to have the college and this place in common, would you like to have lunch sometime? Either venue."

I hesitated.

"No pressure," he said. "I'll see you around."

Around sounded good.

Even though the February 15 protest was two weeks away, and Evan said "no pressure," I didn't sleep well that night. In the morning I dragged myself down from the sleeping loft and sat with my coffee mug at my writing desk. By eleven thirty in the morning I had prepared the writing prompts for my Monday evening fiction workshop, crafted encouraging critiques for the short story elective I taught at the high school, and refilled the paper supply in the printer. I proofed my new ad for the *Women's Times*, then reread the letter from the women's minimum-security prison inviting me to teach a winter semester creative writing class for inmates. My stomach churned at the thought of helping prisoners find their voices. I wasn't sure I wanted to hear those voices.

And I still had no idea what to tell Evan about the demonstration.

I leaned both elbows on the table and looked through the studio windows at the hunchback shape of Mount Tom. The first time Evan visited my apartment, he walked into the middle of the mostly empty room and pointed at the desk facing the inside wall. "You're wasting the view."

He promised it would be worth the extra money to build a desk all along the eastern exposure of the loft, so that I could roll the office chair from computer to writing space to files without losing sight of the mountain. He lugged his tools from next door and constructed the table, taking a day off from his slab-built sculptures that looked like vastly pregnant women or tree trunks with tumors, depending on my mood.

When Evan arrived late that afternoon, I was contemplating a framed series of my mother's paintings, hung on the wall over the one-person table in my kitchenette. About a year after the Loon Lake debacle, my mother started seriously painting again. She'd had some success, a few shows in Northampton and Amherst, and people bought her paintings. Her work was small, less than eight inches square, as if she didn't deserve more space in the world. Most of her paintings were wildlife scenes—there was one of Sadie and Hawkins, one of a deer in the snow.

But my favorites, the ones I hung in my apartment, were what I thought of as her political art, the work she did for the World Peace Org. You know, those holiday cards they sell every year with season's greetings in forty-two different languages? Stylized children holding hands around the ravaged and flooded globe, or dancing in front of the smoking ruins of their refugee camps, or wandering through jungles behind soldiers wearing ammunition belts and carrying automatic rifles. And she had this signature, like Hirschfeld's Nina: a small drawing of an origami crane tucked in the leaves of a tree or hidden in the design of a skirt. Her cards were very popular, especially once people caught on to the cranes and started looking for them in each piece.

I once overheard my parents argue about those paintings. Jake wanted her to charge for her work. "No," my mother told him. "They're my contribution to the movement."

"Contribution?" he asked. "Or penance?"

Despite thinking about it all day, I had reached no conclusion about the demonstration. Or about the prison writing course. Still, I was delighted to see Evan. The pockets of his overalls were stuffed with chilled Pinot Grigio, softened Brie, sesame baguettes, a ripe mango, and a chunk of dark chocolate bark with almonds. We wrapped ourselves in the ratty quilt I kept handy for the frequent failures of the building's heating system and watched the sunset ignite the bare cliffs at the top of the mountain. Evan pointed to a hawk riding the thermals in a lazy spiral. When we were first dating I told him about Sadie and Hawkins and he admitted similar childhood fantasies about flying. I hadn't used Sadie's wings in years.

Evan brushed the crumbs from his overalls, then leaned back, spreading his arms along the back of the sofa. He looked at me. "So. What are you thinking about the fifteenth?"

"I don't know."

He touched my hair. "Talk to me."

"Demonstrations can be risky."

"The NYPD has crowd control down to a science," Evan said. "They keep their cool."

I shook my head. "Things can spiral out of control. Not just the cops."

"You're worried about what *you* might do?"

My mouth felt dry, my tongue enormous. I felt myself awkwardly stumbling into saying things I never talked about. Never.

"People get excited. Angry," I said. "They do crazy things. You know."

"I *don't* know. What kind of crazy things? Tell me."

So I did. I told Evan about my mother and Aunt Rosa and their brave stupid action. I repeated every detail I could remember from Emma and the archives and from the surreptitious reading I'd done at the campus library: the mounted policemen clubbing teenagers, the small hard green apples, the paralyzed cop, the girl wearing a Vietcong flag who'd been hit so hard by a billy club that she never spoke another word, the trials and sentencing. Esther testifying and Rosa going underground. I told him about Rosa going to prison. About two sisters wrenched apart. About meeting Emma at Loon Lake and our fumbling attempt to make it right, and how profoundly we failed. Once I started talking, the whole story spilled out, words tumbling on top of rusty words. In the two decades since learning the family story in the dusty camp archives, I had never told it to anyone. When I finished talking, I felt emptied out, newborn and hungry, and there was only silence.

"Wow," he finally said. "I don't know what to say."

"Maybe that's why I never told you before. Or anyone."

"But you talk about it with your mother, right?"

"She pretends it never happened."

"Your dad too?"

"*Especially* my dad. I think he's even more scared than my mother."

"What about your brother?"

"I think Oliver lives in California. He hasn't been home in years. It's partly my fault; I never said a word to him about what I learned at camp." I rubbed my eyes. "I'm not proud of that. He found out during his freshman year in college, doing research for a history paper on the Vietnam War. He saw the photograph on microfiche, recognized our mother and read her name in the story. When he came home for spring break, he confronted our parents. Really let them have it. 'You taught me to be honest,' he yelled at them, 'but you've lied to me my whole life.' My mom cried and apologized." Was she sorry for what she did, for not telling us about it, or that we found out? I never knew which.

Evan stood at the window, facing the mountain. Dusk had doused the flaming sunset into smolder. "So. Molly?"

"Yeah?"

"Was it worth it, do you think?"

"What do you mean?"

"What your mom and aunt did. I mean, it was spunky and bold and all. But did it make a difference? Was it *worth* it?"

"I don't know." I had to excavate each word from the dark chambers of my heart. "I never asked."

His question was so basic, so profound. Twenty-three years earlier, at Loon Lake, I had tried to figure it out but couldn't. I had never been able to measure the cost of my mother and Rosa's actions, the effects it had on them and our families, and the other people whose lives had changed that day. To balance that cost against what they accomplished, when they stopped cops from beating up protestors. What about the collateral damage? Did the injured cop have kids? I had once asked Emma but she didn't know.

Now I suddenly needed to know what happened to that officer and his family. Why now? The return of my mother's cancer? The demonstration on the fifteenth? Or Evan himself? I didn't know. I took Evan's hand with reddish clay caked around his fingernails, and kissed his knuckles.

"Guess I'd better find out," I said.

The next evening, I drove to my parents' house. Snow followed by freezing rain had transformed the woods, and the roads were crunchy under the tires. I considered turning back, but I wasn't sure I'd be able to summon up the courage again. Besides, the trees in my headlights sparkled with ice. It was magic, if you ignored the brittle branches across the road.

I hadn't told my parents I was coming. I let myself in with my key, maneuvered around Jake's snowshoes and poles in the small mudroom, and hung my parka on top of my mother's wool coat. I stood in the kitchen for a moment, looking at the small alcove desk my mother still used, even though Jake tried to convince her to convert one of the empty bedrooms into a study. On the corner of the blotter stood a stack of my mother's holiday cards, with her crane hidden on each one. On a whim, I took the top card and slipped it with its envelope into my bag. Then I turned toward the living room, toward the murmur of voices interrupted by the staccato noise of television gunshots.

The room was dim, lit only by the cop show on TV and the pulsing coals in the fireplace. My parents were intertwined on the sofa facing the television. My mother's legs rested across Jake's lap. His hands massaged the instep of her foot, plagued by cramps since her first chemo. They both seemed to register my presence at the same moment and turned to me, identical expressions of surprise, then pleasure, then worry legible on their faces.

"Is something wrong?" my mother asked.

I shook my head. "No, but I need to talk to you both." I turned off the television, switched on the overhead light, and sat in Jake's leather recliner, facing them.

My mother struggled to untangle herself from Jake and sit upright. He helped her. They looked at me across the room.

I leaned forward. "Three things."

Jake nodded. "Shoot."

"First, I have a boyfriend. Evan."

Strange, isn't it, that I had never mentioned Evan to my parents? Some other time, when I had a moment, I would have to contemplate what that said about my relationship to my folks, or to Evan.

My parents smiled. "I thought there might be someone," my mother said. "I'd like to meet him."

"When you're ready, of course," Jake added.

"Secondly, Evan and I are going to New York for the big anti-war demonstration." I surprised myself with that. I had meant to say that I was considering going with Evan, but that's not how it came out.

"There could be trouble," Jake started.

I ignored him and continued talking. "But before that—and this is number three—I have a question for you, Mom."

"What is it?"

I slipped off the recliner and sat on the rug near her. I took her hand, the one that wasn't clutching my father's. "Was it worth it? What you did in Detroit, with the horses?"

Jake erupted in protest. "Molly, please. Don't bring up all that old stuff again. Your mother is sick."

"No, it's all right, Jake." My mother took my face in both her hands. "It's complicated. If I had a simple yes-or-no answer, I'd give it to you. But I don't. And besides, it would be my answer, not yours." She released my face and sunk back into the cushions. She closed her eyes. "When I have a little more energy, I want to talk to you about it. And show you some old things, some letters."

That's what I expected. I stood up and smiled at my parents. "By the way, I'm going to Detroit this weekend. Just for a few days."

"That's four things," Jake said.

"Why?" Mom said. "To see your grandmother?"

"I'll stay with her, but I need to talk to the cop who got hurt. Officer Steele."

After a short silence Jake spoke. "That's nuts."

Esther smiled. "Good for you."

CHAPTER 39

Rosa

The last time she was in Ann Arbor, Rosa had lost her baby, almost died in childbirth, and gotten arrested. She had only wispy snippets of memory from that day: the steamy heat, the jangle of Emma playing with her keys, the piling-up of contractions, the metallic stench of fear and blood. Certainly last time there was no guy in a business suit at the airport holding a sign with her name on it, and no one chauffeured her to the campus hotel in a biofuel car. The tweedy academic dean who gushed at her at the cocktail party was a generation younger than the dean who expunged her academic record when she went to prison. Even the January freeze seemed more forgiving. Maybe that was her fleece-lined trousers; in the 1960s she wore miniskirts despite the harsh Michigan winter.

Rosa pushed open the door to Angell Hall and scanned the conference board. There she was, under "Honor Our History: Anti-War Leaders from the Vietnam Era Speak Out 35 Years Later," 10:00 a.m. Auditorium B. Her first anthropology class had met in that room in 1961.

How pathetic, getting so nostalgic about this moldy old place. She checked her watch. She had time for a walk, which was what she had told her student minder after breakfast. "I'm going to wander around campus a bit." She had slid from the booth and grabbed her parka.

"A stroll down memory lane?" the student asked.

"Something like that." Rosa tried to smile. He didn't mean to be snide, and he couldn't help being so young.

Rosa untangled the misshapen scarf Emma had knit her for Chanukah the year she was released from prison, and wound it twice around her neck. She walked across the Diag toward the Engineering Arch. It could be a mistake, returning to the university, but she was intensely curious to see Ann Arbor again. Allen had urged her to accept the conference invitation, saying you didn't often get a chance to return as a hero to a place you left in the back of a police van. The campus looked so different now, ringed by chain bookstores and yuppie coffeehouses. The expansive windows of the Fishbowl were bricked up. The Diag looked small.

Her steps slowed as she reached the Engineering Building and passed under the Engine Arch, where the Ann Arbor police broke up a draft resistance rally with tear gas and billy clubs during her last semester at the university. It had been the first time she saw unprovoked cops attack demonstrators. Methodically, brutally. She had never forgotten the way blood gushed over the face of Esther's friend Nathan, or that he never returned to school after being released from the hospital. At the edge of the wide sidewalk, a tall stone monument with a metal plaque had been erected. For a moment, Rosa imagined that the memorial was for her SDS comrades. She must really be losing it—they didn't build monuments for student activists. Without reading the inscription, she turned back toward Angell Hall and her panel.

Allen was right: it *was* fun to be treated as a hero and an expert, although truthfully she had spent much of the Vietnam War protest years in court, underground, and in prison. Still, the students at the conference took a break from their anti-Iraq War organizing to ask her probing questions about how to stop a war-mongering bully in the White House. Heady stuff. Her afternoon panel was even more satisfying. Following talks by a Black Panther lieutenant and an ex-political prisoner from the American Indian Movement, Rosa was introduced as a distinguished alumna and winner of the 1978 Prison Activist of the Year award. She described how Counter Intelligence agents targeted anti-war activists.

"I was sentenced to fifteen years," she said. "COINTELPRO is responsible for a big chunk of that time. They fabricated evidence, perjured testimony, and conspired with local cops and prosecutors to manipulate the legal system."

"Weren't *you* responsible for a large part of that fifteen-year sentence?" a student asked during the Q & A. "After all, you threw rocks and injured a police officer."

"Apples," Rosa said. "Not rocks."

The student pushed on. "Was that right? Was throwing anything at people or animals justified?"

"I'm not positive it was right." Rosa tried to keep her voice low and even. Tried not to let the student's words burrow into the bloodstream of her own doubts. "We were attempting to stop an unjust war. And right there, right then, we had to stop mounted police from brutally beating unarmed, peaceful demonstrators. Kids, really. Maybe our tactics were wrong, but when you watch people being hurt, sometimes you just react to stop the violence."

"Do you think fighting violence with violence is still okay, in our world today?"

Rosa shook her head. "In 1968, I did what felt right. We did stop the mounted police assault on Grand River Street in Detroit. Our movement did help end the war in Vietnam. But would I do it today? Or advise my daughter to? I'm not sure. Maybe not. I'm planning to demonstrate against the invasion of Iraq on Saturday in New York City, and I don't plan to throw apples *or* rocks."

That got a ripple of laughter, and the student sat down. Rosa sighed. Did she believe her own words? Had throwing the apples been justified, in that context? She no longer knew.

"That's liberal bullshit," a woman's voice called out from the back of the auditorium. "The problem wasn't your puny little apples. The problem is that we want change, but we're afraid to meet the violence of the US government and their corporate buddies head on. Until we're ready to do that, nothing will change."

Rosa couldn't see the speaker's face. "Perhaps you're right," she said mildly. "Many of us in this auditorium probably disagree about tactics. But there's room in the anti-war movement for all of us."

The woman hooted. "That's a cop-out. There's no room for chickens."

Chicken. That's the reason Danny gave for going to Vietnam. "Because I'm no chicken," he'd said. Rosa's face flamed as she remembered her reply: "Fine. Go shoot civilians and napalm babies." If only she could take back her words. *I'm sorry, Danny.* She turned away from the podium.

After the panel, a group of young women wearing Code Pink sweatshirts crowded around Rosa and invited her to join them for pizza before the evening session.

"I'll meet you later." Rosa scribbled the address of the restaurant on the back of her program. Making her excuses also to her student guide, Rosa walked back to the hotel and fifteen minutes later lowered herself slowly into a hot bathtub. Her arthritis was worse in the frigid Michigan air, pregnant with the damp promise of snow. She let her hands soak for a few minutes, then dried them and reached for her phone. She dialed Mama's number.

"I'm in Ann Arbor," she said, "at that conference I told you about."

"So close. And you're not coming to see me?"

Mama never changed. "Not this trip. Allen and I will visit in March."

"I'm eighty-three years old, Rosa. Don't keep me waiting too long."

"March is just next month." Rosa turned the knob to add more hot water. "I have to get back to the city. It's only two weeks until the anti-war rally, and they're still fighting us on the permit. And Maggie's coming to town next week to get an award."

There was a pause. "That's not what I mean and you know it. I want you girls to make things right with each other. That's what I'm waiting for."

After years of insisting she would never "meddle," Mama had started nagging Rosa about forgiving Esther, contacting her. Rosa preferred the old hands-off policy. Did Mama nag at Esther too?

"Got to go, Ma. There's an evening session soon and I'm still in the bathtub."

"Rosa? Promise?"

"I'll try."

Rosa dropped the phone on the bath mat. She balanced her notebook across the white metal tub tray.

Dear Esther,

I just talked to Mama. She made me promise to contact you.

I'm in Ann Arbor for a conference. You'd hate the way this place has changed. Your old art school is gone, moved to a new complex somewhere. I looked but I couldn't find it. And remember the giant black cube in Regent's Plaza where we splashed blood-red paint on the administration building? I pushed it around and around, but couldn't begin to summon up our ghosts. The whole damn square was filled with gray-haired people in Tai Chi positions.

And that house near the hospital, where you and Jake rented the basement apartment the year after Allen and I moved back to the city—it's gone. Demolished. Replaced by a Ronald McDonald House.

So much has changed. We were so young when we lived here, so certain we knew the answers to the big political questions that had eluded our parents and grandparents. Now I'm less sure. Oh, we've learned some things. At least I have. And having several hundred college anti-war activists listening to your every word is good for the ego, but when I think about how far from justice we still are in this country, I feel worn out.

My joints are worn out too. They ache and throb. It's a souvenir of prison—I could never get warm there. The constant damp of the concrete walls invited the dank cold deep into the marrow of my bones. Corroded my joints from the inside out. The specialist claims that the arthritis is an autoimmune disease and has nothing to do with damp. He says my body is attacking itself. He's wrong; this illness is my legacy from prison. There are some things you don't need a rocket scientist for. Or a rheumatologist.

My hands are affected the most. Stiff stick bones connected by swollen knobs of knuckles. On bad days, hot water massage is the only thing that gets me going in the morning. I think of you sometimes when I'm in the bathtub. All I have to do is look down at my left breast, at my drooping red star. Don't worry—I mean that literally, not metaphorically. The tattoo is stretched out with my sagging boobs. Has time been kinder to you, little sister?

Are you okay? I know you had cancer, but I heard you were cured. Sometimes, I'd like to rip my crown of correctness off my head—which is more gray than red, by the way. Sometimes, I wish I were the kind of person who could let it go, could give up the certainty that has protected me from doubts all these years. Then I could forgive you.

But that doesn't sound like me, does it?

Besides, if I weren't steadfast, I might have to conclude that those years in prison were meaningless. I don't think I could face that.

I want to make it clear: I still think what you did was utterly, absolutely, irrevocably wrong. But I miss you. So here I am. Back to a letter that I've written dozens of times in my head but will never, ever mail.

Did we find those answers we searched for on these streets? Would I do it again? I know we made a difference in our world. Our efforts helped end the war, I absolutely believe that. But what a price I paid.

Nine years in prison.

Not being there to raise my daughter.

Missing Pop's funeral.

Losing a sister.

CHAPTER 40

Esther

The new round of chemo hadn't been terrible, except for losing her hair again. At least during her first treatment all those years ago, her bald head had been cool in the summer. This time, she needed a hat. She finally found one that didn't itch and wore the red fleece cap all day, enjoying Jake's lame attempts to compliment her. Since Molly's visit, Jake hadn't made one pathetic pun about her hat or anything else. After dinner, Esther joined him on the sofa.

"You've been so glum. Want to talk?"

Jake pointed at the television. "They're interviewing people about invading Iraq and the February 15 demonstration. Comparing it to Vietnam protests."

The reporter shoved the microphone in the face of the chairperson of the rally committee. "Do you expect crowds of aging *hippies?*" he taunted.

"No. I expect citizens of this country who hate what our government is doing in our name," the organizer answered. "Grandmothers and businessmen and teenagers. Black and white and Latino and Asian. Possibly even a few off-duty television reporters."

The reporter ignored her dig. "But weren't most Vietnam protesters college-aged counterculture types?"

That really pissed Esther off. The newsboys still couldn't tell the difference between political activists and hippies. Everyone got lumped together as longhaired, peace sign-flashing, flower children. Esther yelled at the television screen. "You jerks missed the point. We weren't all the same." If Rosa were watching, she would have hated it too.

The organizer shook her head emphatically. "Certainly the campuses were crucial in the movement against the Vietnam War. And participating in those protests transformed the lives of many college-aged people in the sixties. But let's not rewrite history. There was widespread sentiment against that war among the US population. And that's the case today too. People don't want this war. On Saturday we expect hundreds of thousands of citizens in Manhattan streets to send a strong message to our government: No war in Iraq."

When the segment ended, Esther turned off the TV and snuggled closer to Jake. "This is going to be big," she said. "Maybe we should go, with Molly and her Evan."

He didn't look at her. "Right."

"I'm serious, Jake."

"Me too. That's a really smart thing to do with a compromised immune system. Go mingle with a huge crowd of microbes. Brilliant." He reached for the remote.

Esther grabbed it from him and tucked it into the sofa cushion on her other side. "I feel pretty good. Maybe it's time to pull our heads out of the sand and do something about this war."

"What is it with the women in this family? First Molly, now you."

Esther stroked the back of his hand, clenched in his lap. "Is that it? Why you've been so gloomy?"

Jake finally looked at her. "Why does she want to see that old cop? He'll probably be awful to her. Cruel. Poking at old wounds never helped anyone heal."

"I don't know. Maybe she's onto something. Maybe we should all deal with our ancient demons."

Jake started to stand up. "This argument isn't getting us anywhere."

"It's a discussion, not an argument. Sit down. I want to talk about Rosa."

Jake sank back into the cushion and closed his eyes.

"I know you hate this," Esther said. "You think if we ignore her, she won't haunt us. But it hasn't worked." Her voice thickened. "You're still terrified of the past. And I can't stop thinking about my sister."

"Think what about her?"

"It's taken me over thirty years to realize that I made a mistake."

Jake shook his head. "I know you feel bad about it, but you did what you had to. You had responsibilities. A baby."

"What about my responsibility to my sister?"

"Rosa made her own bad choices, going underground. She would have gone to prison without your testimony," Jake said. "They framed her, remember?"

"I know, but I was complicit. I wish . . ."

Jake leaned closer. "What *do* you wish?"

"That I had done the right thing."

"Refusing to testify? Even if that meant going to prison yourself?"

Esther put her face in her hands. "I'm not sure. But I do know I messed up twice. First by testifying, then by not apologizing. She's my *sister*."

"What about the apples, hurting the cop? The poor innocent horse? Aren't you going to do a *mea culpa* about that too, while you're at it?"

"Nah. That was crazy and it turned out badly and I was scared to death. But I don't really regret it. In fact, I hope I would find the courage to do it again." Esther tried to smile. "But not on Saturday, I promise. Listen to me, Jake. I want to see Rosa."

"I don't want you hurt again. Look what happened last time."

"You mean at camp?"

Jake nodded.

"That was a long time ago but I regret how it ended, every day. I regret that we screwed up so badly. I especially regret we didn't talk about it all with the kids, with Oliver. And you have to take some responsibility for that mess, you and Allen. Anyway, at camp Molly and Emma set it up. Two twelve-year-olds. This time, Rosa and I will make it happen."

"I can't believe you're that naïve. Rosa won't give an inch."

Esther wasn't going to give up either. "I'm sick, Jake. This could be my last chance to make things right with her. To repair the damage and put our family back together. I'm going to do this."

"Then I'll help you." Jake stood up. "Against my better judgement. But right now I need to take a Pepcid and a Valium and make a follow-up phone call on a croupy toddler." Jake started to turn away, then paused. "Do you feel better, getting that off your chest?"

"Yeah, I do. It's not just talk, Jake. It's time." Esther kissed Jake's cheek and watched him leave the room. "It's way overdue," she called after him.

She wandered into the kitchen and sat at her alcove desk. If only she could call Rosa now. They wouldn't have to talk about themselves. Maybe they could discuss the news, unless she had forever forfeited her right to discuss politics with her sister. The newscast did get one thing perfectly right: the activism of the sixties defined their generation. It transformed their lives. How did she lose sight of that?

Taking the red fabric box from her desk drawer, she balanced the cover on its side to reveal the photograph with Rosa. She touched the spiraling curls of the two of them, so young, and then touched her own smooth scalp. Through the frost-sparkled windowpane, a lopsided V of Canada geese flew in the moonlight, one arm curved gracefully, the other lopped off after three lonely birds.

Esther tidied the loose papers, positioning the stapler on top to hold them in place. Lined the frayed spine of her address book along the edge of the blotter. Tucked the oncology clinic appointment card into the blotter's leather frame, showing only the red print reminder to call and cancel if unable to keep an appointment.

Last time, her cancer had behaved pretty well, scheduling itself over the summer so treatment was finished in time for the next school year. But the tumor had returned in autumn with a fierce tingling in her right arm that made writing on the blackboard so awkward she repeatedly dropped the chalk. The tingles progressed to numbness, and slipped down from her armpit to her back, sending tendrils into her ribs, encircling her chest like a persistent suitor. Now that the chemo had shrunk the tumor, hopefully destroyed it, she could write again. If it wasn't too late for letters, after all these lost years.

> *Dear Rosa,*
>   *I've written you these letters for years. I've told you about my life, confided my questions and doubts about my kids and Jake, expressed my worries about Mama. I've never mailed one of them.*
>   *This is my last letter. No more. I have to tell you this stuff in person. Or not at all.*

Esther stuffed the letter into the envelope. She closed the Japanese box and turned it over and over in her hands, tumbling all the secrets she had trusted to it. She placed it on top of the envelope. When Molly got home from Detroit, it would be time to share this part of the family history.

CHAPTER 41

Molly

The taxi dropped me off in front of the Motor City Nursing Home.

"I'm here to visit Martin Steele," I announced at the front desk.

The receptionist's name tag read Tammy. She escorted me down the long hallway to the solarium. Why did a secretary wear white nurse's shoes, and why did the crepe soles creak like a ghost story? And why on earth should I care about her shoes, except that I would rather ponder anything else to avoid thinking about coming face-to-face with the man my mother almost killed. This had sounded like a good plan back in Massachusetts. Evan told me it was when I stopped by his apartment early that morning to drop off Dijon with her litter box, food, and catnip toys. He predicted I'd get some clarity about the whole situation. Now I just wanted to be somewhere else.

I don't know what I expected Officer Martin Steele to look like, but certainly not the shriveled man Tammy pointed out across the room. Tammy touched my shoulder. "I hope it's a good visit. Marty can be a wee bit difficult sometimes."

Officer Steele's gray buzz cut was neat, but his skin was sized for a bigger man, hanging loose around his cheeks and neck. He didn't look up as I approached, not even when I pulled a chair close to his wheelchair and sat. He stared out the plate glass window at the frosty Michigan landscape.

"Mr. Steele?" My voice came out high-pitched and I cleared my throat. He looked at me then, or through me; it wasn't clear. I wondered if he would recognize me. Everyone said the family resemblance was uncanny.

"What do you want?" he asked the air above my head.

"Just to talk to you for a few minutes."

"Talk."

I hesitated. I didn't really have a plan. I had thought the words would just come to me. "I'm trying to understand what happened at the Detroit demonstration in August 1968." Maybe he'd think I was a historian, or a reporter doing a "Where Are They Now" feature story. "Can you tell me what you remember?" That sounded awfully wimpy, even to me.

He looked right at me then, squinting a little.

"Who are you?" His voice was as harsh as I feared.

I took a deep breath. I had promised myself not to lie if he asked this question, not to lie at all.

"My name is Molly Green. My mother is Esther. Esther Levin Green."

He started trembling with what looked like rage. It puffed up his empty sacs of skin, making him seem to grow bigger.

"I'll tell you what I remember," he blustered. His face reddened. His arms waved in the air over his head. "Your mother and her commie sister ruined my life, that's what happened. That bitch got what she deserved. I hope she rotted in prison."

"I'm so sorry you were hurt. I'd like to understand what happened. Will you talk to me?"

"Never. Go to hell."

I stood up and looked around, worried that my presence might trigger a stroke or heart attack or something. "I guess you're still pretty angry at them." I knew I was stating the obvious, but what could I say to this man?

"I'll never forgive them. Now get out of here."

I reached for my backpack. "Do you think citizens ever have the right to challenge their government, when the government is wrong?"

"I don't give a damn about those girls' rights. They attacked us."

"But you . . . the mounted police were beating people, without provocation."

"What do you know about provocation? About defending your country? Life is more complicated than marching and protesting. You're just like my daughter, yapping about civil rights." He seemed to run out of words, out of steam. His ballooned skin began deflating.

Daughter? I had always wondered if he had children.

"What does your daughter think about it?" I asked quietly.

"Leave Becky out of this. And leave me alone. I'm almost seventy years old and I've had enough. Those girls ruined my life, but I got back at them. I showed them good. I ruined that commie Rosa's life right back. And now it's all over. *I'm* over." Mr. Steele's chin fell to his chest. He swiveled his wheelchair around and to the other end of the room.

"Thank you," I said to his back.

I walked slowly back to the reception desk, trying to decide if it was lying to try to get the daughter's phone number. I hadn't known Becky existed until just now. Resting my backpack on the horseshoe-shaped reception counter, I thanked Tammy for her help while I rummaged through my mess of manila folders and airline tickets and scraps of paper.

"Darn it, Tammy. I've misplaced Becky Steele's phone number," I said. "Do you have it handy?"

"Sure thing." Tammy keyed something into her computer and wrote a number on a Post-it note. "Here's her cell. Have a good day now."

I hated tricking Tammy. But I had no choice. I called Becky Steele from the lobby. After hearing my name, there was silence for a few seconds. Then she asked where I was staying and I named the budget chain motel near the airport.

"I'll meet you there at seven," she said. "In the bar."

Becky Steele was late. I sat in the motel lounge, sipping a glass of the house merlot and staring at the card on the bar in front of me. I had addressed the stamped envelope to Rosa Levin, at the address Emma gave me so many years ago when we parted after camp, and used my mother's return address. The painting reproduced on the card was one of my favorites: two women with curly hair marching together down the middle of a city street, surrounded by people carrying signs with peace symbols and No Nukes written in a dozen languages. The crane was hidden in the folds of the rainbow flag held by the shorter woman. It must have broken my mother's heart to paint that. I had no clue what to write on the blank white page inside. So I simply wrote my name and my mother's phone number and licked the envelope before I lost courage.

It was closer to eight when Becky arrived. I had become bored watching myself in the mirror behind the bar. Bored and discouraged. How likely was it anyway that the next generation could untangle the twisted strands of our parents' passionate mess? Clearly I was going to have to figure this out for myself. None of the actors in this very old tragedy were likely to fill me in on the meaning of the play. Still, when Marty Steele's daughter walked into the bar, I studied her face for any resemblance to her father and found myself hoping the woman had some answers.

She ordered a beer and motioned me to join her at a table across the room. For a minute, we regarded each other.

"You're Esther's daughter?"

"Yes."

"You look more like Rosa."

At that moment the hope whooshed out of my body, leaving me as limp and empty as Becky's father. "Listen," I said, "I'm sorry to waste your time. I don't know what I was thinking."

Becky reached across the table to touch my arm. "I'm really glad to meet you. I'm surprised, that's all. I often think about your family."

"Do you hate us too?"

"I used to. I was sixteen when my dad was hurt. I didn't know what the demonstration was all about. I was too busy studying algebra and trying to figure out if smoking weed would rot my brain."

"I've wondered about you for years. You know, whether or not Officer Steele had kids."

"Just me," she said. "Dad was so bitter about his injury, especially after Mom left us. I was pissed off. I had just gotten my driver's license, and all of a sudden I was doing grocery shopping and cooking dinner and driving him to rehab three times a week."

"I didn't know."

"He blamed everything on your mother and aunt. Of course it was more complicated than that. Still, it was tough and he fell apart, tough-guy style. I sat through your aunt's first trial because I wanted to keep tabs on him, more than any real interest in the case. I convinced my American History teacher to give me credit. I had never met anyone like those sisters, so fervent about the world. Even though I didn't agree with them about the war. Then your aunt went underground and the trial ended."

"What happened to your father then?"

"He was furious at Rosa, but one day he stopped talking about it. He looked, I don't know, satisfied. I thought he had accepted things. I just wanted to return to hanging out with my friends and playing softball."

I finished my drink and waved at the bartender for refills.

"When your aunt was caught, I was a senior trying to decide about college. I sat through her second trial, too, and your aunt was still incredible. But this time, it was different." She looked down at her lap.

"What was different?"

"I didn't know the details back then," she admitted. "But my dad couldn't help bragging. He claimed that they were fixing your Aunt Rosa, giving her what the 'commie bitch' deserved."

"COINTELPRO." I had read about the Church Commission findings.

Becky nodded. "Later I read about it too. But at seventeen, all I knew was that justice was anything but. And my father—who I loved and respected—was part of the problem."

"Do you know how it happened, framing Rosa for the bombing?"

"Not exactly. I don't think it was my father's idea. That's not like him. He's very law-abiding. I think when the Feds approached him with their storyline, it fit into his . . . his anger, and his need for revenge. He *knew* Rosa was guilty and deserved to be in prison."

I pictured Mr. Steele in the sunroom. I could see that.

"That trial changed my life. I became interested in politics, went to college, then law school. I'm a public defender." She smiled.

"Wow." It was my turn to be surprised.

"The Levin sisters taught me it's not your family that determines who you become. It's not even your abilities. Your choices define you."

The dark quiet in the bar deepened. I looked into my wine.

"Those choices can be very rough on families," Becky said softly.

"What about you and your dad?"

"One of these years he might forgive me for the kind of work I do. Defending the scum of the earth, he calls it. But we talk on the phone most days, and I cook dinner for him every Friday night. We're okay."

My surprise must have showed in my face because Becky laughed.

"Oh, there's a worldview chasm between us for sure. And sometimes it's a challenge to love each other across that gaping hole." She paused. "But we're family."

I folded my cocktail napkin into an origami crane. Was it ironic that Esther and Rosa's victim and his daughter, who disagreed so strongly, had made more peace than the sisters had?

Becky took the crane from my hand. I guess she also read my mind. "What about your family? I saw that Rosa was pardoned. Have she and Esther forgiven each other?"

I shook my head, remembering the aborted reunion attempt at camp and the years of silence since then. Running my finger across Rosa's address on the card, stuck in the outside pocket of my bag, I wondered if a recurrence of cancer was enough to get these two stubborn women to forgive. "I wish they would. Could. Not yet."

"I'm sorry to hear that." Becky handed me back the floppy cocktail napkin crane, then stood up. "I'm glad you called. But I've still got to prepare for court tomorrow morning."

"And I've got to be at my grandmother's early for breakfast," I said. "Thanks for seeing me."

Gran lived with her sister Miriam and Miriam's husband Max, the three of them shoehorned into a two-bedroom apartment in a senior complex Gran called Geezerville. They shared the space with eighty-odd years each of framed family photographs, paintings, and prints, chipped china tea cups with fussy painted flowers, and their collections. Miriam collected salt and pepper shakers, which she arranged behind glass-fronted cabinets. Max's World War II metal soldier figures faced each other in battle formation across the coffee table. Gran's passion was small porcelain dog statues, hundreds of them, mostly cocker spaniels. Settled on the sofa in their overheated living room, I amused myself by imagining reconfiguring the armies of their treasures: the salt shakers and the cavalry defending against the onslaught of the peppers and the spaniels.

"Your mother loved that one best." Gran pointed to a large framed print half visible in the hallway. "Before we moved to this place, all my paintings had to stay in my bedroom, like a ghetto. Here, I insisted that my things be out here with theirs. But Miriam refused to have *that* one in the living room, says it's too depressing."

I stood in front of my mother's favorite. A crowd of old-fashioned-looking people in drab brown and gray work clothes marched toward me. They looked solemn and stern, especially the young woman in the front row, holding an infant.

"Esther named her Hannah." Gran shrugged. "She used to have conversations with her, about unions and strikes."

"Tell me about my mother and Rosa." I returned to the sofa and my coffee, wrapping my hands around the warmth. I tried not to stare at the family photographs on tables and shelves and walls. Later, I hoped Gran would identify every single stranger.

"It's hard to remember," Gran started.

My face must have reacted, because Gran gave me a sharp look. "Don't worry. I'm not senile yet. It's just hard to make myself revisit the painful parts." She paused. "For years I wasn't allowed to talk to you about any of this. How much do you know?"

"I know what they did. I know that my mother testified against Rosa, who went underground, then to prison. I'm trying to understand their action. Was it brave or stupid? That's why I came to Detroit, why I wanted to meet the cop. Not that he was very helpful."

"No, I don't suppose he was. Don't you want to go downtown, revisit the scene of the crime, as part of your investigation?"

Was Gran being sarcastic?

"Not really," I said. "I want to know what you think."

"Your problem is that you don't know your own history. You come from a long line of activists—revolutionaries and trade unionists and suffragettes and Gray Panthers. Your mother tried to protect you and ended up robbing you of your heritage. I didn't like it, but I went along with my daughters' craziness. Both of them. Every year, before you and your brother came to visit, I hid away the pictures of Rosa and her family, just like your mother insisted." Gran shook her head. "I've been thinking about it a lot recently. I shouldn't have helped Esther hide the truth from you kids."

I sighed. Would things have been different if I had known, had grown up seeing pictures of my aunt and uncle and cousins?

"You don't even know the little things." Gran touched my lips. "When you get angry, your lips get thin and they almost—"

"—disappear. I've been told. So what?"

"Your Aunt Rosa's lips do that too."

I stood and started pacing the living room. I hadn't come to hear about family resemblances. Was Gran going to avoid talking about the truth too? "What *about* Esther and Rosa? Was their activism worth the price?"

Gran picked up one of Max's soldiers, a rusty green infantryman with rifle held across his chest. "It's worth fighting even when we lose. Which often happens when your enemies hold the power. But you've got to choose your battles. In my book, throwing rocks at horses was plain dumb."

"Apples. They threw apples." I stopped pacing in front of the crowd of strikers in the painting, explaining the facts to Hannah as well as my grandmother.

"Whatever. Throwing things at an animal in the midst of a street fight and hurting a cop was tactically wrong. *Cockamamie*, your Grandpop would say. But people do stupid things under pressure. Even my smart daughters."

"It ruined their lives."

"Come here, Molly. Sit. The world can be a pretty nasty place. Either you're a person who hides from the ugliness, or a person who fights back. Fighting back is what we do in this family." Gran grinned and added, "Well, not everybody. Your Uncle Max is a Republican."

I sat on the arm of her chair and leaned over to rest my cheek on my grandmother's hair. "So what should I do about Esther and Rosa?"

"Nothing." Gran patted my arm. "That's their battle, Molly. Get on with your life."

Two hours after my plane landed in Hartford, I was at my parents' house. My mother looked marginally less gaunt than the week before, and her smile, when I walked into the kitchen, was radiant.

"Feeling better?" I asked.

"I'm starting to," my mother said. "Still no hair, though." She tapped the red fleece hat. "How was your trip?"

"Where's Jake? I want to tell you both."

"With his birds, no doubt." She called to him.

Sitting across from my parents on the sofa, I had a momentary flash of visiting day at camp. Was I meddling again, in something I couldn't fix? Well, this time it was up to them.

"I went to Detroit because of Evan. He's been trying to convince me to go to New York on the fifteenth. I was totally scared, freaked out about going, but couldn't tell him why." My throat started to ache and I could feel my voice thicken. "I was doing the same thing you did, the thing that I hated. I was keeping secrets, as if they were shameful."

"I'm so sorry, Molly."

I put up my hand, palm out, holding my mother's apologies at bay. "Let me finish, okay?"

Esther took Jake's hand.

"When I told Evan about our family, he asked me whether it was worth it, what you guys did. I realized I didn't know. I went to Detroit looking for answers. I talked with Martin Steele, and his daughter."

My mother's voice was small. "Was Steele awful to you? What was he like?"

"Angry," I said. "And pathetic. I felt sorry for him. I talked with his daughter, and she was helpful. I liked her."

"Did you find your answers?" Jake asked.

"A beginning. Next is the February 15 demonstration."

"Yes." Esther looked at me hard. "Will you see Rosa?"

"Should I?" That reminded me of the card, still in my bag. I made a mental note to mail it.

"I want you to read something." Esther went to her desk in the alcove off the kitchen and carried back a small red box covered in fabric that had once been embroidered with a design of some kind, and a thick manila envelope. "Look at these, then decide." She put them in my lap.

The fabric was see-through thin. I eased the cover off, spilling folded pieces of notebook paper, some folded with age, the torn edges caught on each other. Under the papers were four smaller boxes and a short braid of tri-colored hair. Gray and red and brown. Creepy.

"That's our hair," Esther said. "Rosa and me and our Grandma Leah. I've probably never told you about Leah, have I? She was a freedom fighter in Russia, against the czar."

You come from a long line of activists, Gran had said. I hugged the red box to my chest and added, "There's one more thing."

They both looked at me. Jake's bald forehead lined with worry. Esther looked expectant, and no longer scared.

"I want you to come with us to New York," I said. "Both of you."

CHAPTER 42

Rosa

"Damn." Emma glanced at her watch as they hurried along the Chelsea sidewalk. "We're late."

"I don't see any numbers," Rosa said. Maggie had warned that the meeting hall was poorly marked.

"I bet that's it." Allen pointed down the street. "Picketers."

"Big surprise." Emma hurried her parents along. "Come on. It's after eight."

A scraggly line of demonstrators blocked the entrance to the union hall. "Human rights for the unborn," a young man shouted at Rosa. He pumped his picket sign up and down in the air, making the image of a bloody fetus dance a macabre jig.

"How about human rights for all people?" Rosa shouldered past him. She frowned at a middle-aged woman wearing a sandwich board proclaiming ABORTION IS MURDER.

They found three empty seats in the back of the auditorium as a woman draped in purple scarves stepped up to the podium and spoke into the microphone. "Welcome to the National Pro-Choice Coalition's annual Roe v. Wade program. Every year we honor people who make significant contributions to women's reproductive health."

Rosa hadn't seen Maggie often since her friend returned to school. Even after her release from prison, their visits were rare.

"This year's award goes to a nurse who moved to the South in 1976 to work with under-served rural women who had few options for reproductive health care in general, and almost no access to contraceptive and abortion services. When she couldn't find a job in a women's clinic, because there weren't any clinics, she went back to school and became a Physician's Assistant. She learned to perform abortions and started a women's center. Please welcome Maggie Sternberg."

Maggie had always been into women's health, dragging Rosa to abortion rights rallies in the late sixties. Rosa remembered her own eloquent arguments against going, that it was imperative to spend all their time fighting against the war. Maggie refused to yield, insisting that there was also a war against women who died on the battlefield of botched illegal abortions. It was a rally at the city morgue that finally convinced Rosa that Maggie was right. Hundreds of women dressed all in black—long robes and scarves or hats, some shrouded with veils. They carried only twisted coat hangers, thrusting them at the sky as a symbol of the brutality of self-induced abortions. No picket signs. No chants or songs. Instead, they keened. They cried and wailed, a cacophony of female voices wordlessly mourning their sisters and mothers and lovers and friends and daughters.

Next to her, Emma leaned forward in her seat and clapped loudly. Emma talked with Maggie every week, and she insisted that they attend this ceremony. "They picket her clinic every day," she had explained to Rosa. "She gets death threats. The clinic was firebombed last summer and a week later the doc she works with was beaten half to death. Maggie deserves ten awards."

Rosa massaged her aching knuckles and listened. She had missed so much of her friend's life. She didn't realize her cheeks were flooded until the woman seated on her other side patted Rosa's arm and offered her a hanky smelling of gardenia. The woman leaned close and whispered in a heavy drawl that Maggie had performed her abortion, too. Saved her life because she would have killed herself if she had to have another baby by that jerk.

After the ceremony Rosa, Allen, and Emma waited by the door for Maggie.

"Come home with us," Rosa asked Emma, "and visit some more with Maggie?"

"I can't." Emma pulled on her stocking cap and gloves. "Jeff's in DC until Friday, Clara's babysitter has a geometry exam tomorrow, and I have to be in court in the morning. Plus, they're still fighting us on the parade permit for Saturday. The cops claim they can't ensure *order* if we march, so we can only rally at the UN. Can you believe that?"

Allen made an expression of exaggerated shock.

"Okay, so big surprise," Emma said. "We'll win, but not without a fight. Besides, it looks like Maggie is ready, and you three probably have a lot to talk about."

Gathering Rosa and Maggie into a three-way hug, Emma kissed the warm cave of each neck. "My two moms."

An hour later, Rosa saluted Maggie with her wineglass. "*Mazel tov.* You are amazing."

Allen echoed the toast and sipped his wine. "An award well deserved. You knew back in the sixties what you wanted to do, and you kept going until you got there. Very impressive."

"Hardly." Maggie waved her hand back and forth. "We're nowhere near *there* yet. Poor women still can't get services. Men slap women around every weekend. Abortion providers get shot in the clinic parking lot." She raised her glass to Allen. "Besides, you're still fighting the good fight too."

"Guess I'm the only one who screwed up." Rosa looked back and forth between Allen and Maggie. "Got derailed and spent a decade in prison."

"COINTELPRO helped push your caboose off the tracks," Maggie said.

"No." Rosa shook her head. "I messed up."

Maggie lifted her glass to Rosa. "You sure didn't mess up with Emma. Or your work in prison."

"You get a lot of the credit for how Emma turned out," Rosa said.

"Can you believe she's a lawyer with a six-month-old daughter?" Allen said. "That I'm a grandpa?"

Rosa clasped Maggie's hands across the table. "Please stay an extra few days? You could spend time with baby Clara tomorrow and come to the demonstration with us on Saturday—it's going to be huge."

Maggie traced the swollen joints of Rosa's thumb with her finger. "I have patients scheduled. An extra week makes a big difference in my business. Hey, how's that friend of Emma's doing? Poose?"

"Poose from camp and Swarthmore?" Rosa asked. "Is there a problem?"

"Oops," Maggie said. "Forget it. How about some more music?"

Allen wandered to the stereo in the living room. "We've already heard every single Dylan song ever recorded," he called out. "Do we start over or branch out?"

"What's wrong with Poose?" Rosa asked again.

"I shouldn't have said anything," Maggie said, then called to Allen, "Anything's fine with me." She poured herself more wine and held the bottle over Rosa's glass.

Rosa shook her head. "Tell me about Poose."

"Dylan or Billy Bragg?" Allen asked.

"I can't discuss it," Maggie said. "I'm sorry. I assumed you knew."

"No more Dylan," Rosa yelled. And no Baez, either. That would invite Esther, now lurking in dark corners, into the middle of the room and right up to the table, and Rosa couldn't bear it. Not yet.

The opening chords of "All You Fascists Bound to Lose" filled the silence hovering over the table. Rosa closed her eyes and let her head spin with the music and the wine. Poose must have needed an abortion. It was reasonable for Emma to seek Maggie's advice. Allen must have known, too, the way he left the room. Why was she the only clueless one?

"I'm going to bed. It's after one and I have work tomorrow. Today." Allen stood behind Rosa's chair and put his arms around her. He leaned forward to kiss her forehead, then kissed Maggie's cheek. He pointed at the wine bottle. "Should I open another one?"

Maggie put her hand over her glass. "I've had enough."

"I'll just finish this." Rosa emptied the dregs of wine from the bottle. "So, how's your love life?"

"I'm still with Sarah. We're good."

"I'd like to meet her sometime."

"So come visit us. It's not Siberia, you know."

"It's hard." Rosa sighed. "I can never thank you enough. I'm not good at grateful."

"No, you're not." Maggie grinned.

Or at forgiving, Rosa thought.

"Let it go," Maggie said.

"You practically raised my daughter. You were a comrade to Allen, a sister to me."

"Now you're getting maudlin." Maggie laughed, then stopped. "What about your real sister?"

"What about her?"

"You haven't mentioned her." Maggie swirled the last deep red drops in her wineglass. "Are you in touch?"

Rosa shook her head.

"Wasn't she sick? Breast cancer? Is she okay?"

"I don't know."

Maggie put the palms of both hands on the table and pushed her chair back. "This is so stupid. I can't believe you guys. Let's just call her."

Rosa pointed to the clock on the kitchen wall. "Now? It's too late."

"You are really something." Maggie pulled her cell phone from her pocket. "Do you know what town she lives in?"

Rosa pointed to the basket in the center of the table. "In there."

Maggie thumbed through catalogs and newsletters, grocery receipts and coupons. She lifted a square envelope. "From Esther?"

"Her daughter signed it. Molly."

Maggie removed the card and looked at it. Her hand jumped to her mouth. "It's you guys."

"Did you find the origami crane?"

Maggie brought the card close to her face and studied it. "Oh," she said. "There."

"But why didn't Esther write something?"

"She didn't have to." Maggie smacked the card on the table. "That picture? That's the best apology you could ever expect. It's your turn."

She nodded. Maggie was right, but Rosa's mouth and throat were filled with tongue and cotton, with no room for air. "Help me."

Maggie dialed, placed the phone between them on the table and punched the speaker button.

The ringing filled Rosa's head. The sound spiraling. Her head spinning.

"Hello?" His voice sounded groggy.

"Jake?" Maggie spoke quietly toward the phone.

"Who's this?"

"Maggie Sternberg. I'm here with Rosa."

"Oh."

"Sorry," Maggie said. "I know it's late."

"I was asleep. Is something wrong?"

"Nothing's wrong. We want to talk with Esther."

There was a pause, then rapid words. "She's sleeping. She's been sick. A recurrence. She just finished chemo. She's weak."

"We just want to talk to her, Jake. Please."

"I don't think it's a good idea to wake her up."

Rosa grabbed the phone. "Please wake her up."

"Is that you, Rosa?" Jake's voice sounded tight with emotion, but Rosa couldn't identify it. Anger? Fear?

"I really need to talk to my sister." She squeezed her eyes tight, feeling the enormous truth of her own words. "Please. Please wake her up."

Jake hesitated. "Give me your phone number, Rosa. I'll tell her you called. I promise."

Rosa drooped forward until her forehead rested on the table. Jake had always tried to get between them. "Please tell her I'm sorry."

"We're sorry too," Jake said quietly.

Rosa recited her phone number. Then she left the kitchen and stood just beyond the doorway. She leaned her head against the doorjamb. Listening.

"Are you still there?" Maggie asked Jake.

"Yes."

"It's time, don't you think?"

"I don't want Esther to be hurt any more," he said.

"How bad is she?"

"It's hard to tell. Not great."

"Jake," Maggie said, "Rosa's ready."

"So is Esther. I'll give her Rosa's number."

"Thanks."

"And Maggie," Jake added, "give Rosa and Allen a message for me. Tell them we're coming to New York on Saturday for the demonstration. Molly and Esther and me."

The next afternoon, the smell of lasagna greeted Rosa in the hallway.

"We're about to eat," Allen called from the kitchen.

"Told you I'd be home on time," Rosa yelled back. Allen had called twice, reminding her that Emma was coming to dinner with Jeff and Clara. "The wind was practically a tornado—if they have tornados here in the Arctic—but I'm here."

She draped her coat over the bicycles by the front door and dropped a shopping bag on the counter. She accepted a glass of wine from Maggie, who was setting the table.

After her conversation with Jake, Maggie had decided to stay for the demonstration. "I wouldn't miss this for anything."

"How's it going?" Allen asked Rosa.

"The press conference was fine, and everything for tomorrow is as ready as we can make it."

"Did you write your speech?"

Rosa shrugged. "It's only three minutes."

"Three minutes in front of a million people," Allen said. He pointed to the bag. "What's that?"

"I need your help with a project tonight. You too, Maggie, and Emma and Jeff."

"Sure, just take the bag off the dinner table," Allen said. "What kind of project?"

Rosa looked at him, then at Maggie. "Cranes," she said. "We're folding origami cranes."

When the dinner dishes were washed and put away, Rosa brought the shopping bag to the table, along with a sealed cardboard carton. Emma settled Clara on the rug with her stacking cups. "What's in the box?"

"Relics from my past. Schmaltzy things I thought I'd never want to see again. Stuff Allen didn't throw away like I told him to."

Maggie grinned. "Getting sentimental in your dotage, Rosa?"

Rosa ripped the tape away, leaving a mud-brown stain on the cardboard. She opened the cardboard edges and lifted out a bundle of folded pages of notebook paper.

"Letters to Esther." She put them aside. "Never mailed."

She reached back into the box and brought out a short tricolor braid. She touched it to her lips and squeezed her eyes shut, picturing the women who grew the gray and brown hair. She handed it to Emma.

"The red's yours," Emma said. "Whose are the others?"

"The brown is Esther. The gray is our grandmother Leah. The one from Russia."

"Who had a printing press in the outhouse—how could I forget?" Emma laughed.

"Hey, I remember this." Maggie reached into the box for a small blue button with Go Michigan. Beat Thailand printed on it in yellow.

"Thailand?" Jeff asked.

"Maybe my biggest contribution to the anti-war movement." How weird was that—after all she'd done, maybe designing a silly button was her most important role. Rosa pointed to her chest, over her heart, right over her tattoo, and Maggie pinned the button on her sweater. Rosa turned to Emma and Jeff. "We discovered that the university was developing counter-insurgency devices for the Defense Department to use in Southeast Asia. This button made *Newsweek*."

Rosa fumbled in the box for a wrinkled yellow concert program. She handed it to Maggie.

"I remember that, too." Maggie showed it to Allen, then to Emma and Jeff. "Rosa and I went to this Grateful Dead concert in Berkeley, the summer before the demonstration and arrest." She looked at Rosa. "The summer you got the tattoo."

"Esther too." Rosa pulled a tube of posters, silk-screened on heavy paper, from the box. She unrolled them on the kitchen table, anchoring each corner to hold them flat. Esther's favorite was on top: two Vietnamese figures carrying rifles, walking through shallow water, rice fields probably, morphing into a scene of shouting, angry protestors on a US city street. Iridescent scarlet and blue shimmered on the page.

Allen ran his hand over the rice paddies. "I haven't thought about this poster in thirty years."

Rosa looked at Emma. "Esther designed this for the graphics collective. My sister was very talented."

"I know, Mom. Like the cranes memorial at camp."

In the corner of the carton was one last item, a folded peace crane with "Happy 22nd Birthday and A Long Life" written with Esther's signature flourish on the crane's wing. Rosa put the origami bird on her hand and displayed it to the group. She removed a stack of brightly colored square paper wrapped in cellophane from the shopping bag, and a printed instruction sheet.

"Here's our project. Esther's cancer is back. She has always loved cranes and we need 1,000 of them. I never did learn to fold these things."

"Why don't you talk to her? Apologize?"

Rosa shook her head. "This is better. She'll understand."

Emma muttered something under her breath. Rosa couldn't hear, and didn't want to anyway. While the others read the instructions and began folding, Rosa lined up the cardboard backing from the origami package with the corner of the silk-screened poster. She drew pencil lines along the edges of the small paper, dividing the poster into eight smaller squares.

"What're you doing?" Maggie asked.

Rosa wasn't sure she could explain, could even talk. Her swollen fingers struggled with the scissors. Then she looked at Maggie. "Don't you think my letters would make powerful cranes?"

"No. Use these." Emma handed Rosa a stack of origami paper. "Save the letters for Esther to read."

Rosa hesitated, then nodded and started folding the patterned papers. Deep blue with silver stars. Orange striped sunshine reflected in green seas. She wasn't the artistic sister, but she could picture what these peace cranes would look like when they were done. And she could imagine the reaction on Esther's face.

CHAPTER 43

Molly

Fortified with layers of silk and down and fleece and wool, Evan and I emerged from the subway station into the brittle cold of Columbus Circle. The icy air sparkled with anticipation and pulsated with street music.

It was still three hours before the scheduled start of the rally, but already the crush of people on the sidewalk threatened to overflow into the streets. At the top of the subway steps, I tugged on the sleeve of Evan's jacket, pulling him off to the side to wait for my parents. I was worried about my mom.

"She's still not very strong," Jake had warned that morning. He admitted that they had argued fiercely about the trip to New York, debating the dangers, health-wise and cop-wise and cosmic. Finally Jake gave in. I asked what made him change his mind, but he wouldn't say. Not taking the bus was Esther's concession to her weakened immune system. So we drove to the city, my parents peppering Evan the whole way with questions about his family and his work. Of course, they really wanted to know his "intentions" but would never ask. We parked on the Upper West Side and took the subway to Fifty-Ninth, Esther embarrassed behind the medical mask Jake insisted she wear.

We huddled out of the wind in the shelter of a newsstand wall. I held Evan's gloved hand in mine. Jake took Esther's backpack and transferred it onto his shoulder.

"Got any apples in there?" Evan teased.

I frowned at him, but Esther laughed, shoving the mask into her parka pocket. "No way. Apples aren't tough enough for this administration." She looked at the helicopter patrolling the sky and added, "Just kidding."

"So, do we have a plan?" I asked.

Evan opened the map he'd printed from the Internet. "The rally site is First Avenue and Forty-Ninth Street. We're at Seventh and Fifty-Ninth, so let's..."

I interrupted. "I mean about meeting up with Rosa."

"Let's get to the rally site first." Jake pointed at the red circle on the map. "Then we'll call her and figure out how to meet."

"No. Let's call her first," Esther said, speed-dialing her cell phone. She half-smiled at Jake. "I programmed her number last night. Is that pathetic?"

"It's hopeful. Scary but hopeful."

Esther listened, then whispered, "Voice mail." She hesitated, then spoke into the phone. "It's me. Esther. We're at Columbus Circle, heading for the UN. Call me, okay? So we can plan a meeting place."

Evan looked around. "Let's just follow the crowd." He pointed to the people surging around a deep blue banner with white letters proclaiming HISTORIANS AGAINST THE WAR. "Everyone's going to the same place."

We slipped into the cross-town flow along Central Park South, behind a woman in an ankle-length fur coat. She carried a poster with a peace sign and the message, BACK BY POPULAR DEMAND.

"That's real mink," Evan whispered in my ear. "My great aunt had a coat just like that."

"Is that real Army?" The young guy walking next to mink lady—her son maybe—wore full army camouflage, boots, flashlight and walkie-talkie hanging from his belt and all. I read his sign, Frodo has failed, Bush has the ring. I laughed. This was *fun*.

Waiting for the traffic light at Sixth Avenue, I stamped my boots to restore feeling to my toes. My mom pulled off her thick mitten, dug in her pocket for a tissue, and blew her nose.

"Are you okay, Esther?" Jake asked. "Should we stop and rest?"

Esther shook her head. My mother would never ask us to slow down. When the light changed, we stepped into the street.

People joined the crowd at every intersection, swelling our numbers, making it almost impossible to stay on the sidewalks. We tried anyway, reminded by marshals with armbands to obey the traffic laws and the cops. More cops than I had ever seen before. Dozens at every intersection, reinforced by police cruisers and vans and motorcycles, even this far from the rally site. But the crowd didn't act intimidated. We chanted and sang. "Give peace a chance." "No blood for oil." "George Bush, military hack; out of Afghanistan, hands off Iraq."

We defied the debilitating cold, boogieing to the beat of drummers, clapping thick-gloved hands. All of us, an astonishing mix of ages and colors. Kids bundled in strollers and great-grandmothers pushed in wheelchairs. Even a clown on a unicycle riding tight circles in the street. A man wearing a business suit entirely covered in duct tape waved a sign announcing, Department of Homeland Security's Spring Line. Next to him, a guy dressed in green with an ivy crown and a praying mantis hand puppet held a sign, Earth Be Weary of War. At Third Avenue, a troop of puppeteers with giant paper mâché effigies of Bush and Cheney and Rumsfeld zigzagged through the crowd, accompanied by a brass band playing a jazzy arrangement of "This Land is Your Land." We clapped and shouted our appreciation. It got even more crowded. The four of us linked elbows to stay together.

Despite the numbing cold, I felt intensely alive. Also frightened and woozy and tingly and angry and totally wired. I squeezed Evan's elbow against my breast, excited through all those layers.

I turned to my parents. "The energy is amazing. Was it like this in Detroit, that day?"

"No," Jake said. "It was damned hot."

"You weren't there." Esther pressed her lips together.

"Was it, Mom?"

"Yes." Esther smiled. "It was amazing. Just like this."

I smelled something odd. Like firecrackers laced with hot peppers. "What's that stink?"

"Tear gas, right?" Evan asked.

Esther nodded but didn't speak; I was wordless too. Then she tightened her grip on my arm and pointed just ahead, at a group of young men and women—the age of my community college students—brandishing a red and black banner with three giant letters: SDS. "Stop the war, yes we can," they sang. "SDS is back again!" She wiped a smudge of tear from her cheek.

By Second Avenue, my toes were thick and numb despite fur-lined boots. A line of policemen prevented us from continuing east, even though the street was empty beyond them. Instead we were turned south, inching along, merging awkwardly with the thousands of people already filling the street in that direction. Our progress was glacially slow. At each block, the cops funneled us into an enclosure of metal police barricades. We stood, feet stamping, until we were released into the next pen.

A woman nearby asked one of the cops why we were being herded like cattle.

"For your own safety," the policeman answered. "We're on high terror alert."

"Bullshit," the woman replied. Then she turned to the crowd and shouted, "Whose streets?"

"Our streets," the crowd answered.

Back and forth, we asked and answered. The yelling kept us warm. Whiffs of tear gas came and went, along with another smell I couldn't identify. It was earthy, like ripe barn.

For a while, we walked behind the new SDS contingent. As they chanted, I watched my mother take off her mitten and dig again for a tissue. Jake kissed her forehead. Crossing Fifty-Third Street, inch by slow inch, I tried to imagine what this demonstration must have felt like for her.

"Damn it. My mitten," Esther said. "I must have dropped it."

We all looked down, trying to spot a blue mitten among shoes and boots.

"We'll share," Evan said. "Wear mine for awhile." He offered his thick glove.

Esther shook her head, slipped her hand into the deep pocket of my parka. I pulled my glove off and slipped my bare hand in the pocket to massage my mother's icy fingers.

Her phone rang. Esther looked at the caller ID for a moment, biting her lip, before handing it to me to answer.

"Rosa? This is Molly."

"Where are you?"

"Second Avenue, between Fifty-Third and Fifty-Second."

"We're at the rally site," Rosa said. "Good luck getting here. It's crazy."

"Who's with you?" I hoped to see Emma again.

"Allen, Emma, her husband Jeff. And our friend Maggie."

I remembered Emma talking about Maggie. Her almost-aunt. "I hope we can get to you."

"It's an astounding crowd," Rosa said. "And this is so ironic. They wouldn't give us a permit to march. But what do you call all those people on the streets?"

I laughed. "I'm certainly no expert, but this looks like a march to me. How do we get there?"

"Not easily. The cops are penning people into 'protest zones,' keeping them from getting to the rally."

"Yeah, that's where we are, moving from one pen to another. Moo."

"They're not letting anyone onto First Avenue. You might have to just hop across the barricades so you can walk east."

"Do what?"

Rosa laughed. "You sound like your mother. Tell Esther I can't wait to see her. And, I have a present for her. Call me again when you get closer, okay?"

"Okay." I snapped the phone shut and handed it to Esther. "She can't wait to see you."

Jake put his arm around Esther. "What did she say about the rally?"

"That it's huge and the cops are trying to keep people away."

At Fifty-Second Street, we were stopped by a double row of barricades, fortified by a wall of police officers, standing shoulder to shoulder. Batons and plastic handcuffs were displayed in clear view in their gloved hands, a silent warning. I scanned their faces under fur-lined hats with earflaps. What were they thinking? Especially the guy on the end, with twin bars pinned on his uniform and a regular cap. His ears were bright red. They must have hurt.

Esther pointed out a Loon Lake banner way to the left and we tried to get closer, but it was too hard to move.

"Damn," Jake said. "We'll never get there on time. I really wanted to hear Richie Havens. He's supposed to sing 'Freedom.' That's how he opened Woodstock."

"Wow," Evan said. "Were you there?"

"No way," Esther said. "That was for the counterculture types. We were serious revolutionaries." Her smile was crooked—self-mocking and proud at the same time.

"Harry Belafonte and Pete Seeger are supposed to sing, too." I stood on tiptoe to see why we weren't moving, but no luck. "Can you see anything?" I asked Evan.

He jumped and craned his neck. His red wool hat bobbed above the heads and signs. "People," he said. "People everywhere." Then his grin faded. He pointed to the roof of a brick building where three uniformed men surveyed the crowd with sniper rifles and binoculars.

By the official start time of the rally, we had made it to the corner of Fifty-First Street. The police seemed more agitated, and the firecracker smell was stronger. The earthy smell was stronger, too, and I recognized it—horses—as a battalion of mounted police rode toward us. The crowd tried to make room but there was nowhere to go. Jake pulled us back, inch by inch, toward the metal barricades on the east side of the street. Maybe they would offer some protection.

One of the young men holding the SDS banner shouted at the cops and stood his ground as the horses approached. The mounted officer on the end of the line raised his baton overhead in warning. I imagined the boy crumpling to the frozen asphalt.

In my pocket, Esther's fingernails dug into my wrist.

The mounted cops were so close that I could see their deadpan faces. One horse glanced my way in passing. Chocolate brown eyes and a white star on the forehead.

Evan's hands gripped my shoulders, pulling me further back against the metal barricades, alongside my parents. Jake looked stunned. Esther held his arm, seemed to be whispering into his ear. The crowd surged forward, screaming at the mounted cops and the police in riot gear who followed them. The four of us inched back, away from the action. Esther pointed at the barricades and the block beyond, empty except for a few scurrying people taking advantage of the cops' attention elsewhere. In one fluid moment, we climbed over the barriers and ran east.

We snuck under barriers at First Avenue to rejoin the demonstration, avoiding the line of police in riot gear. Over loudspeakers and hand-held radios, crackling with static electricity and interference and cheers, the voice of Archbishop Tutu welcomed the crowd. "We are members of one family, the human family," he said. "What do we say to war?"

"No," the demonstrators roared. We roared.

Esther called Rosa again. She turned slightly away and talked for a minute, then hung up. "They're next to the Bring Down the War Machine banner."

I could see the enormous sign near the stage, near the giant puppet of the President holding buckets of blood and oil.

"Did she say anything else, Esther?" I asked.

My mother stared at me, open-mouthed. I realized what I had said. "Esther," I repeated.

Esther smiled. "That she's wearing a red wool hat."

"Like me," Evan said.

We locked elbows and pushed through the crowd. Evan led. "Keep your eye on that other red hat," Jake said, bringing up the rear. With difficulty we snaked through the tightly packed demonstrators. "Please excuse us," we murmured. "Sorry."

The Archbishop's voice rose. "President Bush, listen to the voice of the people. They are asking you to give peace a chance." The crowd exploded in applause as my family reached the double row of barriers around the stage. The banner whipped in the wind, tethered by a line of people holding the elaborate frame of ropes and grommets. Under the banner stood Rosa, with a red Speaker badge pinned to her coat, and Allen, his beard speckled with gray. Emma stood next to a blond man wearing a Siberian fur hat and a stocky woman who had to be Maggie. Emma waved, motioned us closer, then leaned to Rosa and pointed. Rosa waved, then turned away and walked backstage.

Emma walked to the barrier and whispered something to the cop on guard. He moved the metal gate aside to let our family through. "Come," Emma said to Esther. "My mom is waiting. She has something for you."

I took Esther's hand and we followed Emma around the corner of the stage. A deep voice came over the loudspeakers, singing about government lying and drifting toward war. Jake walked close behind us, his mittened hands resting on our shoulders. "That's Havens," he said, "singing Jackson Browne's song."

Rosa stood alone at the back edge of the stage. Esther dropped my hand and turned to Jake, her face questioning.

"Go," he said.

Esther walked forward and faced her sister. Jake and I followed her, a few steps behind.

"I made something for you," Rosa said, reaching for Esther's hand. "We all did."

"Now?" Esther asked.

"It's long overdue."

On the narrow platform behind the stage, Emma and Allen had opened two large trash bags. They grabbed handfuls of colored objects and flung them into the air so they fell onto Rosa and Esther. I climbed up next to them, and then Jeff and Jake and Evan and Maggie joined us, each of us burrowing our hands deep into the bags to launch folded bits of patterned paper into the icy air. Hundreds of wings shimmered. Pink sparkly birds tumbled over yellow striped ones and purple swirly ones and orange flowered ones and Kelly green paisley ones.

Havens's voice danced among the folded birds, powerful words about struggles around the world. Esther and Rosa stood face-to-face, clutching each other's hands, eyes locked and cheeks glistening. Glittery birds speckled with crimson promises fluttered for a moment, then spiraled onto their parka shoulders. Clumsy ones made from poster paper that didn't take the folds right plummeted onto the frozen ground. Over and over, until the bags were empty, our family flung paper birds aloft. An updraft caught a few flimsy ones made of thin notebook paper and carried them soaring over high in the air above the sisters, where they hovered before drifting out into the crowd.

Acknowledgments

This book has been twenty years in the writing, and many people have shared their memories and knowledge in support of the work. I am particularly grateful to Marnie Mueller and to Gail Hochman who both offered early encouragement to a very green writer, and to my Stonecoast MFA buddies, the "Vanettes"— Ginnie Gavron, Perky Alsop, Sarah Stromeyer, and Sharon Arms.

The women in my critique group have read multiple versions of this manuscript over two decades with patience and care. Thank you so much, Jacqueline Shee-han, Lydia Kann, Rita Marks, Brenda Marsian, Maryanne Banks, Patricia Riggs, Kari Ridge, Celia Jeffries, Kris Holloway, and Dori Ostermiller. I am grateful to those who offered their expertise about the legal and political issues critical to this story, including Chris Pyle, Bill Newman, Karen Shain, and Rachel Meeropol. Many of my friends, writers and readers, have read and given feedback on the manuscript. Thank you, Ann Ferguson, Jon Weissman, Jane Miller, Karen Shain, Alice Levine, Holly Bishop, Céline Keating, and Liz Goldman.

Once again, I deeply appreciate the experience, wisdom, and energy of publicist Mary Bisbee-Beek, and the team at Red Hen Press—Kate Gale, Mark Cull, Tobi Harper, Monica Fernandez, Natasha McClellan, and Rebeccah Sanhueza.

An earlier version of the first chapter was previously published as a short story titled "Her Flammable Sister" in *DoveTales, an International Journal of the Arts*, in their 2013 "Occupied" edition.

For readers interested in learning more about the anti-Vietnam War and second wave women's movements, I recommend *Sisterhood is Powerful* by Robin Morgan; *SDS* by Kirkpatrick Sale; *Underground* by Mark Rudd; *Fugitive Days* by Bill Ayers; *To Be of Use*, poems by Marge Piercy; and the film *She's Beautiful When She's Angry* directed by Mary Dore.

I am deeply grateful to the women with whom I shared the socialist-feminist struggles of the late 1960s and 1970s. Our sisterhood changed and defined me.

My family has lived with Rosa and Esther's story for decades, reading many versions and offering their support and feedback. This book is for you, Robby, Jenn, and Rachel.

Biographical Note

Ellen Meeropol is the author of three previous novels: *Kinship of Clover* (Women's National Book Association Great Group Read and literary fiction finalist for the Best Book Award), *On Hurricane Island* (semi-finalist for the Massachusetts Book Award), and *House Arrest*. Her recent essay publications include *Ms.* magazine, *Lilith* magazine, the *Boston Globe*, and *Guernica*. Ellen's dramatic script telling the story of the Rosenberg Fund for Children was produced most recently in Manhattan featuring Eve Ensler, Angela Davis, and Cotter Smith. A founding member of Straw Dog Writers Guild, Ellen leads their Social Justice Writing project. She lives in Northampton, MA.